Glass Princess

M. Lynn

Fantasy and Fairytales

Edited by Melissa Craven
Proofread by Patrick Hodges
Cover by Covers by Combs

Also by M. Lynn

Fantasy and Fairytales

Golden Curse

Golden Chains

Golden Crown

Glass Kingdom

Glass Princess

Noble Thief

Cursed Beauty

The Hidden Warrior

Dragon Rising

Dragon Rebellion

Queens of the Fae

Fae's Deception

Fae's Defiance

Fae's Destruction

Fae's Prisoner

Fae's Power

Fae's Promise

Legacy of Light

A War for Magic

A War for Truth

A War for Love

For Robin and Mackenzie.
The reason I know how to write meaningful sibling relationships. I learned the easy way - by having sisters who would fight for me if anyone ever tried to tear us apart.

The Six Kingdoms

One

Thunder split the sky, crashing down around Helena. The roar echoed among the trees, but she didn't turn back.

Freezing rain pelted her pale face as she made the daily trek.

Thirteen long days. They'd been in Bela too long, and all she knew to do was wait.

"Len!" Dell ran to catch up to her, his long strides matching hers. "You can't keep doing this."

His words barely made it past the drumming of the rain, but she knew what he meant. It wasn't the first time.

Her feet picked up speed. "I have to," she yelled back.

A bolt of lightning lit up the gray morning sky.

"No." He grabbed her arm, yanking her back. "You don't."

She turned to face him, pushing at his chest until he released her. "My brother is out there. Quinn is the only one left besides me and Kass."

He didn't say the words they were both thinking. He didn't have to. His eyes said it all. *If he's not dead. If he hasn't joined his twin's side in Madra, then where is he?*

She shook her head. "No. He'll come."

She turned and trudged up the hill to Bela's lookout post.

Before he betrayed them, she'd thought Cole would always be by her side. How well did she really know her brothers?

Her fists clenched at her sides. She couldn't think that way. Estevan gave his life to save her and Kassander, he was too good to betray his family. She knew them. She knew Quinn.

He'd come.

At the top of the hill, a small shack sat with a deck surrounding it. Helena had spent each excruciating day since her arrival sitting there. Waiting.

She wiped the rain from her face and yanked open the door. Aron turned at the sound of her entrance, a grim set to his handsome features. Shaking his sopping chestnut curls out of his face, he regarded her with surprise.

Dell pushed through the door behind her. "I thought you'd finally gain some sense and stay inside today."

Helena moved to one of the windows spanning the far wall. "I've never claimed to have sense."

Aron nodded as if that was a perfectly acceptable answer.

"I tried to stop her." Dell wrung water from his dripping tunic.

Helena grunted.

A scowl marred Aron's face. "She has her own mind. Let her use it."

Helena barely heard their continuing conversation as her eyes scanned the countryside. She'd never seen anything so beautiful as Bela, but it wasn't the vast thriving forests or plains of wildflowers she searched for today.

"Anything new?" she asked.

"Nothing more than a few traders from Dracon. The

roads are clear." Aron stepped closer to her near the warm hearth. "We're unlikely to see much on a day such as this. Even with my gifts."

Helena would never grow used to the incredible powers existing within Bela. Aron's gift allowed him to see things others could not, and at great distances. Queen Persinette enlisted him to watch for the last Rhodipus sibling in case he did not arrive as a friendly visitor.

Still, Helena had faith in Quinn.

Aron moved around the small room with confidence, sliding chairs out of the way as he set about to stir up the small fire attempting to thrive in the stone fireplace.

Dell's gaze held thinly veiled hostility. He'd never warmed up to the young man, and Helena knew he didn't trust him. Then again, he didn't trust anything in Bela, much to her annoyance.

Helena couldn't fault him for that. She had a hard time believing Persinette and Alexandre had no motives other than helping them.

Aron turned from the fireplace. "I really should get back outside."

"But it's pouring rain out there." Helena gestured to the window.

"I have a job to do and I see much better outside. My queen has entrusted me with this and I will do what I must." He dipped his head once before slipping out just as another crack of thunder shook the walls.

"That man is crazy." Dell flicked his eyes to the window.

Helena couldn't disagree. The people of Bela had an unwavering loyalty to their king and queen. She'd seen nothing like it. It was... unnatural. In Madra, the people obeyed her father, but only because they feared what would happen if they dissented.

Was Cole now ruling with the same methods?

Anger seared through her blood when she thought of Cole. Her breath clogged in her throat. "I can't stay here." Before Dell could stop her, she ran out into the storm, finally able to breathe once she was outside. She dropped to her knees, her entire body shaking as images returned to her.

Flames. Flames. They seared across Helena's vision until she saw nothing else.

Death. Her family was dead. Mother. Father. A sob caught in her throat. Estevan.

Arms wound around her, but they couldn't hold her together.

Her ebony hair stuck to her lips as she sucked in a breath. A single rebellion had torn down everything she'd known in one night. Had it all really been that fragile?

"Helena." Dell's words warmed her otherwise icy skin. "Len, it's okay. You're here. We're in Bela. It's over. We don't have to fight anymore."

His words were meant to soothe her, to stop the panic clawing at her chest.

But he was wrong. Nothing was over. Their fight had only just begun.

BY THE TIME they returned to the village, the storm had moved on to ravage some other unsuspecting landscape.

Another day. Another disappointment.

Every morning, Helena woke with a small hope in her heart that it would be the day Quinn came for her.

Every night, she went to bed with the weight of defeat crushing her.

Dell walked beside her, a silent companion. They'd struggled to find much to say to each other. Both lost their families, but he didn't feel it the way she did. His family wasn't dead. They'd joined Cole in betraying the king, in killing her parents.

The palace of Bela sat on the edge of great white cliffs, across a small stream with a bridge connecting it to the rest of the village. Calling it a palace was generous. In truth, it only comprised four small bedrooms, a common space, kitchen, and a throne room lacking in any kind of grandness.

Just like the rest of Bela, its beauty lay in its simplicity.

Queen Persinette, who insisted on being called Etta, allowed Helena, Dell, Kassander, and Edmund to stay with her and her husband, King Alexandre.

The queen's horse, Vérité, grazed outside the door as they walked up and Helena headed toward him. Dell walked by her without a word and went inside.

Vérité raised his head, fixing her with a golden-eyed stare that calmed her for the first time all day. The horse had taken an immediate liking to her as soon as she'd met him.

And she'd fallen for him when he'd bitten Edmund.

"Hey, buddy." She reached out to dig her hand into his damp mane. "You stay safe in the storm today?"

Vérité stepped forward to nudge the side of her head with his nose.

A tear slipped from her eye as his understanding gaze pulled every bit of emotion she'd pushed down right up to the surface. Vérité dropped his nose to her shoulder.

"I'm okay, Vérité. Or I will be. One day." She shook her head. "Why am I talking to a horse?"

"From my experience..." Etta stepped from the doorway. "It's because there's no better listener than Vérité. No judgment. Only comfort." A smile curved the queen's lips. "And he'll never repeat anything you say. He's honorable that way."

Helena met Etta's soft gaze. She'd heard the stories of the Belaen queen who'd fought La Dame... and won. Anyone who had doubts of the tales need only to look at the woman and they'd become a believer. Fierceness emanated from her.

In all honesty, Etta terrified Helena.

When Edmund appeared behind Etta, Helena's shoulders relaxed.

"Supper is ready," Edmund said, his voice as lifeless as it had been since they'd arrived on Bela's shores.

At least one person felt the loss as strongly as Helena did.

She nodded to the queen as she walked past her to wrap her arms around Edmund's waist. He stiffened in surprise before returning the hug and resting his chin on her head.

"No luck today, then?" he asked.

Helena shook her head against his chest. "Sorry I'm getting you wet."

Helena could feel Etta's eyes burning into her back. The two royal women experienced a strange tension every time Helena was around Edmund. Was the queen jealous of their friendship?

Edmund hadn't told any of his Belean friends what Estevan had truly meant to him, and his morose demeanor put a barrier between them because they couldn't understand the gravity of what he'd lost.

She walked further into the palace, one arm still hooked around Edmund's waist. King Alexandre, Dell, and Kassander sat near the fireplace with full plates of boar steaks and some kind of leafy vegetable in front of them. Alexandre said something that made the other two laugh.

Helena's arm tightened around Edmund.

"I know," he whispered. "I feel it too."

She tried not to hate them for their joy, but it had already entered her mind.

"I'm not hungry." She released Edmund. "I think I'll just change into something dry and lay down."

He brushed a hand over her hair and placed a kiss on the side of her head. "I promised Stev I'd keep you safe, Len. Just remember, whether or not Quinn comes, Kassander isn't the only brother you have left."

She turned away before he could see the tears shining on her face. "Thanks for saying that, Edmund."

After rushing into her room and shutting the door, she leaned up against it, whispering to herself.

"I'm not alone. I'm not alone."

She stripped the wet clothes from her body and pulled on a sleeping gown before collapsing into her bed. Her mother would have chastised her for planning to sleep the day away, but she didn't have it in her to rise again.

Tomorrow would be another long day of waiting for someone who might never come.

Two

"Use your sword, Dell, not your body!" King Alexandre rubbed his side where Dell had rammed him.

Dell stopped. "Shouldn't I use anything that will help me win?"

"Of course. But in most fights that's going to be the blade you have in your hands."

"Unless I'm awful with the blade."

Alex grinned. "Unless that. Take it from someone who knows, you don't want to be awful with the blade."

Dell groaned. He was a boxer, a brawler, not a swordsman. "Why are we doing this again?"

"Why indeed." Etta clapped from her position at the side of a large oak that had shielded her from their view.

"Here we go," Alex grumbled. "Aren't you supposed to have meetings all morning?"

"Still no word from Ty, so Matteo and I postponed a few until tomorrow." She turned to Dell. "Did you know, Mr. Tenyson, that you have the great pleasure of being trained by Alexandre Durand, worst swordsman in Bela."

Alex shook his head. “I’ve trained for years to get rid of the title and she won’t let me.”

Etta walked toward him and patted the side of his face. “He’s lucky he has a wife who can protect him.”

Alex trapped her hand against his cheek. “Very lucky.”

She grinned and kissed him before disarming him and shoving him away. Picking up his discarded sword, she passed it between her hands.

Dell backed away as she advanced.

“Sword up,” she commanded. “Stop staring at the blade. It can attack from any direction before you get the chance to react. Watch my feet and my body position. They will give you warning.”

She shifted her feet forward and lunged. Dell only had enough time to block the attack before she made her next move. He ducked out of the way, almost falling to the ground.

Dell had never considered himself unskilled and had even done okay against Alex, but Etta moved with the stealth of a cat while using the strength of a boar.

She peppered him with attacks before finally stepping back and wiping sweat from her brow. “I never feel right if a day goes by where I don’t hold a sword in my hand.”

Dell chuckled. “Bet that works great as the queen of a peaceful kingdom.”

Etta’s smile spread across her face. “I like you, Dell. Come. You and I need to have a talk.”

He looked to Alex, but the king only shrugged.

Etta started down the forest path without glancing back to make sure he was coming.

“I don’t have much time.” She pushed open the palace door. “But we can’t go on as we have been.”

He followed her inside. “I don’t know what you mean.”

“Sit.” She pointed to the table on her way into the

kitchen. When she returned, she carried two mugs brimming with ale.

"Thanks." He chuckled.

"What's so funny?"

"I may have been fathered by a powerful man, but I basically raised myself on the city streets. Now I'm having an ale with a foreign queen."

"And protecting a princess." She raised an eyebrow.

He took a long drink, avoiding her gaze. As much as he tried to help Helena, the princess wouldn't let him. It was as if she'd forgotten everything that happened before the rebellion. He no longer existed for her.

"Look, Dell..." Etta sighed. "Bela has been through a lot, lost a lot. So, I know the toll it takes. It hasn't been easy rebuilding our kingdom, but this peace is our reward. I lived most of my life beholden to others, but more importantly, beholden to my own secrets. I recognize the signs. I have tried everything I can think of to get my Edmund back. There was a time when he saved me, kept me sane. When he chose to become our ambassador to Madra, I felt every moment of his absence. But it's as if he's still gone. He returned to us, but part of him is still across the sea."

Dell almost told her. Of Estevan and his relationship with Edmund. Of everything Edmund had done to prevent the rebellion.

But those weren't his secrets to tell.

"I'm sorry, your Majesty. I can't help you. Just... don't give up on him. Edmund is the only reason I'm sitting here today. He's the reason Helena and Kassander made it out of Madra. I've never met anyone like him... but the sacrifices he had to make..." Dell shook his head. "I know what it's like to watch someone you care about lose bits of themselves."

Etta put a hand on Dell's arm. "Then I'll tell you the

same thing. Don't give up on her. She'll come back to you." She drained the rest of her ale and stood. "I must attend to a few things. Thank you for this."

Before she made it to the door, a frazzled Matteo rushed in, his blonde hair disheveled from the wind and his cheeks rosy from the cold. "Tyson has returned."

"About time." Etta followed him to the throne room.

Dell joined them as the young man burst through the door and rushed to his sister, throwing his arms around her.

Was nothing formal in Bela?

Helena appeared at Dell's side. "I was with Aron when they rode through the valley. For a moment, I thought it was Quinn."

"I'm sorry." Dell gripped her hand. She stiffened but didn't pull away.

Alexandre appeared and reached Tyson is three long strides. "You were supposed to return two days ago."

"You know mother." He grinned. "She wanted to fatten me up."

Dell would never wrap his head around the dynamics between Bela and Gaule. Alex and Tyson were the sons of the Gaulean queen but had different fathers. Tyson shared a father with Etta who married Alex. And then there was Camille who was still in Madra and the sister to both princes.

Alex's smile dropped. "You went to see *her*, didn't you?"

Dell had spent most of his time either following Helena to the lookout post or among the people of Bela. It was there he learned everything he needed to know about the family they now relied on for protection.

The young prince Tyson was in love with a girl who'd only ever been his friend. Once Dracon suffered defeat, the girl returned to Gaule to run her family's estate.

Tyson studied the ground. "Amalie wasn't at her estate. I tried, but..."

Alex put a hand on his shoulder. "I'm sorry, brother. What word do you have from Gaule? Does mother know of the happenings in Madra?"

A guilty expression flashed across his face. "She knows of the takeover. The new king has reached out to her and assured Camille's safety and the continuation of the treaty. Mother intends to honor it."

A stream of curses flitted through Dell's mind, but he didn't voice a single one as Helena squeezed his hand, the first sign she wanted his support.

The only hope they had of a peaceful resolution to this problem was if the other kingdoms put pressure on Madra. Gaule was the key to that.

"It's happening again," Edmund said. When had he arrived?

"No." Etta's braid slapped her shoulder as she shook her head. "We can trust Queen Catrine."

"Can we?"

"Watch it," Alex growled.

Edmund held his hands in front of his chest. "Look, I don't mean to say Catrine is against magic-folk in the way your father was. But you have to see the signs. Non-magic kingdoms allying in fear of us? If Cana or Andes joins the alliance..."

"Cana will never ally themselves with anyone." To Dell's surprise, it was Helena who spoke up.

"We can't know that," Matteo chimed in.

"Actually, I'm the one person in this room who probably does. You say your friend is in Cana?"

"Ara," Etta confirmed.

Helena continued. "That doesn't mean you know anything about it. Most of the kingdoms live in blissful ignorance of what goes on beyond those borders because foreigners rarely make it out." She breathed deeply. "Cana has no loyalty to one king or queen. They are separated into clans who are too busy fighting one another to worry about other kingdoms. You should certainly fear the individual Canaans with their assassin's skill, but don't worry about them signing any treaties."

"How do you know all that?" Dell asked.

"It's not important."

Etta eyed her curiously. "Okay then. We need to maintain a close watch of Gaule and Madra. We have another matter of import." She nodded to Tyson.

Tyson pulled out an unsealed letter. "They allowed Camille to write to my mother." He held it toward Helena.

Helena snatched the paper, unfolding it rapidly. Dell read over her shoulder, his eyes only catching parts of it.

...

honor the treaty, mother. It's the only way to ensure peace with Madra. The new king is an honorable man.

That didn't sound like the princess at all, at least the Camille he'd met. "She didn't write this."

Most of the letter meant nothing to him until he came upon the words he knew would break Helena in two.

Prince Estevan died in his cell three days ago of illness. Cole was going to let his brother live.

The paper fell from her fingers, fluttering to the floor as tears cascaded down her face.

Dell tried to pull her to him, but she put up a hand to stop the movement.

"You could fix this." Helena's voice was so quiet, Dell wasn't sure anyone else heard her until they all stopped. She lifted her eyes to scan the room, finally settling them on the queen. "Madra would be no match against Bela."

"No," Etta cut her off.

"But your magic—"

"I said no."

"You won't help? You'll let me sit here idly for what... the rest of my life?" Helena straightened her spine, sending the queen a scathing look. "Madra is mine. Not Cole's. Mine. My father is dead. They murdered my mother as I hid. I'm not hiding anymore. I am now the heir to the Madran throne."

"We can't." Remorse mixed with stubbornness filled Etta's eyes. "We have a responsibility as magic-wielders not to use our magic to overrun other kingdoms. We aren't tyrants."

"They. Killed. My. Brother."

Edmund dropped to the ground at the words, needing to see the letter for himself. A strangled cry escaped his lips.

They'd all assumed Estevan wouldn't live much longer, but the confirmation brought every emotion they'd hidden since the rebellion crashing into the room.

Edmund held the letter to his chest for a moment before ripping it in two, standing, and stalking from the room.

Etta and Alex's gazes both followed him.

"Oh." Understanding lit in Etta's eyes.

"Len," Dell whispered.

She shook her head, stumbling back until she reached the door. Dell didn't follow her as she disappeared.

"I wish we could help them." Etta leaned into Alex.

"Would it really be so bad?" Tyson asked. "We can't let Camille marry a usurper."

"Ty." Alex fixed him with a stare. "If Bela marches into kingdoms to fix them or use the magic to subdue them, it sets expectations. Etta won't live forever. We won't begin down the road of dictatorship. That was how La Dame became so powerful. Magic cannot be used against non-magical folk. It isn't right."

Tyson sighed. "Sometimes, I wish you guys didn't always do the right thing. I want to march into Madra and gut the king who killed Edmund's boyfriend."

Alex reeled back in shock. Matteo turned away.

Tyson looked between them. "You guys didn't know?"

"You did?" Etta asked.

"From the first time I saw him. I know Edmund almost as well as I know myself. He loved the prince."

Alex cursed. "I need to go find him."

Dell blocked the door. "Your Majesty, the only person on this earth right now that Helena will let in is Edmund. Let them be there for each other. Just for right now."

Alex looked as if he'd protest.

"He's right," Etta said. "If Edmund wanted us to help him, he'd have let us. That girl means as much to him now as you or I."

Alex's shoulders dropped.

Dell left them in the throne room to find some solace of his own. Estevan's confident face flashed through his mind. Dell went against his family and joined Edmund because Edmund was so sure Estevan would do great things for Madra.

He'd been the hope for many people.

And now, like a candle in the night, he'd been extinguished, and all Dell could see of Madra's future was darkness.

Three

For weeks, Helena assumed Stev was dead. She'd seen Cole taking him prisoner in the moments before she'd succumbed to her injuries. One of Cole's men had stabbed her, and the last thing she'd seen was Dell hovering over her, shielding her from her brother's wrath.

But something nagged at the back of her mind. She had to know what really happened in that hallway. Every excruciating detail. Estevan was really gone, and she had to know why.

Why didn't he escape with them? Why did he stay? Why did Edmund let him?

The questions were the only things keeping her from dipping her head under the current of her grief and refusing to surface again.

A freezing wind whipped her hair from her shoulders, and she pulled her cloak tight around herself. In the distance, a lone figure sat at the edge of the cliffs with his legs dangling over the side.

Edmund hunched his back, collapsing in on himself. As

Helena neared, she took in the sound of violent waves crashing on the rocks below. *Fitting.*

She approached Edmund silently and lowered herself beside him, glancing over the edge of the cliff before inching back. "How are you not terrified of falling?"

Edmund continued to stare out at the churning sea. "I fear many things, Lenny. Falling to my death is not one of them."

"That's... morose."

He finally turned to face her, but his eyes held a faraway look. "My greatest fear has already happened."

"Mine too."

His lips tugged down, and he ran a hand through his blonde hair. After a beat of silence, he slid back from the edge of the cliff and pulled Helena against his side. She buried her face in his shoulder as he stroked her hair.

"I wasn't only afraid of losing Stev," he whispered. "It's anyone I love. So much has happened in the past few years. Bela's war with Dracon. Turmoil in Gaule. The Madran rebellion. I've been living in constant terror of the people around me dying. Etta, Alex, Tyson, Matteo, Stev, You... Even Camille. At this point, I'd probably even get upset if Vérité died, and I hate that blasted horse."

A sound between a laugh and a cry escaped Helena's mouth. "I've never experienced fear like that. My entire life, I've been protected, shielded. Now it's all I can think about. How do you live like this, Edmund? With your heart ripped out of your chest again and again."

"I'm still trying to figure that out." A tear tracked down his face, and Helena wiped it away with her thumb.

"I keep wondering if it would be better for Quinn to be dead or for him to have chosen Cole."

"Not dead." Edmund shook his head.

"But if he betrayed us too… I can't live with that."

"Yes, you can. It's amazing the kinds of things we can live with." He sucked in a breath and fell silent.

Helena shivered, and Edmund pulled her closer.

The words she wanted to say next clogged in her throat. Edmund's eyes held so much pain. Was it right for her to make him relive it?

His entire body shook, and she knew he was reliving it anyway.

"Edmund."

He didn't respond for a long moment as he got his breathing under control. "Yeah, Len?"

"I don't remember being taken from the palace. My final moments with Stev are just… gone." It took all her effort to keep a quiver out of her voice. "I need to know everything."

He sighed. "Honestly, I'm kind of surprised you haven't asked before now."

"My brother wasn't dead before now."

Edmund's gaze wandered away from her again. "Don't fool yourself, Len. He's been dead to us since we left that palace. We always knew we wouldn't get him back."

She pressed her lips together. "Please, just tell me."

"Cole…" He cleared his throat. "He was going to arrest us all. You and I had been captured. One of Cole's men threw a knife at you." He rested his cheek on her hair. "I thought you were dead."

He stopped speaking, and she squeezed his hand, urging him to go on.

He did. "Stev thought you were gone too. But Kassander wasn't. He and Dell had hidden him. Once the healer said you wouldn't live, Stev made a deal."

Helena tilted her head up to look at him. "What kind of deal?"

"If Cole allowed me, you, Dell, and Kass to leave, he'd give himself over willingly and tell his people to stand down."

Helena leaned away from him and scooted back. "It's all my fault. He's dead because of me." She got to her feet.

Edmund followed her. "No. He thought you'd die whether we got you to Corban or not. Stev sacrificed himself for me and Kassander. Every bit of fault lies with me."

Helena couldn't hear any more. She turned on her heel and ran back to the palace. Etta and Alex stared at her as she sprinted toward the room she was staying in. She searched under the mattress for the only piece of her mother she had left.

Her knives.

Two golden-hilted blades came free, and she tucked them into the bodice of her simple shift dress before leaving the same way she'd come. Anger churned through her veins, and if she didn't let it loose, she'd do something she regretted.

She reached the clearing behind the palace and pulled the knives free. Centering her body with the base of a tall pine tree, she raised one arm. Inhale. Exhale. Flick the wrist. Release.

The knife stuck in the tree with a thunk. She didn't pause before sending the second in the same arc.

She ran to the tree and yanked them free before finding a second target. Anger and desperation fueled her drive, making her forget everything but the weight of the blades in her hands.

As Helena released the first knife again, someone screamed, ducking out of the way. The knife hit a tree and clattered to the ground.

Kassander's dark head appeared in the clearing, his eyes wide.

Had she been so focused, she hadn't seen her brother there? She ran forward. "Kass, you okay?"

He lifted his head, a grin spread across his face. "How did you learn to do that?"

In that moment, Helena realized Kassander didn't know. No one told him about Stev. She pulled him off the ground and hugged his lanky frame, ruffling his familiar curls.

"Hey." He pulled back. "What's wrong, Len?"

Her face fell. Even her little brother could read every emotion in her eyes.

"I need to tell you something, Kass."

"If it's about Quinn..."

"It's not. It's about Stev."

Kassander's brow furrowed.

"He died, Kass."

Kassander grimaced. "We already knew he was dead."

"No, we'd only assumed."

"I don't see the difference." Tears welled in his eyes. "I thought you were going to tell me we lost another brother."

Helena bent to peer into her brother's eyes. She took his chin between two fingers, forcing him not to look away. "Do you have faith in Quinn?"

He nodded.

"So do I. And Kass, if he never comes, you still have me. Okay, kid? You'll always have me."

He wrapped his arms around her. "You'll always have me too."

Every bit of anger she'd felt seeped out of her at those words. She wasn't alone. Madra hadn't only been her kingdom. She wasn't the only one who would one day want it back.

NOTHING CHANGED in Bela as the days turned into nights. Helena continued watching for Quinn alongside Aron, but he never came. Edmund still went off on his own most days, but in the evenings, he'd sit with Alex and tell him of his time in Madra.

Kassander and Corban had taken to following Alex around, fascinated by the confident king, the man without magic who lived among the magic-folk.

Dell improved with the sword. Not like he'd ever get the chance to use it.

And each moment they sat across the sea, the people of Madra were ruled by a usurper, a bastard prince.

Helena tried to push thoughts of the brother she'd loved from her mind. Still loved? Was that even allowed? She couldn't reconcile the brother she'd grown up with and the man who killed her parents.

She turned over in bed as light streamed through the window. The smell of bacon hit her as soon as she opened her eyes. The normalcy of that smell was like a shock to the heart. Nothing was normal.

After pulling herself from the bed, she changed into a pair of woolen pants and a heavy shirt before padding across the cold stone floor to the kitchen.

The king of Bela stood shirtless in front of the stove, sweat dripping down his back as he turned over griddle cakes and bacon.

Helena froze, her jaw falling open. Alexandre Durand was a beautiful man. In Madra, the royal family had a host of servants preparing every meal. It had taken quite a bit of getting used to over the last few weeks to have the king and queen do everything for themselves.

It was the way of Bela. Etta may lead, but she did not

rule. And her people were more loyal because of it. Because she was one of them.

The queen in question stepped up to Helena's side. "He wanted to cheer you guys up, make you feel more at home, after..." She didn't need to say it. *After they learned of their brother's death.*

Edmund appeared behind them. "So he decided to walk around shirtless? That's one way to cheer us up."

Etta pushed his shoulder. "No. He made breakfast."

Edmund laughed, the sound making them all pause. He'd been in such pain he hadn't so much as cracked a smile recently. He froze as if realizing what he'd done. That for just a moment, he'd forgotten what he was supposed to be feeling.

Alex turned. "If I knew all it took was bacon to hear that sound again, I'd have made it every morning."

Etta covered her mouth with her hands and pretended to cough. "Wasn't the bacon."

Helena smiled, thankful for the lightness she'd missed so much. She'd always joked around with her siblings, but never had friends of her own.

Edmund blushed, but shrugged as if he wasn't ashamed. Helena wished she knew herself so well. She spotted Dell sitting near the fire, his gaze trained on her. His eyes darkened, and Helena pulled hers away.

What would it be like to give in to her desires like everyone else around her? Stev had been so brave, so strong in being with the person he loved. She could only imagine what their father's reaction would have been. The two men would have been separated at the very least.

What had Helena ever been brave about? She lived her life behind a mask, never showing who she really was.

Stev lived freely. He may have been stiff and formal at

times, but he defied their father to give food to the people. He fell in love with another man. He protected her at all costs.

She turned to Etta who still stood ogling her husband. "Are you busy today?"

Etta raised an eyebrow. "Nah. I'm not the queen of an entire kingdom or anything."

"I'm done watching for someone to come help me. Quinn may be out there still, but I can't keep wasting time. You say Bela won't aid Madra, but Madra isn't alone. They still have me. Train me to fight."

Dell choked on a laugh. "Len, what do you know about fighting?"

She scowled, swinging her gaze around the room. Tyson, Alex, and Matteo glanced away. Edmund stayed quiet.

Etta considered her response. "When I turned eighteen, I had to enter a tournament, fighting to the death to protect that oaf." She pointed to her husband. "Every single man I met laughed at me." She leaned forward. "And you know what I did?"

Helena shook her head.

A gleeful glint entered Etta's gaze. "Beat them." She turned to the others surrounding them. "Matteo, clear my calendar. I will be occupied today."

The queen's cousin shook his head. "Not today, Etta. We have meetings all day with the traders from Dracon and Gaule. Then you're scheduled to hold court this afternoon."

Etta waved his words off. "You can handle the meetings, oh trusted one. Alex will join you. Take Edmund too. He knows this kingdom as well as anyone and it'll occupy his mind."

Edmund started to protest, but one look from Etta shut him up.

"Grab some food, Helena. I don't intend to be easy on you."

Helena piled food onto a plate and took her seat next to Dell.

"You sure about this?" he asked.

"Never been more sure of anything."

"Persinette Basile is one of the greatest fighters there is."

"Then there's no one else I want training me to return to Madra." She bit into her food.

"You really want to go back?" He eyed her skeptically.

"Do you believe in me, Dell?"

He nodded without hesitation. "Of course I do."

"Then please... shut up."

One corner of his mouth tilted up. "Well, okay then. But I get to watch."

Four

Dell sat with his back resting against a felled tree and bent one knee. The chill of the ground permeated his clothing, but it didn't bother him as he focused on the piece of soft wood in his hands. He didn't know what it was to be yet, but that wasn't unusual. He never looked too far ahead of himself. His hands knew what to do. They'd create while his mind was elsewhere.

He gripped the knife between his thumb and forefinger as he dug in.

Etta and Helena stood facing each other. Etta held two long staves in her hands. She tossed one to Helena.

Helena snatched it out of the air.

Etta nodded in approval. "I've seen you out here with your knives, Helena. You have good hand-eye coordination."

Knives? What was the Belaen queen talking about? Len was about as unthreatening as a princess could get. What did she know of knives?

"Thank you." Helena's fingers loosened and squeezed in anticipation.

"I wouldn't thank me yet. Coordination is only the beginning. To best someone in a fight, it takes quick thinking, agility, and anger."

"Anger?"

Etta twirled the staff in one hand. "Oh yes, that's the most important part. We aren't made to fight one another, to hurt each other... unless given a reason. The difference between someone who has what it takes and someone who doesn't is the ability to channel that anger, to use it and mold it."

Len's jaw tightened, and she swallowed. "I have plenty of anger."

Dell had seen the darkness growing within her for weeks. His entire life, he'd been mistreated and betrayed by his family. To him, it was life. To her, it was a tragedy and a betrayal.

A slow smile spread across Etta's face. "Are you ready?"

"Yes."

The intensity in Helena's gaze hadn't existed before. Dell remembered the softness in her eyes even when she fought with him on the beach. The sweetness when he kissed her at the ball. But then, he'd never truly known her. The girl who roamed the city streets was not the same one who hid behind a mask for most of her life.

Yet, he couldn't take his eyes away from her.

He set the wood aside and leaned forward against his knees.

Etta circled Helena and Len turned to face her once more, letting her staff drop just enough to give Etta an opening.

The Belaen queen smacked Len's weapon away, and the wood cracked against Len's stomach.

"I asked if you were ready," Etta yelled. "Do not lower your weapon. Ever."

Helena bit back the pain Dell knew she must have felt and raised her staff. Etta's next attack didn't take her by surprise. She knocked it away only to be smacked across the back.

She fell onto her hands and knees.

"Get up," Etta demanded.

Dell jumped to his feet. Helena was no warrior, and Etta went too far.

"No, Dell," Helena wheezed. "I'm okay." She released a ragged cough. Picking up her staff, she stood at the ready again.

Etta advanced with a flurry of moves. Helena stumbled back, blocking them as best she could. Etta kicked out with her foot, catching Helena's stomach and sending her onto her butt.

Helena grimaced, her breath wheezing in her chest.

"Are you angry yet, Princess?" Etta asked. "Or has that been bred out of you too?"

Dell tried to move forward, but Etta pinned him with a glare. "If you interfere, we will find out just how inadequate with a sword you are, boy."

Even with Alex training him, Dell knew he'd be no match for Etta. The stories of her skill had spread through Madra like wildfire. But he didn't sit down until Helena stood.

"I'm okay, Dell." She trained her eyes on Etta. "Again."

Etta lunged forward, but Helena twisted out of the way.

"Come on, Princess," Etta taunted. "Forget all the decorum they have taught you. Don't hide your emotions in a fight. Show me your anger."

Helena struck but there was no force behind the blow.

"You can do better than that." Etta scowled. "Do you know how I won my first tournament?"

Helena shook her head.

"I hated them. Every blasted one of them—including Alex. Including Tyson. I wanted to kill them all. The only person I've ever shown mercy to is Edmund when I chose not to kill him."

Dell gaped at her. The stories were true? Etta fought for her life in order to take up a position in the royal household of Gaule. But Edmund... why had he been in the tournament? And now she was married to Alexandre Durand.

Priest, he needed an ale.

Etta continued. "Mercy is not something you give your enemies. It's something you give when you decide someone is not your enemy. Who are your enemies, Princess? If the time comes, will you be merciless?"

A war raged in Helena's eyes, but she did not speak.

Etta advanced. "Your brother betrayed you. He killed your father. Your mother." She leaned in. "Estevan."

Tears tracked down Helena's face.

"Quinn isn't coming to help you, Helena."

Dell saw the moment those words registered. Helena lashed out, bringing her staff down with such force the collision with Etta's weapon echoed among the trees.

Helena didn't stop there, pushing Etta back and swinging the long weapon over her head. Etta blocked each move, grinning as she did.

She was insane. There was no other way to describe this foreign queen. She pushed and pushed, goading Helena into action.

After a while, Etta lowered her staff, her chest rising and falling rapidly. Sweat gleaned on both women's faces.

Helena wiped her brow on her sleeve.

"Okay, Princess. Now I believe you're more than a pretty face." Etta pushed her golden hair away from her sticky face.

"Don't call me Princess. I may have lived my entire life

behind the high walls of a palace, but I'm not there anymore. I can't be that girl in the pretty dresses who throws knives in secret and hides from the world. My family deserves better than that."

Etta laughed. "We just might make a warrior of you yet, Pr-Helena."

Dell stood but vines crept over his legs, holding him in place. "Stay there, boy," Etta commanded. He gaped at the growing greenery.

"Magic," he whispered. He'd only witnessed Edmund, Mari, and Corban using their powers, and it never shocked him any less.

Etta tilted her head. "We aren't done yet. Now that we know you have the will to fight, I can teach you how. I could have dealt a killing blow at least ten times during your burst of attacks."

Helena seemed to deflate, her unsure eyes seeking his.

"You can do this, Len." He offered her a smile. "I know you can."

She gave him a nod. "No one will ever best me again." She turned to Etta. "I have to be able to protect Kassander. He is all I have left."

"Then let's begin." Etta gestured to the center of the clearing and took up her stance.

THE LAST TIME Dell had ridden a horse, it was just after a fight he'd lost and it had taken everything he had just to stay on the beast. But he'd had Helena to hold on to.

Now, it was just Dell and the open land. When he'd borrowed the horse from Alex, he hadn't had a destination in mind.

Helena and Etta were practicing every evening now, and he left them to another night of sparring and bruises. Len refused to allow Corban to heal them. She'd said she wanted to feel everything, that it made her a better fighter.

But he hated seeing her porcelain skin mottled with stains of blue and purple. He couldn't stand another night of watching the women battle.

He hadn't planned a visit to the lookout post, but he soon found himself on the winding trail through rock and underbrush. Aron sat at the top of the hill outside the small shack. A lilting melody drifted from the miniature guitar in his lap.

He kept his eyes on the horizon where the sun sank beneath the trees.

"Isn't there supposed to be a different watchman at night?" Dell asked.

Startled, Aron's hands stilled on the guitar. "I enjoy this time of night. As soon as the sun disappears, I'll head down to the village. This outpost is useless at night, but the night watch rides through the woods near town until daybreak. They're already out there, I'm guessing."

Dell nodded as he scanned the trees below. "Has there been anything?"

What was he expecting? New word on Quinn? If Aron knew anything, he'd tell Etta and Alex.

The big man sighed. "I wish I had better news for Helena."

Dell had long since lost hope in her reuniting with Quinn. The man was either dead or a traitor to his family.

A commotion below had Dell and Aron both jumping forward to get a better look. Two horses thundered through the forest as if their tails were on fire.

"Dell," Aron said calmly. "You brought your horse?"

Dell nodded.

"I think it'd be a very good idea for you to beat those travelers to the queen and king. One of those riders is wearing Madran red."

Dell didn't hesitate. He sprinted around the shack to where he'd tied Alex's horse and untied the knot before climbing on.

He kicked his heels into the horse's flanks and took off down the now dark path, slowing along treacherous turns and tilting too far to the right in the saddle. For a moment, he didn't know who was in charge – him or the horse. As soon as he reached the bottom of the hill, he nudged the beast into a canter, regaining his balance.

As he neared the village, torches illuminated the night. The few people who still lingered in the streets scrambled out of the way.

When he reached the palace, he slid down, not bothering to tether the horse before pushing inside.

Etta and Alex were the only two present near the fire. Upon seeing Dell's face, Etta sat up from where she'd reclined on her husband's lap.

"Dell, what is it?"

Dell swallowed. "Two riders are making their way through the forest. Aron saw them through the trees. One of them is Madran."

Etta shot to her feet, the mask of a queen firmly in place. "Do not speak to Helena of this. Not until we know who these riders are." She turned to her husband. "Find Edmund. I think he's at the tavern in the village. If he's done drinking his sorrow away, tell him I need him by my side."

She rushed to the door. "Dell, come with me."

He scrambled after her. They walked across the bridge and waited until they heard the sound of horses making their way through the village.

Where were the guards? In fact, he couldn't remember ever seeing Etta with guards. He guessed when loyal magic folk surrounded her, she had enough protection.

As the riders left the cobblestone street of the village, tall grasses sprung from the ground halting their advance. Dell's eyes widened as vines snaked up the horse's flanks.

"Your Majesty," a voice called out. The darkness hid their faces.

Etta froze. "Simon?" She ran forward as the vines and grass receded.

A brawny man with chiseled features slid down to face her. They stared at each other for a long moment.

"What are you doing here, Simon?"

Dell watched in confusion. Who was that man?

The second man dismounted and Dell stepped back. Him, he recognized. Landon Rhodipus. A distant cousin of Helena's who was famous for leading the Madran units in the war against La Dame.

"General?" Etta looked between the two men.

"I am sorry, your Majesty." Landon bowed his head. "But we must intrude on your peace here to speak with you. We've ridden for days, abandoning our posts to be here."

Etta nodded, glancing back at the small palace. "Come inside. It's cold out here." She walked past Dell and the two men followed. "I'll have someone tend to your horses."

"Thank you, your Majesty." Simon inclined his head.

She led them into the great room, walking straight to the table along the far wall where a pitcher of wine sat beside a tray of goblets. She poured one for each of them as they all sat.

"This is Dell Tenyson." She pointed to him.

"Tenyson?" Landon's eyes flicked to his. "Your Majesty,

are you aware that the Tenysons have aided in the takeover of Madra?"

"Yes, General," she snapped. "I will explain his presence once you explain yours. Dell, meet General Landon and Simon, personal guard to the queen of Gaule."

Dell reeled back. His appearance couldn't mean anything good.

"Has something happened to Catrine?" Etta folded her arms across her chest.

"Other than her daughter being held by a usurper?" Simon pinned Etta with a stare.

"It is my understanding that Camille is still in Madra because Catrine has chosen to honor the alliance."

Simon shook his head. "They're using Camille as a pawn."

"It's true," Landon piped in. "Her safety is a bargaining chip Cole Rhodipus is using to bring his brother Quinn home." When Cole stole the crown of Bela, his twin was in Gaule with his army unit. He'd had no role in the takeover and no one knew which side he'd choose.

A new voice entered the room. "Are you saying the queen of Gaule has my brother?"

Dell's eyes snapped to Helena in the doorway. Fire burned in her gaze. The sudden silence from Simon and Landon was answer enough.

HELENA WAITED for someone to voice what she now knew. She'd recognized Landon as soon as she peered into the room. It'd been years since she'd seen her cousin and they'd never been close, but he was still someone from home, someone who'd known her without the mask.

"Helena." Her name slipped from his lips like a prayer as he stood. His eyes widened. "The reports said you were dead." He swallowed thickly. "That everyone was..."

"Dead?" she finished for him. "Tell me, cousin, are you behind Cole? He had the support of the army, your army."

"No, Helena." He took a step toward her.

She stepped back.

"I would never betray your father."

Her father's loyalists weren't much better than Cole's. They still tore the kingdom apart.

But those loyal to her father would be loyal to her.

"I believe you." She wrung her hands together. "Now, tell me where Quinn is."

Simon rubbed a hand across his face. "That is why I came here with Landon."

Landon returned to his seat and nodded. "I heard rebellious rumblings among my troops long before they revolted. By the time Quinn arrived in Gaule, they'd already chosen their sides. The rebels received orders to make haste back to Madra. Their mission was to return Quinn to his twin's side. So, they attacked. Most of the loyalists were killed outright, but I escaped with Quinn. We sought refuge from the queen of Gaule."

Simon scratched his face, exhaustion drawing down the corners of his eyes. "Word reached the new Madran king that his brother was in Gaule. He sent a messenger to inform Queen Catrine should she choose not to return Quinn to his rightful place, her daughter would suffer for it."

"Camille." Helena covered her mouth with her hand. They'd had no choice but to leave Camille in Madra, thinking she'd be safe as long as Cole needed the Gaulean alliance.

Before anyone got another word in, the door burst open, revealing two stumbling men and a third holding them up.

"Found Edmund." Alex grinned. His smile dropped as he took in their companions. "What's going on? Simon, is my mother..."

"She's sitting on the edge of a moral precipice, but otherwise in good health." Simon stood to greet the king.

Confusion flashed across Alex's face as he shoveled both Edmund and Tyson into chairs. "Sorry about these two. They're both going through rough times." He reached out and clasped Simon's hand. "Tell me what I've missed."

Helena wrapped her cloak tighter around her sleeping gown and leaned against the doorway, trying to process everything they'd said. One thought rose above the rest. Quinn was alive.

Ire snaked through her veins and she slapped the door, jolting everyone in the room. "So the Queen of Gaule will send my brother back to Madra?"

"Yes, Princess." Sorrow filled Landon's eyes. "We were welcomed into the palace of Gaule and safe there for about a week before guards came to arrest Quinn and place him in the dungeons. I haven't seen him since."

There was one question she was scared to ask because the answer could break her. But she needed to know. "And Quinn... does he want to go back? To Cole?"

Landon's eyes softened. "He fought with everything he had to keep himself from that fate."

Helena released the breath she'd been holding.

"Was he planning to come to Bela?" Dell asked.

Landon shook his head. "There was nothing for him here. He thinks every member of his family died in Madra."

Etta narrowed her eyes. "Then why are you here?"

Simon took a long drink before setting his goblet down.

"Catrine is facing choices that only lead down a dark path. I will not let her compromise her character."

Helena didn't know the man, but she understood the look in his eyes. He betrayed the queen because he was in love with her.

Edmund lifted his head. "Simon, nice of you to join us."

"Ignore him," Etta said.

Tyson released a snore.

"And him." She sighed.

"What would you have us do?" Alex asked.

"Talk to her." Simon met the king's gaze. "I didn't come to Bela because I need the king and queen's help. I came because I needed Catrine's sons. Quinn isn't scheduled to leave on a Madran ship for another week."

"And if she won't listen?" Dell asked.

Helena kicked away from the doorframe and strode toward them. "Then, we fight. Quinn will not be returning to Madra while I still have breath in my lungs. I'll be ready to leave in the morning."

She slapped the side of Edmund's face. "Wake up, you drunkard."

He startled awake. "What? What's going on?"

"Sleep this off because you're coming with me." She turned to Alex, flicking her eyes between him and Tyson. "Decide which one of this queen's sons can change her mind and prepare to ride." She strode to the door.

"I'm coming too," Dell called after her.

"Of course you are."

Five

Helena slipped into her room and put a hand against her throat. Her pulse hammered against her fingers. What was she doing?

Elation took control, drowning out any doubt. Quinn was alive. Not only that, but he wasn't rushing to join his twin. The two had always had a bond that nothing on the outside could encroach upon—not even her.

A tear slipped down her cheek. She'd felt so alone—even when she'd still had Kassander by her side as well as a handful of others who cared about her. But Quinn... he truly was alone in a dungeon.

A groan came from the bed she shared with Kass and he thrashed.

"No," he said. "You can't take them. Helena!" His eyes shot open, landing on his sister.

Helena rushed to the bed and sat on the edge, pulling Kassander onto her lap. "Shhhh." She stroked his hair. "It's okay. I'm here." For now. She'd have to leave him come dawn.

Kassander's wide eyes lifted to hers. "I dreamed of that night."

She dropped a kiss on his forehead. It wasn't the first time any of them dreamed of burning castles and sword fights in the halls. Every time she saw it, a phantom pain seared up her arm where she'd been stabbed.

"It's over, Kass. We're safe."

"Are we?" It was a question she'd asked herself many times. Would Cole come after them? He thought Helena was dead, but Kass...?

No. She knew with sudden certainty, Kassander wouldn't be harmed. At least not by Cole. Their brother may have hated their parents and despised Estevan, but he'd loved his youngest sibling. She'd seen it. Not everything could have been a lie, could it?

She laid back on the bed with Kassander. "I need to tell you something."

"Hmm?" He turned to bury his face in her shoulder.

"I have to leave tomorrow."

"Where are you going?"

Could she tell him about Quinn? No. By the time he woke, she'd be gone. If she was too late to help Quinn, Kassander would never know. She couldn't bear his disappointment again.

"Just promise me you'll keep yourself out of trouble until I return."

She waited for an answer, but he'd already fallen asleep.

THE SUN HAD BARELY RISEN when Helena saddled her horse. She wasn't comfortable in a saddle, but she supposed she'd learn quickly. There was no other choice.

Edmund grumbled beside her. "It's too early, and my head is killing me."

Helena knew he meant nothing by what he said. He wanted to find Quinn almost as much as she did. He was just Edmund, a complainer.

"Maybe if you hadn't forced so much ale into me," Tyson began, leading a horse up beside them, "We wouldn't feel so rough this morning."

Edmund snorted. "Forced." He narrowed his eyes as he finally took in the beast at Tyson's side. "No. Ty, you go put that horse back right now."

Helena leaned around Edmund to catch sight of Vérité.

Tyson crossed his arms. "Unlike you, Vérité likes me. Etta told me to take him. He can help us."

"He's just a horse," Dell said.

Simon joined them, shaking his head. "You don't know Vérité. He's more than a horse, but he only listens to Etta."

"And me." Tyson sent a glare toward each one of them.

"Fine." Edmund took a step back. "But keep him away from me."

As if he knew they were speaking about him, Vérité lunged for Edmund, snapping his teeth and catching the edge of the blonde man's cloak.

Edmund released a high-pitched squeal and jerked away.

Dell laughed, but Helena didn't join in the hilarity. She only had the mission on her mind. Get to Gaule. Confront the queen. Free her brother. Then take her revenge on Cole.

Landon helped her onto her horse, and she gripped the reins as if her life depended on it. Maybe it did.

The rest of their group mounted up and without a look backward, they left the village behind.

Helena kicked her horse to keep up with the rest, wobbling before righting herself and straightening her spine.

Dell pulled up beside her, a knowing look on his face. "You okay?"

She only nodded, her lips folding in to a grim line.

Sensing her need to not talk, Dell called up to Tyson. "How'd you get stuck with this mission instead of your brother?"

Ty shrugged. "Alex is king in Bela now. Plus, mother is more likely to listen to me. Alex and Camille have had a... tough relationship. Mother wouldn't take anything he says about Camille to heart. Me, on the other hand, I love my sister. I also love my mother and know she doesn't hand innocent people over. We will help Camille, but not this way."

For the first time, Helena considered how hard it must be to hold the title of prince in two kingdoms. It had been difficult for her to be a princess of one.

But she didn't think for one second that a queen could be swayed simply by talk. Not one who was said to be as strong as Catrine. What would it really take to free Quinn?

Landon rode beside her, looking as though he was trying to find something to say. "We'll reach the border by sundown tomorrow."

Helena only nodded.

"Is it true?" he finally blurted.

She turned to pierce him with her gaze. "Is what true?"

"The young prince Kassander. He lives as well? I heard rumors at the palace."

She faced forward once again. "He does. He was sleeping when you arrived."

A smile spread across Landon's face. "That's good. Really really good."

"Estevan is still dead." Her voice held no emotion.

"Yes." He ducked his head. "I had heard that."

"And Cole doesn't have long to live."

His brow furrowed at that, but he nodded.

"Two brothers dead or traitor," she continued. "One

imprisoned. One a child. Do you believe in vengeance, General?"

"I do."

"What about killing one's own family?"

He shifted his eyes away from her and didn't answer.

Dell met her gaze with worry, but didn't speak.

Weariness seeped into her bones by the time they stopped for the night. She dismounted, an ache creeping up her spine. She stumbled as she tried to walk after spending all day atop a horse.

Dell gripped her arm. "You'll get used to it."

She shrugged and freed her pack tied to the saddle before walking away.

Simon and Landon got a fire started. Tyson passed around a tin of the dried meat Etta had sent.

"Quinn should have chosen a better time of year to get imprisoned," Edmund said, pulling his cloak over his mouth.

Tyson shoved him. "You can't make jokes, asshole."

It was a side Helena hadn't known of Edmund. Flippant and uncaring. In the year she'd known him, he'd always had a joke in him, but it wasn't like this. Had the loss of Stev stolen the man he'd become?

She shook her head and lowered herself onto the bedroll she'd laid out, pulling the wool blanket up to her chin. The nighttime chill seeped through the cover and she scooted closer to the fire than was safe. She wasn't the only one.

A faint breeze suddenly stopped, throwing them into utter stillness. At least Edmund still had his magic.

Without the wind, the cold grew more bearable.

The men chatted as Helena let her eyelids droop. Tomorrow night she'd reach Gaule.

I'm coming Quinn.

SOMETHING BRUSHED HELENA'S ARM, jolting her awake. Her eyes snapped open to find Dell hovering over her.

"What are you doing?" She pushed the blanket off to sit up.

He sat back on his heels and scratched his cheek. "You were shivering. I... uh..."

It was only then she noticed there hadn't only been one blanket covering her. Both now lay crumpled to the side. "You were giving me your blanket?"

He shrugged, suddenly at a loss for words. That wasn't like him.

"Dell..." Whatever she'd wanted to say, something else left her mouth. "I don't need you to take care of me."

His jaw clenched. "You've made that rather clear." He stood and stalked away.

Helena kicked off the rest of the blankets and jumped up to run after him. "Dell, wait."

He turned so quickly, she collided with him. "For what, Len?"

"I'm sorry."

He pushed out a breath and dipped his head to meet her gaze. "You have nothing to be sorry for. Come here." He pulled her against him and wrapped his arms around her. "I'm only here because of you, Len. You may not need me, but that doesn't mean I'm going anywhere."

She pulled away. "What do you mean you're here because of me? You had to run from Madra for your own safety as well as mine."

He ran a hand through his hair and looked to the sky. "Do you know why I defied my brothers to help Edmund?"

"Because you trusted Edmund."

"I did... but Len, I became a spy. I risked everything... that's not something you do just because someone you respect asks you to."

"Then why?"

He lowered his gaze until it settled on her once more. "I knew what would happen to those inside the palace if a rebellion broke out."

"But you didn't know I was the princess." It couldn't have been all for her.

"No. I thought you were the prince's mistress."

Embarrassment flushed through her. "And you still wanted to save me?"

The rough pad of his thumb scraped across her cheek. "From the moment I met you, it didn't matter who you were behind the palace walls. When you were with me, you were Len. I never stopped thinking about you."

He rested his forehead against hers.

Helena's heart lurched at his touch. She wanted more than anything to give in to the emotions swirling inside her.

"Do you ever wish we could go back to the ball?" she whispered. "To when you realized who I was and no one else existed but us?"

"Every day... without our families imprisoning us beforehand."

She closed her eyes, a tear escaping. Life behind the mask seemed like so long ago, yet she found herself missing it. Days spent with her mother. Nights spent joking with her brothers. She hadn't needed the rest of the world. She'd had them.

For a short time, Dell had given her everything they couldn't. He'd shown her what kind of life she could have had. One of adventure... one of love.

"Helena," he breathed. "I-"

He leaned in, his lips brushing hers.

"We can't." She pulled away. "That's the problem, Dell. We can't go back. Those people don't exist anymore. If I'm going to do what needs to be done, I need to forget about the girl I was." She stepped out of his arms.

He let them drop to his sides. "Len, don't do this. Don't let the anger consume you."

"Didn't you listen to anything Etta said? That's how I'm going to fight."

Six

Rain enveloped the group on the second day's ride. Dell pushed wet hair from his face and kept his eyes trained on Helena's back. She was wrong. Anger wasn't the only way to fight. He'd heard everything Etta taught Len, but didn't think anger was the point of her lessons.

"Ty," Edmund barked. "Aren't you going to do something about this?" He glanced to the sky as another deluge struck them.

"Oh." Tyson shrugged. "I guess I could."

Dell startled as the rain stopped. No, it didn't stop. The patter of it hitting the ground still sounded around them but it was as if the water bent out from where they rode. Like a shield had been placed around the group.

Helena gasped moments before Dell too felt the water drain from his clothing.

"Are you doing this?" he asked the young prince.

Landon cursed and looked around wildly. "You Belaens," he grumbled.

Tyson shrugged. "I can be useful sometimes."

What did that mean? Tyson's power with water was the coolest thing Dell had seen in Bela.

Edmund shifted in his saddle. "Ty... of course you're useful."

Tyson looked down at his hands. "Nah, it's okay. I know my role in Bela and in Gaule. I'm the messenger. Belonging to neither kingdom wholly. You haven't been here the last year Edmund. After..."

"You left Amalie," Edmund finished.

"Yeah, that. I spend most of my time on the road. Don't worry though; I'm the best person to navigate Gaule. That's something I can do."

"Navigate Gaule?" Dell looked between the two men.

Tyson sighed, but it was Simon who answered. "Gaule has become a treacherous place, lad."

Helena slowed her horse to move beside Dell. "No. I've studied Gaule with my palace tutors. It was a place of peace for many years."

Simon fixed his stare on her. "It was a false peace, but that isn't something they'd teach in Madra. Gaule hunted down those with magic within their borders for many years. For non-magic folk, they had peace, yes. But it came at a cost."

"And then Alex happened." Tyson rubbed his eyes as if it hurt his head to think of this.

"What did Alex do?" Dell flicked his eyes between each of those present.

Simon grimaced. "Nothing that should have cost him his throne. He wanted to halt the persecution. Many of the nobles acted out of fear and didn't stand behind their king when the common folk rebelled. His own council took the crown from atop his head."

"A council can't do that," Helena scoffed. "The only ones with the power to remove my father were the priests."

"There are no priests in Gaule. The council and king ruled in conjunction with each other. They realized the people would never end their rebellions with Alexandre as their king. He was a magic lover."

"Darn right." Tyson crossed his arms.

"Wait." Dell couldn't fathom how this could happen. "Queen Catrine took the crown from her own son?"

"Alex let her." Tyson's voice held a defensive note. "This was at the same time Etta was marching to war against La Dame. Alex needed to join that fight and he never could have when his duty lay with Gaule."

"Did Catrine's coronation quell the rebellion?" Helena asked.

Dell wondered if she was thinking of the rebellion in her own kingdom. That too resulted in a new ruler.

Simon blew out a breath. "We'd hoped it would, but the kingdom was already divided. There are still many who are loyal to the queen, but others continue to sow unrest. Years of rebellions have resulted in food shortages, only adding to the unease."

"That's why she needs the Madran alliance," Helena breathed. "My father said we promised her troops."

Tyson grit his teeth. "And it is the only reason my sister would agree to marriage in a foreign kingdom."

"They won't release Quinn." She gripped her reins, speaking only to Dell this time.

Dell couldn't negate the truth in her words. If Gaule needed Madra why would the queen risk the alliance to release a single man?

Simon, overhearing Len's words, brushed a hand over his

head nervously. "You don't know Catrine. She does the right thing no matter the cost. Her integrity is below none. That is why I came to Bela. There has to be another way. Gaule cannot be beholden to a king who killed his own family to take the throne."

Helena flinched. Dell reached out to grip her hand in reassurance, but she nudged her horse to widen the gap between them.

He pressed his lips together.

Tyson looked to them. "Simon is right. This is bigger than handing one man over to Madra. Once mother does this, what's next? Will they hold Camille's safety over us always?"

They sank into silence, considering the implications of those words.

After a while, the rain disappeared and Tyson released his magic, slumping in his saddle from the effort.

The sun sank on the horizon as Simon stopped. "If we go much farther, we'll be crossing into Gaule and I prefer not to do that in the dark of night."

Edmund gazed at the expanse before them. A valley stretched into the night, white coating the grasses. "Snow. We don't get much of that in Bela." A smile slid across his face. "Could we not ride to the Moreau estate? It can't be far and a soft bed sounds nice right about now."

Dell didn't miss the stricken looks flashing across both Tyson and Simon's faces.

"Edmund," Tyson began. "I keep forgetting you've been in Madra with little news of home."

"Only what the traders brought us."

Tyson nodded. "Duchess Moreau lost her lands soon after you left for Madra."

Edmund's eyes widened. "How?"

"Duke Ferenz has built quite a force. He laid siege to the great house. You've been there. It's built for fighting since it sits close to the borders of both Bela and Dracon. But they stood no chance. The duke's men ravaged her villages. We won't find friends there."

Edmund sat back in his saddle, stunned. "And the duchess?"

"Safe. She now resides at the palace full-time."

He blew out a relieved breath.

Dell didn't know the people they spoke of, but their grave expressions said enough. Gaule would not be friendly territory.

HELENA PATTED the sword sheathed beneath her saddle before climbing on, pride blooming within her for doing it without aid.

She'd slept fitfully through the night, unable to rid her mind of Gaule's tragic story. A people torn apart by something as simple as magic. In Madra, the few with magic were feared. Most of them took ship to Bela as soon as word of Persinette's return reached their shores. Some stayed for various reasons.

But she didn't know if they'd been hated. It was just one of the many things she didn't know of her kingdom. How long had the Madran rebellion been brewing? Did the people support it? Had they loved her father or brother at all?

They didn't see the first village until they crested the rise of the valley.

A watchtower stood tall with the black mark of fire stretching up its stones.

The wall surrounding it had crumbled in many places. They led their horses through the deserted streets. Food and personal items scattered along the cobblestones as if a mass of people left in a hurry.

"The duke's army is camped near here." Landon took the lead. "We must hurry and be off the Moreau lands quickly. There's a Madran force patrolling the zone between here and the palace. Once we leave this village, we'll no longer be able to stick to the road. The forest paths are treacherous for horses so keep an eye out."

He barely got the words out before something slammed into Helena, knocking her from her horse.

"Len!" Dell yelled, but he couldn't get to her because in that moment, a dozen riders appeared from the alleyways.

Helena shoved at the man who'd overtaken her. He grappled for her wrists, and she twisted beneath him.

She caught sight of his crimson uniform. Madrans. Rebels. Ire zipped along her skin until all she saw was an enemy trying to subdue her. She slammed her knee up, catching him in the groin. His hands on her loosened just enough for her to yank one free and pull the knife from where she always kept it in her bodice. With one jerk of her hand, he fell over sideways.

She scrambled to her feet, pulling her knife free, and prepared to face the next attacker. A woman ran for her and Helena ducked the slice of her sword. She looked for her horse to retrieve her own sword, but the animal was gone.

Blasted beast.

Tyson reared up on Vérité as the horse kicked his legs out at his attacker's horse. It was as if the animal thought he too was part of the fight.

Helena turned once again to face the woman who came after her. She judged the distance between them, calming her breath before hurling her knife with deadly accuracy. It struck the woman between the eyes. She toppled from her steed, and the horse ran off.

A ringing sounded in Helena's ears as the fight died down around her. The Madrans had been no match for the smaller but more skilled group they attacked.

She stumbled back. The last time she'd been in a fight... images played in her mind. Fire. Estevan. She shook her head, trying to free herself from the grip of the past. Would she have to do this again and again to secure the throne? Kill?

Dell jumped from his horse and sprinted toward her. "Len, you okay?" He gripped her shoulders, eyeing her up and down as if looking for injuries.

"We need to get away from here." Simon grunted.

Dell dipped his head to peer into her eyes. "Len, look at me."

The scene came into focus again.

"You okay?" Dell asked once more.

She shrugged him off and retrieved her knife from the dead woman as coldness seeped into her. "Fine." Wiping her blade on her pant-leg, she rejoined the others. "They were Madran."

"Deserters, Princess." Landon's lips tugged down. "The turmoil within the troops gave many a chance to break away. Bands of deserters now travel the roads, no better than ordinary robbers."

"Why haven't they returned to Madra?"

"How, Princess?" Landon shook his head. "They have nothing, no money for ship's passage. Madran troops are sent to foreign countries with no knowledge of when they'll return home. They enlist under the promise of food for their families. But your father and his wars... He kept many of them in war zones for years."

Helena glanced at the dead men littering the street. She

used to wonder what could drive a person to kill, to rob. But they hadn't one day woken up and just decided to live their life that way. Circumstances, many of them created by her father, turned people into who they became.

How had she lived her life blind to her father's faults? He'd failed his people. Cole hadn't been wrong in believing he no longer deserved to be king.

She could forgive her brother for wanting the crown.

But her mother? Estevan? No, those were the deaths he had to pay for.

Once outside Moreau territory, they were on land owned by the Gaulean crown and patrolled by the Madran force.

Branches whipped Helena in the face as she rode across the snow dusted forest floor.

Each day, they drew nearer to the palace. What was she going to say to the queen to make her see?

Uncertainty curled her stomach, but it was Quinn. She couldn't let him down.

THE WALLS of the palace of Gaule were grander than any Helena had seen. They loomed above her, brushing the sky.

Simon rode toward the small gatehouse that looked newly constructed. He spoke with the guards in a low tone.

Edmund's eyes never left the gates. "Last time I was here, Etta blew these gates apart."

Helena's eyes widened. "She has such power?"

"Not anymore." He tore his eyes away. "There was a time when Etta held all the power of her ancestors. She destroyed her own magic to best La Dame. Now she only had that which she was born with. The power to make things grow."

Dell scratched the back of his head. "It would have been

amazing to be there for the battle of Dracon. To see that kind of magic."

A new man emerged from the gatehouse and Edmund turned his horse away from them. "Be glad you weren't." With that final word, he dismounted.

An older guard in a crisp blue uniform approached.

"Father." Helena had never heard such ice in Edmund's tone.

So, this was the man who'd scorned Edmund his entire life. Helena scanned his stern face, instantly disliking him.

"You shouldn't be in Gaule," the man stated. "It isn't safe for your kind even if the queen supports you."

Edmund shrugged. "It's never been safe for me, has it? We must see the queen."

As if noticing them for the first time, Edmund's father surveyed their group with a scowl.

Simon returned. "Anders." He held out his hand. "I bring important guests."

Anders refused to shake his hand. "You abandoned your post, Simon. I should have you thrown in a cell."

"Anders, I have been and always will do what is best for the queen."

The man sighed. "I know. She has been in a rather bad mood since you left. She'll be glad to see you safe at least. Come. She has already retired to her rooms for the night, but she'll want to see you straight away. Your guests can have their audience tomorrow."

Helena opened her mouth to protest, but Simon held up a hand.

"Has the Madran ship arrived yet?"

Anders nodded. "This afternoon. It's anchored outside the cove. They're scheduled to leave in the morning with the prince."

Each word stabbed into Helena's heart. Tomorrow. They were almost too late.

The gates opened, their gears sending a screech into the night.

Simon hesitated for a moment. "Then our guests cannot wait. They must see the queen now."

Anders didn't stop them as they rode straight through into a town with rows of homes and shops along cobblestone streets. In the distance was another high wall separating the palace from this outer part.

Growing up in a Madran city, the villages of Gaule and Bela seemed small in comparison. She didn't understand how their population could live so spread out.

At the stables, two lads took their horses.

They walked through the open inner gates into a courtyard. The steps up to the palace entryway stood at the far end, arches guiding the way. Torches stood on either side of the doors. Guards nodded to Simon, not stopping him to question those with him.

She didn't know what she'd been expecting after the humble palace of Bela, but it wasn't the ancient splendor surrounding them now.

They walked across the marble floor, turning many corners until she wasn't sure she'd be able to find her way out. Her heart beat faster the closer they got to the queen's quarters. This was it. Her moment to save the one member of her family she could. Yet, she didn't know what she would say.

They stopped outside a carved mahogany door. Simon paid no attention to the guards stationed there, and they didn't hold him back. He knocked and waited.

"Enter," a voice called.

One of the guards pushed open the door revealing a lush, velvet-carpeted suite.

A tall woman with dark hair and clear eyes appeared. Her brow furrowed, and she crossed her arms over her chest. "Simon."

"Your Majesty." He bowed.

"That's it?" Her voice rose an octave. "That's all I get? Your Majesty?"

"Mother." Tyson pushed past Simon and she saw they weren't alone for the first time.

"Ty?" She softened. "I wasn't expecting to see you until winter left us." She held her arms out, and he sank into her embrace.

Helena averted her gaze, tears burning at the back of her eyes. She'd give anything for her own mother to hold her like that again.

The queen looked to the rest. "Edmund?" She released Tyson. "Oh, dear boy. It's been years."

Edmund received a hug as warm as Tyson's. He buried his face in the queen's shoulder and his back shook as if the woman broke through every wall he'd built with one embrace. She pulled back.

"Edmund." She tilted his chin so he'd look at her. "I was worried about you when the news out of Madra reached us. Are you..."

"Okay?" A tear slid down his cheek and he pulled away. "I..." He shook his head as if deciding against telling her. "We're here for a reason. No matter how much I've missed you, that is not why I've come."

Catrine's queenly mask returned, and she gestured them into the room, eying the strangers.

"Landon," she greeted him. "I did not think we'd see you again."

"Your Majesty." He had nothing else to say to her.

Catrine spoke to the guards at her door. "Find someone

to fetch us some tea."

"Wine," Edmund corrected. "We will need wine."

Catrine's voice hardened. "Tea."

"Yes, your Majesty." The guard disappeared and Catrine shut the door before turning toward the sitting room.

Two long couches faced each other in front of a crackling fireplace.

"Sit," she said. "Please. Then you can tell me who you have brought to my kingdom, Tyson."

Tyson swallowed thickly as he took his seat.

Helena remained standing. She faced the queen. "I am Helena, Princess of Madra."

Queen Catrine's only reaction was to raise an eyebrow. "Well, I certainly wasn't expecting that. Seems we may need that wine after all."

"Told you," Edmund grumbled.

"We don't have time for drinks or pleasantries." All uncertainties from moments before faded away, and Helena knew everything she needed to convey. She lifted her chin, peering into Catrine's hard eyes.

"No." Catrine crossed her arms. "That is my answer to you. You've come about my prisoner."

"My brother," Helena growled. "You will release him to me."

"I'm sorry." The queen averted her gaze and stepped around Helena to sink onto the couch beside Tyson. "I can't do that. My daughter is at stake. My kingdom's alliance."

Helena turned to face her once more and opened her mouth to speak, but Simon cut in.

"And what then? We hand over an innocent man to the usurper and he comes back to us asking for more next time. Camille will never be safe while she's there. You're putting all of Gaule at risk."

"Their troops," she said. "We need them. I cannot continue to hold back the rebels on my own. Etta refuses to send help, so what am I to do?"

"Mother." Tyson gripped her hand. "Etta can't send magic folk into Gaule. Even if she tried, her people would refuse, and she'd let them. They will not come to the aid of the kingdom that persecuted them."

The queen breathed out slowly. "I know. It is why I cannot release the prince. I'm sorry you have come this far. Madra is my only hope."

"Then you will fall just as my father did." Helena strode to the door and left them staring after her.

Seven

The palace of Gaule was foreign to Helena, yet so familiar. Servants bustled by, preparing for the next morning's duties. Guards watched her, always aware of the stranger in their midst.

She'd felt someone following her as she left the royal wing and knew who it was without turning around.

"They sent you after me?" She said, not stopping.

Dell appeared from the shadows. "You shouldn't have left."

"I said what I came to say. She spoke her own words. I've lived my life around people who make decisions in a kingdom and I can read the signs of a lost cause. We all needed a moment to breathe."

"Len." He gripped her arm to halt her steps.

"We have to get him, Dell." She turned, conscious of the eyes on her.

Heavy steps thudded down the hall and Edmund's grim face appeared. "Not here." He brushed past them, turning the corner into another hall. It came to a stop at a door that led into a practice yard. Wooden targets stood on one end, but no archers or swordsmen practiced at the late hour.

"There won't be any unwelcome ears out here." Edmund turned to them. "Tyson will continue to speak with the queen. That's why we needed him. We probably won't see him until the morning so we need to go to our second plan."

Helena's shoulders relaxed. She should have known Edmund wouldn't rely on only talk to save her brother. He'd do what it took... even if it meant betraying a queen who was obviously like a mother to him.

Edmund scanned the surrounding area before settling back on Helena. "If the Madran ship has already arrived, we need to prepare ourselves for the possibility that there are Madrans staying at the palace."

"Would the queen tell us of this?" Dell asked.

Edmund's shoulders rose in a half shrug. "Catrine keeps her secrets. She would not want unrest within these walls. We're no longer in Bela where the people trust their queen, nor Madra where the king has immense power. Ruling Gaule is like sitting on the edge of a knife. Many people see Catrine as having stolen the crown from Alexandre, but she saved him from this fate."

Helena felt for the woman sitting in those lavish rooms. She knew what it was to feel caged by circumstances. But that didn't mean Helena wouldn't fight her with every breath she took.

She hardened her jaw. "It doesn't matter what good she's done. She has Quinn. Tell me, Edmund, are you on my side or on hers?"

Edmund closed his eyes, shielding her from the war raging in their depths. "Catrine has always taken care of me as if I were her own." His lids slid open, allowing Helena a glimpse into the pain behind his words. "But she's wrong now. And I have to do this. I have to protect you, protect your brothers."

"For Estevan?" she whispered.

He shook his head. "For you. You're my family as much as Catrine... as much as her sons."

Helena held back the emotions threatening to spill forth. She wasn't the girl who could break down anymore. Not when so much was at stake.

Dell stepped forward. "What do we do?"

"Ask him." Edmund gestured behind them.

Helena and Dell turned to see who had arrived. Reed stood near the doorway listening to their hushed conversation.

Dell reached for his sword instinctively, forgetting they'd been disarmed before being allowed into the palace. Helena felt the weight of her hidden knife, secret within the fabric of her dress. She didn't want to pull it, but if he made a move, she wouldn't hesitate.

Reed threw his hands in the air seconds before Dell ran at him, slamming him up against the wall. He pressed his arm to Reed's throat. "He heard everything. We can't just let him go."

Reed coughed. "If you release me," he rasped, "I have information you want to know."

"Dell." Edmund clamped a hand on Dell's shoulder.

Dell ripped his arm back and stalked to the other end of the training yard before returning. "Okay, brother, what do you have to tell us? Speak before I ask Helena here to slit your throat with the knife I know she has hidden somewhere."

Reed's eyes widened, and Edmund cursed.

Helena turned to hide her face.

"Princess?" Reed hadn't ever seen her without the mask.

If it hadn't been for Dell's blathering tongue, he wouldn't know she stood before him. "They said you died."

She turned to face him and her lip curled up. "They said a lot of things. Like that they were loyal to their king. Or that they loved their kingdom. Lies. Believe nothing that comes out of a rebel's mouth."

Reed pushed himself off the wall. He approached Helena, but Dell stepped in his path. "What are you doing in Gaule, Reed?"

"The king sent me to fetch his brother. He trusts no one besides me and Ian. And well, Ian never leaves his side."

"The king," Helena scoffed. "The king is dead."

"Look." Reed rubbed a hand across his face. "I saw you arrive today and have been following you since. I'm probably not the only one who saw. Luckily, the rest of Cole's men who are with me would only recognize Edmund." He faced Dell. "As soon as I saw you... we didn't know if you'd made it out or where you've been since."

"I'm surprised you cared," Dell bit out.

"I didn't." The statement shocked Helena, but Dell didn't even flinch. "But Cole... Madra is suffering. Bela refuses to trade with us and Gaule has nothing of value such as food."

Helena glanced at Edmund. "Did you know Etta cut ties to Madra?"

"No." He looked just as dumbfounded as her. The Belaen queen wouldn't send forces in to help, but she'd bleed them dry. Bela had rich farmlands helped by magic. Since regaining their kingdom, they provided much of the food to the six kingdoms.

But this wasn't Cole suffering. It was the people. Helena's people. They were hungry before. Now...

Reed went on. "Cole has grown paranoid that someone will try to take his throne. It's why he sent me to retrieve

Quinn. Even if the brothers don't agree on this now, Cole thinks his twin is the only person he can trust."

"Camille." Edmund clenched his jaw. "Is she..."

"She's fine." Reed averted his eyes. "For now. Cole hasn't been the same since the day he took the crown." He fixed Helena with a stare. "He blames himself for your death, and it's the one thing in all of this that's eating him from the inside out."

Helena didn't believe Reed's words. In order for him to feel guilty, Cole had to have a heart, and she knew now that was the one thing he lacked. A brilliant mind. An iron will. He could have made a good king if he possessed the final piece.

"Cole is not my concern tonight," she bit out. "Tell me of Quinn."

Reed rubbed a spot on his head. "We're set to leave tomorrow on the morning tide."

"Can we break him free of the dungeons tonight?" Dell's eyes bounced excitedly as if about to embark on some grand adventure.

Edmund brought him back to reality. "No. I've spent a considerable amount of time in those dungeons. I've even escaped them once with Etta. But they've been fortified since then as have the top of the walls. Do you see this?" He pointed to rows of spiked wire lining the walls stretching around the palace. "There's no way out of the inner palace now if they don't want you to leave. It's late, so they have shut the inner walls. They'll reopen at daybreak but will be heavily guarded."

Helena studied Edmund for a moment before her eyes rested on a rack of arrows behind him. "How are you with a bow?"

His brow rose as if not expecting the question. "Decent."

Skepticism rang strong in his voice. "But if whatever plan is formulating in your mind hinges on accuracy, you'll want Tyson's aid."

"Will he defy his mother and risk his sister?"

Edmund nodded reluctantly. "Ty will always do what he thinks is right. Gaule is his kingdom. If Camille becomes Queen of Madra, Tyson rises to heir of Gaule. If he believes this Madran alliance will plunge Gaule into further trouble, he will stop it."

Helena faced Reed. "I don't trust you Reed Tenyson, but I'm short on allies, and I know what you did for us in Madra. You helped Dell protect Kassander. For that alone, I will not kill you. But I will let Tyson shoot you."

"WE CAN'T TRUST HIM." Dell pulled Helena away as Edmund kept his eyes trained on Reed.

"I know that." She turned her back on him and put her hands on her head. "But tell me another way, Dell. Please, tell me how we're going to save Quinn without his help."

When she turned to face him again, the first emotion he'd seen in her other than anger since they began this journey broke through. Her eyes shone, but she didn't let a single tear fall.

Without thinking, he pulled her into a hug. She stiffened for a moment before relaxing into his arms.

"Dell," she whispered. "Reed is the one who told Edmund where Ian trapped you." She tipped her head back to look up at him. "I know you want to think of both your brothers as evil creatures, but without him, you wouldn't have been able to come to our aid in the rebellion. Without him, I'd be dead."

Dell blew out a breath as the truth of her words hit him. His eyes roamed her face, and his hand came up to cup the back of her head. When he thought of that night and what almost happened, he couldn't breathe.

Helena had made it clear where things stood between them, and he would abide by her wishes. But he'd never lose the feeling she'd struck in him since that day at the beach when they had escaped the demands of their lives.

He hadn't known the true extent of everything she ran from that day, but for him... his brothers. His step-mother. His life.

But that was no longer Dell's life. She'd changed his fate. It now lay here, in a foreign kingdom, with her.

He released her with a nod. "Okay, but we have to take precautions."

"Agreed." He followed her back to where Edmund and Reed stood in an uncomfortable stand-off. Despite his help, Reed still worked for Cole.

Helena crossed her arms, eying their temporary ally. "Tell me everything. Your entire plan to get Quinn to the ship."

Reed rubbed his jaw. "There are tunnels."

Edmund let loose with a string of curses.

"Care to share?" Dell asked.

"Queen Catrine showed them the tunnels." He rubbed his eyes as if he couldn't believe it. "She's so bent on this Madran alliance, she's giving away the kingdom's secrets."

On some level, Dell understood the queen's thinking. A usurper king held her daughter captive and signing his treaty was the only means to save her daughter. It seemed so simple. Trade one man for the princess' safety. But he also understood why Simon had come for them. Why Etta had sent them. Why even Tyson didn't want to trade for Camille.

What would be next? Would Gaule lose itself to Madra piece by piece? This was no longer about Quinn Rhodipus.

Reed clasped his hands behind his back. "We don't want Quinn to be seen making his way to the cove where our ship is anchored. We'll extract him from the dungeons and take him through the tunnels that lead to the sea. There, we will row out to the ship."

Helena bit her lip, lost in concentration. Dell watched her consider Reed. He could practically see her mind working.

How had she only been an ornamental princess? Madra would have been better off with Princess Helena on the council rather than as the traditional head of merchants after her marriage.

Helena stepped forward, scanning Reed from head to toe. She tapped his leg while glancing at Edmund over her shoulder. "If he takes an arrow here, will he bleed out before he can get to the ship?"

Reed froze.

Edmund considered the question. "He should be fine." He directed his next words to Reed. "Just don't remove the arrow. Do you have a doctor on that ship?"

Reed nodded, taking a step back. "You want to put an arrow in my leg?"

"How else would we rescue Quinn without raising suspicion?" Helena lifted her eyes to his. "Are there fighting men on your ship?"

"Only a handful. There are two men here with me in the palace."

"Do you care if they're killed?" Her voice held no emotion, only a cold logical tone.

Dell's jaw fell open.

Reed straightened. "They're loyal to your brother."

"Were they there that night?"

Everyone knew which night she spoke of. The rebellion.

Reed's silence was answer enough.

Helena clenched her fist, but didn't speak again before the door to the courtyard opened and Tyson appeared, a grim set to his mouth. He didn't bother to ask who Reed was because his gaze locked onto Helena.

Helena rushed to him. "Have you made any progress?"

His eyes dropped, giving them the answer.

"I'm sorry," he said. "I will continue to try."

Helena's eyes hardened, glowing in the torchlight. "You have to know, Tyson... we're going to keep Quinn from getting onto that ship no matter your mother's decision."

He nodded as if he expected no less. "I convinced my mother to allow you to visit the dungeons."

Helena froze, her words choking her on the way out. "I can see him?"

Eight

A row of guards stood at attention at the bottom of the narrow dungeon staircase. The first thing Helena noticed was that each cell had some poor soul trapped inside. Did Gaule have this many criminals? Maybe they were rebels.

Their harsh screams and moans sent a shiver down her spine as she sidestepped the arms reaching out for her.

How could Quinn be in a place such as this? Her sweet brother, the best of them all. And this was his fate? Sorrow churned within her, turning over and over until it hardened into anger chilling her heart.

This too was Cole's fault.

"There was a time," Edmund whispered, "When these cells stood mostly empty. But Gaule has changed."

Helena wasn't interested in hearing of Gaule's past. She scanned each face she passed until the guard leading them through the dank passageway stopped in front of a set of rusted iron bars. He took a knife from his belt and slammed it against the metal, jolting the man inside.

"Oy, Prince." The guard sneered. "Seems like someone came to say goodbye."

Quinn lifted his bruised face and Helena sucked in a breath. His hazy eyes drifted over her, and she wasn't sure he truly saw her. The beginnings of a beard coated his sharp jaw, giving him a darker look than she was used to. But it was still him. She stepped back, for a moment feeling as if Cole sat in front of her with his identical looks.

Not Cole, she told herself. *He's not here.* The fear subsiding, she sank to her knees on the dirt-covered floor to get closer.

Quinn's eyes cleared, and he shook his head as his gaze locked onto her. He mouthed her name, not making a sound.

She nodded.

Ignoring the presence of the guard, Edmund, and Dell, Quinn scooted across the cell on his butt. "Helena." His voice sounded as if he hadn't used it in days.

"I'm here." A tear tracked down her face, and she reached through the bars.

His eyes widened, and he gulped back a sob. "You're dead."

She shook her head; dark curls falling loose from her low tail. "I'm here," she repeated.

Her strong brother shook as sobs wracked his body. He buried his face in his hands. "I thought..." He couldn't get the words out. "I thought it was just me. And Cole..."

"Don't speak his name," she said, hardening her jaw. "He is no longer our family."

He lifted his glassy eyes to her. "You found me?"

She nodded.

"You came for me?"

She reached farther into the cell, needing to touch him.

He squeezed her hand as if still not quite believing she was real.

"I was so scared that in the end..." He sucked in a breath. "That you died thinking I betrayed you along with Cole."

She wiped a tear from her face. "No, Quinn. I know you. I know what's inside of you. You loved us... you loved them."

"Father." He shook. "Mother. Stev. Kassander—"

"No." She squeezed his hand to stop him. "Kass is alive."

It was as if a light entered his eyes. "Both of you? I never imagined. Where is he?"

"Waiting for us in Bela."

"Us? They tell me the queen has agreed to allow the Madrans to take me."

"We have a plan, Quinn." She gestured to Edmund and Dell.

"Did you help her?" Quinn asked Edmund.

Edmund shook his head and jabbed a thumb toward Dell. "It was all him."

Color rose in Dell's cheeks as Quinn climbed to his feet, legs wobbling beneath him. He stuck his hand through the bars.

Dell took it. "Helena was hurt. I wouldn't have left her behind. If she hadn't been injured, she'd have saved us all."

"I know." Quinn's eyes bore into Dell for a moment longer before he released him.

"Quinn." Helena regained his attention. "Tomorrow, when you hear someone yell your name, duck."

"Be careful, Lenny." He leaned his head against the bars. "I can't lose you again."

SHE HAD HIM BACK. Before seeing Quinn in person, the idea of him still existing was like a dream. She'd waited for so long to just hear him say her name, but the dream didn't even compare to reality.

The palace of Gaule was a contradiction. The people treated their group as unwelcome guests. The queen planned to send Helena's brother to her enemy. Yet, they'd been given lavish rooms. Servants had brought trays of cheeses and meats along with pitchers of burgundy wine stronger than any offered in Madra.

So much for Gaule being a starving kingdom.

But this was how it always was, wasn't it? The average person went hungry while those higher up feasted. She'd lived her life on one side, always having more than enough food. Always receiving the best of the trade from neighboring kingdoms.

Locked inside her castle, she hadn't known it could be any other way.

But now she saw it in the faces of the men who'd tried to rob them. She heard stories of the rebels who only wanted to eat.

Her mask no longer shielded her from the world.

And it was terrifying.

She rolled over in the four-poster bed that could have fit three people. Plush white blankets insulated her from the cold many of the Gaulean children would experience that night.

Overhead, a deep purple canopy hid the window from view. She pushed back the curtains and sat up to gaze down upon the sleeping castle. Her room looked out on the outer castle. The people who lived there were the lucky ones. The crown took care of them.

But what about the rest?

What about people like Quinn who were nothing but pawns to those with power? Who took care of them?

She let her legs hang over the bed, her bare feet grazing the soft white carpet. Before bed, a palace servant had brought water for her to bathe and provided her with a silk, pink sleeping gown. She hadn't experienced such luxury since leaving Madra.

Back then, she'd expected it. She was a princess.

Now, it irritated her.

She slipped her hand under the pillow where she'd stashed a knife. Having it nearby gave her some sense of strength. But if they came under attack, she'd be no use against a host of well-trained guards.

Would the Gauleans give her up? If Cole found out she still lived and that his supposed allies were harboring her...

She tossed the knife into the air, catching the hilt with her other hand before throwing it toward the door. It started to open moments before the knife stuck into the intricate woodwork.

Dell froze. "Was that meant for me?"

Helena shrugged and stood from the bed. The sleeping gown only reached the tops of her thighs and she tried to pull it down as Dell's gaze slid over her. A blush stained his cheeks, reaching all the way to the tips of his ears.

"Thanks for knocking." Sarcasm dripped from her words.

He didn't take the bait. "I had an idea."

"It's the middle of the night." She gestured to where silver moonlight filtered in through the window.

"Yet, you're up throwing knives about the room."

She walked to the table in the sitting area where two pitchers sat. Pouring herself a glass of water, she lifted it to her lips without offering any to Dell.

With a sigh, she set the glass down. "Do you know why I throw knives? Why my mother taught me that one skill and kept her others from me?"

He shook his head and crossed the room, taking her cup. He sipped it as she narrowed her eyes.

"Throwing a knife requires great concentration. It's almost as if it takes you into an entirely new world, one where life or death can be decided with the flick of a wrist." She snatched the cup back from him. "My mother thought I needed something that allowed me to pretend nothing else existed. No expectations or limitations. Just me and a blade. It was never about protecting against others. She thought I needed protection from myself. From the doubts in my mind."

Dell reached for the pitcher and poured himself his own glass. "Your mother sounds like an amazing woman."

Helena averted her gaze. "I wish Madra had gotten to see more of her. My father and his priests placed her into the role of figurehead. She was a queen who was only noted for her beautiful dresses and the children she bore, but she was so much more than that."

"I've never heard you talk of her."

Helena rounded the white settee and sat, pulling her legs up under her. "Sometimes I forget."

"Forget what?" He moved to a torch along the wall, pulling it free to dip into the smoldering fireplace. It lit, and he replaced it on a hook, his face now bathed in an orange glow. But it wasn't just the flame. Dell shone from the inside out. She'd noticed it the first time she'd seen him, and it had never gone away.

He sat beside her.

Helena bit her lip. "That she's gone." She flicked her eyes to the fire as if ashamed of her words. "I've been so focused. I want to avenge her death, but I never really processed the fact she's gone."

"I was young when my mother died." Dell twisted his hands together. "And then my father soon after."

She sat up straighter, reaching for his arm. "I'm sorry, I didn't even think. Sometimes I forget I'm not the only one who has lost people."

He placed his hand over hers. "That's not why I'm telling you. It took me a long time to feel normal again. To stop looking around every corner for the next event that would further destroy my life. I didn't let myself get close to anyone or believe in anything. My brothers... Ian has always been a lost cause. But Reed? I spent a lot of years just looking for a fight. And I found plenty. Maybe we could have been there for each other if things were different."

Her hand squeezed tighter. "If you weren't a street fighter, you'd never have met me. Or Edmund."

A smile slid across his face. "I like to think we'd have met no matter the circumstances."

Energy zipped along Helena's every cell. The hair on her arms stood on end as she lost herself in the depth of Dell's crystalline gaze.

She wedged her lip between her teeth, unable to move any further. He trapped her in his power.

They broke apart when someone pounded on the door. Helena jumped to her feet and ran to open it, desperate for a moment to breathe.

Tyson greeted her on the other side. "I have news."

She gestured for him to come in. His eyes swept the room and one eyebrow rose when he saw Dell.

"I'd feel bad for interrupting, but this is important." He crossed the room in a few strides and fell into a large wing-backed chair with a self-satisfied smirk on his face.

"What are you waiting for?" Dell asked.

"Edmund. I sent a messenger to rouse him and bring him here."

Edmund barreled through the door, sleep still dogging his steps. His scowl softened as he shook himself awake. "What's going on?"

Tyson leaned forward, his elbows on his knees. "My mother will not tell Madra they can't have Quinn."

Helena deflated. She'd gotten her hopes up when Tyson arrived.

Tyson held up a hand to stop their questions. "But, if bandits were to overtake him somehow, she would not send her men to hunt them down."

A smile spread across Edmund's face. "She'll let us go?"

Helena sat once more. "You told her our plan?"

"Yes." Tyson directed the first answer to Edmund before turning to Helena. "And no. My mother is a bright woman. And she knows me. She also recognizes something in the speech you gave her. It sounded very much like the self-righteousness Etta once carried around here."

Edmund laughed. "It did, didn't it?"

"Self-righteous?" Helena's lips drew down.

Tyson was the one who answered her. "Most of the people in Gaule hated Etta. But, there was one thing we all learned." He smirked. "She was always right. She knew what the right thing to do was before the rest of us."

Helena couldn't decide if their description was a compliment or not, so she ignored it. "So, your mother assumed we'd try to get to Quinn, anyway? And go against her wishes in doing so?"

Tyson nodded. "She was blessed with insolent children."

Edmund grunted in agreement. "We need to prepare. We won't return to the palace. Landon will meet us with the horses once we have Quinn. If we are to be at the cove before the morning tide, we must leave soon. We have a trek ahead of us. The castle gates won't be open yet, but that's not the only way out of here."

Secret tunnels. Hidden entrances. Maybe Gaule wasn't so different from Madra after all.

Nine

Helena eyed Tyson in question as he laughed and turned into a chapel that looked like it hadn't been used in a century.

"All these years and mother still hasn't cleaned this place up." He ran his fingers along a dusty altar before jumping onto the small platform to push at a door that groaned with disuse.

Helena started losing faith he'd get it open, but Tyson reached for a hidden panel. He pulled a latch, and the wood groaned as it turned on its hinges.

Bits of rock rained down as Tyson pushed it far enough for a person to slip through. He shook dark curls out of his face and turned to them with a grin. "Cool, right? I love this palace."

Edmund patted his shoulder. "Bela will have its fair share of secrets one day as well."

Tyson gave him an appreciative smile as if that had really been a concern of his.

Who were these people? Helena's father would consider them the wrong sort to get mixed up with, but she imagined her mother would have liked them. Tyson was as tall as a man and as muscular too, but he had this childlike glee she hadn't seen since... she glanced toward Dell. Since she'd met the boy of Madra who took nothing seriously.

She hadn't seen that side of Dell since they arrived in Bela.

But then, she'd changed as well.

She shook her head. Her father would be wrong. Tyson was exactly the kind of person she needed by her side. While she and Edmund mourned, he reminded them there was still something worth fighting for other than vengeance. It wasn't a childlike glee. She saw it clearly now. Tyson was just good.

He waved each of them through the secret door before shutting it behind them.

"We're in the wall right now," Edmund explained of the short tunnel.

"In the wall?" Dell's voice was close in the darkness.

Ahead was a second door, illuminated by a sliver of dawn light.

Edmund reached it, turning back to them. "There's a part of the castle where the inner and outer walls connect. We've used this many times with Etta and Alex. This hall takes us straight from the inner castle to the outside. We'll exit on the eastern side of the walls. As soon as we get out, we have to run for the forest."

They each nodded in understanding before Edmund pushed through the door, letting them out onto a grassy hill. Helena glanced back as the door shut. From the outside, no one would even know it was there.

Edmund took off, and she followed him, pumping her arms in time with her steps. The darkened forest stretched in the distance. Over the trees, the beginnings of a sunrise highlighted the morning.

Dell ran beside her, his chin down as his lithe frame moved gracefully.

By the time they reached the tree cover, Helena struggled to breathe. She put all her energy into not collapsing as she bent, air wheezing in her chest.

"Everyone okay?" Edmund asked.

"Never better." Tyson grinned. Did nothing affect him?

He looked as if he'd only gone for a leisurely stroll and Helena almost hated him for it. At least Edmund and Dell had the decency to be short of breath.

She sucked air through her teeth and straightened. They had to move. Quinn was counting on them. She began walking, but stopped when she noticed no one followed her.

"Len," Edmund called. "You're going the wrong way."

She groaned and turned to walk past them once more. "What do you expect from me? I spent my entire life in the same set of hallways."

Tyson took the lead, claiming he'd made this trek many times before. "Last time," he began, "Gaule was besieged. Alex and I arrived to save the day, of course. This was right after we helped drive La Dame from Bela. Well, not Alex. He was sort of under her power. The git. But when we got back to Gaule, our mother was surrounded. Alex was still king. We led our people through the woods to reach the tunnel entrance and save everyone."

"*You* saved everyone?" Edmund scoffed.

"Oh, shut up. You weren't even here." Tyson leaned close to Helena as if telling her a secret. "He stayed behind in Bela when Etta was being a right jerk."

Edmund pushed him. "She'd just had the curse broken."

Tyson shrugged. "She was still a jerk. Well, it wasn't really her. She had all this power inside her that controlled a lot of what she did, but that power left her once we defeated La Dame for good."

Dell shook his head. "I'm so confused."

Helena only knew the stories brought back to Madra from soldiers and traders. They had never told her the details behind the great magic war—as the non-magical folk of Madra called it. She'd never imagined she'd be traveling through a foreign kingdom with two men who were not only there, but deeply involved.

She knew nothing of war, but they did. "When I return to Madra, will you two join me?" She didn't include Dell because she already knew he'd be at her side. It was his way. But with Tyson and Edmund... maybe she could take her brother down after all. Maybe she could avenge her family.

Both men were silent for a moment, the only sound coming from their boots hitting the soft pine of the forest floor.

Edmund swung his arm over her shoulders. "You don't even have to ask, Lenny. I told Stev I'd watch out for you and that promise doesn't end at crossing the sea."

She smiled up at him. It was the first time he'd mentioned Estevan without stuttering over his name or shutting down completely. Progress.

Tyson shook his head. "I'm sorry. As a prince, I understand what you might be going through. If someone took Alex or Etta or my mother from me, I'd want revenge as well. But, I can't go against my queen's wishes and she wants magic kept out of this fight."

Something inside her told her he didn't mean his mother. Tyson wouldn't disobey Etta, the queen who instilled such loyalty. Her heart sank.

Edmund squeezed her tighter to his side and leaned in to whisper. "I've never done what Etta tells me to."

Tyson barked out a laugh. "No truer words."

She wished Tyson would reconsider, but it didn't change her plans. When she walked through Madra once more, she'd have Dell, Edmund, and Quinn at her side and her faith rested in them. She felt for the knife at her waist. A sword Tyson had procured from one of the guards hung from a scabbard she'd tied there as well, but it didn't give her the same comfort as the shorter blade.

As they walked, she went over and over the plan in her mind. They hadn't fully trusted Reed. He thought they planned to follow him through the tunnels and overtake him as soon as he stepped outside.

He was wrong.

They would still overcome the Madran party at the cove, but the attack would come from the forest.

As they neared the water, the trees thinned. The forest stretched to the edge of land right before the coast curved inward toward the cove.

They reached the edge of the trees, stopping where the ground fell off over a small cliff. A white beach sat below where the waves crashed, foaming toward the shore.

"This way." Tyson's voice brought Helena back to the matter at hand.

She glanced at him over her shoulder.

Tyson jerked his head to the side, telling them to follow him. He put a finger to his lips. They were close now.

Helena forced her tired limbs to trudge the rest of the way. They ceased moving as the rocky cove came into view. Still hidden among the twisting branches and thick trees, they watched. A ship sat at the mouth of the cove with its arched Madran style. Long oars stuck out from a dark wooden hull. Helena sucked in a breath. It was one of her father's ships. The royal flag of Madra flapped in the stiff breeze.

Helena hugged her cloak around her shoulders tighter and pulled her knife free, not bothering with the sword.

A small boat approached laden with two men in Madran officer uniforms. As the water grew shallow, they jumped overboard, crashing through the sea as they pulled their boat onto the sandy shore.

"Only two," Edmund whispered. "Reed kept his word."

She heard the danger in his tone. Saw him fingering the hilt of his sword. Those two men wouldn't live through the day.

And she couldn't summon a single shred of remorse. Traitors deserved to die.

"Where are these tunnels?" Dell shielded his eyes against the morning sun.

Tyson pointed toward a curved gap in the rock face. "There's a door through there. It can only be opened from the inside."

Edmund retreated farther back into the trees. "Time to take our positions. All that's left to do is wait."

AS THE SUN rose high above their heads, the two soldiers on the beach stood from the rock they'd been sitting on and approached the tunnel.

Helena met Dell's gaze, answering the question in his eyes with a nod of her head. She was ready.

She crouched low in her spot behind a boulder at the tree line and gripped a knife in each hand. Tyson knocked an arrow, leaning against the base of a towering pine as he watched the tunnel entrance.

Edmund pulled his sword in one fluid movement, holding it as if it weighed nothing at all.

Silence filled the space between them.

Finally, the men reappeared. Reed walked behind them, his hand clamped around Quinn's arm.

Helena gasped. They'd tied his hands behind his back and a trickle of blood ran from his hairline. Did he fight back?

Who was she kidding? Of course he did. It was Quinn.

A slow smile spread across her face, halting when another movement caught her eye. More soldiers poured from the tunnel, surrounding Quinn and Reed.

Soldiers they hadn't expected or planned for.

"Well, what now?" Dell muttered.

"We can still get him." Her voice hardened as she looked Edmund's way. "We can fight."

"They outnumber us three to one." Tyson lowered his bow.

Edmund's eyes spoke of defeat.

"No." She clenched her fingers tighter around her knife. "Edmund, if this was Stev, you'd do it. We have to try. I won't just leave him. If you won't help me, I'll do it myself."

Helena jumped from her spot and ran, Edmund's curses trailing after her.

Quinn's eyes jerked up as she broke from the trees. The soldiers watched her in confusion until she launched one of her knives full speed. It struck the center of the Madran royal crest on the nearest man. He stumbled back, blood soaking his uniform.

That spurred the rest into action. The clatter of swords rang in her ears, but she blocked it out as she ducked the first attack, dropping low and slicing her knife along the back of the man's knee. He collapsed, a scream she couldn't hear on his lips.

Another soldier made for her, and she wasn't fast enough to twist out of the way as he swung his sword toward her. It stopped mid-air as an arrow struck him through the eye. The blade fell from his grasp, and he dropped.

Edmund and Dell reached them, engaging their own attackers. Dell barely avoided a blade to the arm before he tackled his man to the ground.

Edmund twisted on his heel and swung his sword in a graceful arc as he fought two men at once. Helena had never seen a man fight with such grace before. She spared him one final glance before engaging.

Catching sight of Reed dragging Quinn to the small boat, her heart beat painfully. She had to help him.

Quinn bucked and fought against Reed, but two others joined them to lift him into the boat. Helena stood in a daze, warm blood spraying her face as Edmund fought beside her. Everything happened too quickly for her to help any of them. Tyson took out one of the men with Quinn as two arrows appeared sticking out of his chest. He toppled into the water.

Reed and the other men didn't spare him a glance as they pushed the boat into the water.

"No," Helena roared, running into the sea, trying desperately to reach her brother.

But he was too far.

Something bumped into her as she waded in waist deep water tinged with red. A sob caught in her throat as she looked into the face of a dead soldier. Revulsion swirled in her gut.

She lifted her eyes to the beach where Edmund and Dell had dispatched most of their foes. An arrow sailed overhead but landed in the water next to the boat.

Helena lifted her arm into the air, launched her knife with as much force as she could muster. Every lesson her mother taught her rang in her mind. *A knife can be as deadly as an arrow at a distance granted you know how to make it so.*

A scream ripped through the air as the knife stuck into Reed's arm. Overwhelming despair quickly overcame any satisfaction of hitting her target.

She pushed the body floating beside her away and ran from the sickening stench coating the air. Dead soldiers littered the beach, but that wasn't what caught her attention.

Edmund fought with the confidence of a seasoned warrior. Dell fumbled with his sword as his attacker advanced. Their blades clashed and Dell's flew from his hands as he fell to his knees, driven by a kick to the stomach.

A scream lodged in Helena's throat as a blade sliced into Dell's side, steel biting flesh. A Belaen blade tip appeared through the attacker's chest as Edmund pierced him from behind before kicking him to the side, leaving them alone on the beach once more.

Helena fell to her knees beside Dell as Tyson joined them and fired every last arrow he had toward the small boat. It was halfway to the ship when one of the arrows struck Reed in the leg as he stood to force Quinn's cooperation.

"I'm out." Tyson watched the boat reach the ship, unable to do anything more.

A tear slid down Helena's cheek. They'd lost him. Quinn was gone.

But Dell was still there, and he'd been hurt. She turned her attention to him as his eyes slid closed.

"Dell." She ripped at his clothes, searching for the wound. "Don't you close your eyes. Stay with me. Please."

"Len." Every breath rattled in his chest as if it was a great struggle. "Trying."

Edmund knelt beside him and gripped her hands to still their shaking. "Let me look."

She nodded and Edmund lifted Dell's shirt to find a deep cut. "We need to stop the bleeding."

Helena tore the cloak from her shoulders and handed it to Edmund. He pressed it to the wound.

Dell jerked and sucked a breath through his teeth.

"Is he going to be okay?" Fear surged through Helena as she thought of the possible answers to her question.

"He needs a healer." Edmund searched for any other injuries. "And soon. We don't have time to return to Bela." He lifted his eyes to Tyson as if waiting for permission.

Tyson ran a hand through his wild hair, emotions warring in his eyes. "Yeah. Okay. We can go."

"Go where?" Helena leaned closer to Dell until she could hear his breathing. As long as that sound filled her ears, he was still with her.

"I have a friend," Tyson began. "Here in Gaule. She has a Draconian healer in her household."

Edmund tore strips from the bottom of his shirt. "We can't move him until we wrap the wound. Ty, I'm gonna need water to clean it."

Tyson ran forward as Helena helped Edmund bunch Dell's shirt up to the broad span of his shoulders.

When Tyson poured a drop of water from the bag at his waist and it expanded over the wound, she jumped to her feet, her heart pounding in her ears. "What are you doing?"

"Cleaning it." Tyson's brow furrowed in concentration. "I can send the water in and then call it back, dragging any impurities with it."

She shook her head. Magic.

Tyson and Edmund finished cleaning Dell's wound and wrapped it tightly. Dell hadn't opened his eyes.

Helena couldn't stare at his still face any longer, but

when she turned away, all she saw was the expanse of sea and the ship where her brother was now a prisoner.

She added Reed Tenyson to the long list of people who'd betrayed her family.

Rustling came from the trees and Helena turned just in time to see Vérité burst free. He ran across the beach until he stopped at Tyson's side and dipped his head.

Tyson breathed a sigh and rubbed the horse's nose. "Perfect timing as ever, buddy."

Landon appeared a few minutes later with the other horses in tow. His eyes widened when he took in the dead soldiers. When he settled his gaze on Dell's prone form, he slid from his horse.

"Is he okay?" Landon ambled his thick frame over.

Edmund set his hands on Dell's chest. "We need to get him to the Leroy estate."

Vérité stepped to Helena's side, nudging the side of her face with his nose. A sob shuddered in her chest and she turned to bury her face in the beast's soft neck. He rested his nose on her shoulder as if wrapping her in an embrace.

That was stupid, he was a horse. But Helena needed some kind of comfort.

She'd failed. Again. It seemed she couldn't save any of her brothers. A feeling of uselessness sank deep into her chest. Recovering Madra was a far-off dream with no hope of ever coming true. She'd never get to look Cole in the eye and take it all back from him.

It would have been possible with Quinn. Her brother could do anything. She gripped Vérité's mane, needing something to hold on to.

"Put him on Vérité," Tyson said.

Edmund started to argue, but then cut himself off.

"You're right. Vérité will take care of him. That horse takes care of everyone... except me."

Landon and Edmund hoisted Dell onto Vérité's back before Tyson slid up behind him. Helena pulled dry clothes over her wet ones as quickly as she could before mounting her own horse, never taking her eyes from Dell's face. A peace settled over him, but she refused to let him keep it.

They'd get to the healer before he disappeared altogether. She couldn't save Estevan or Quinn, but she wouldn't lose Dell.

Her heart clenched.

No, she couldn't.

Ten

"I'm not going to die," Dell said simply.

"The illegal fights. Stealing. Do you even have a head on those shoulders?"

An angry flush rose in the young man's face as if he was preparing to explode. Helena grabbed Edmund's arm. "Edmund, leave him be."

Dell's anger snapped away in an instant as his eyes fixed on Helena, seeing her for the first time. "Who do we have here?" He sat up to peer closer. "You don't think you're fooling anyone in that getup, miss, do you?"

Helena ripped the hat from her head. Her dark curls spilled out, and she turned to Edmund. "Am I that obvious?"

The first time Dell had seen Helena, he'd wanted to get under her skin. He'd wanted to test her, challenge her, to make her face flush with anger. She was the most beautiful person he'd ever seen.

"Dell." Her voice floated through the air as if in the dream itself. "Dell, are you still with me?"

Always, he wanted to answer. *He'd never leave her.* But

the words wouldn't leave his lips. He couldn't speak, couldn't move.

As reality crashed in around him, a spearing pain shot through his side. A scream ended in a gurgle on his lips as something beneath him moved. Was he on a horse?

He could hear the people around him, but his body no longer followed the commands from his brain.

"Will they help us?" Helena asked, desperation plain in her voice. "I trust nothing in Gaule."

Tyson sighed. At least, he thought it was Tyson. "Yes."

"Who are these people?"

When no one answered Helena, her voice rose in anger. "We've been riding into the night to reach this estate and the mysterious people who live there. I deserve to know what we're walking in to."

Tyson grunted but didn't answer as he kicked his horse and rode on ahead.

Edmund's voice filled the silence. "The Leroy estate was once owned by Lord Leroy, the man Alex had executed for treason. His daughter now resides there."

"Can we trust her?"

Edmund hesitated. "More than anyone else in Gaule. Amalie... she grew up with Tyson. They were the closest of friends even when she was betrothed to Alex. After the war with Dracon, Tyson stayed in Gaule for a time to be with her but returned to Bela about a year ago. Amalie felt she had a duty to return to her family's estate. The people in the villages nearby needed someone to get them through these hard times. Tyson loved her. That was never a secret. Yet both of them chose duty over that love, and it didn't end well."

The words filtered through Dell's hazy mind, but he only wanted to sink back into the darkness. Not allowing himself that mercy, he latched onto everything Edmund said as a way to maintain his hold on his conscious state.

"So, things aren't amicable between them, yet she'll help us?" Skepticism rang in Helena's voice.

"You don't know Amalie. She'd help anyone who showed up at her door. That's just who she is."

"And this healer in her household?"

Edmund paused for a moment. "Maiya. She was once an agent of La Dame. We all knew she didn't have a choice in any of it, but after the war ended, she didn't feel as if she could stay in Bela among the people she'd betrayed."

They fell quiet and Dell wanted to tell them to keep talking, to keep filling his mind, to keep the darkness at bay.

Instead, he focused on the pulse of pain, letting it leech into every cell.

Without the pain, he feared he'd disappear.

THE GUARDS SPOTTED them before they reached the Leroy estate. Helena watched them approach warily.

"Prince Tyson," one of them called. "You shouldn't be on the roads this late."

"We've been lucky, Cameron. Haven't seen a soul for hours." Tyson rode up to the guard and stuck his hand out.

Tyson must have been here many times before.

"Lady Leroy is away for the night."

The tension in Tyson's shoulders relaxed. "That's okay. Is Maiya at the estate house?"

The guard spotted Dell for the first time. "Yes, of course. We'll escort you to make haste."

He asked no questions before motioning to the rest of the guards and turning to gallop down the road into the village.

The road winded between storefronts and homes before coming to a dead end at two massive gates with a small door at the base of them.

Cameron yelled to one of his guards. "Go wake mistress Maiya and bring her here."

The door opened, and another guard appeared. "Prince Tyson? We weren't told to expect you tonight."

Tyson slid down. "It's been a long time, Calvin. We must catch up, but right now I need a bit of help."

Helena jumped to the ground, her tired legs almost giving out beneath her. A hand gripped her elbow, keeping her upright. "Careful, Len." Edmund pulled her to lean against his side and wrapped an arm around her waist.

The guards lifted Dell down and carried him through the door.

Cameron gave orders to have their horse's taken care of, but Helena barely heard him over the roaring in her ears. She sprang free of Edmund and followed the guards to where they laid Dell on the ground in a stone courtyard.

She knelt and pressed her fingers to his neck, needing to feel his life for herself. When his pulse thumped against her hand, she pulled back with a sigh.

They'd made it. Tears cascaded down her face as the day's desperation washed over her. What if someone had stopped them on the dangerous Gaule roads? What if Dell hadn't been strong enough? So many possibilities rolled through her mind, and she closed her eyes.

A gentle hand on her shoulder had them snapping open to find a dark-skinned young woman with black corkscrew curls standing at her side in a long sleeping gown.

Helena wiped the back of her hand across her eyes. "Please, save him."

The woman offered her a smile. "You're the princess?"

Her eyes widened as panic built in her chest. No one in Gaule was supposed to know who she was. She scanned the faces of the guards surrounding them, her chest rising and falling rapidly. Finally, her gaze settled on Tyson.

"The people here can be trusted." His face pinched as if it hurt him to say.

She remembered what Edmund had said of the lady of this estate. Tyson had loved her once.

"Don't worry, Princess." The healer's soft voice held a musical quality that soothed Helena's nerves. "You're safe here."

Helena's shoulders sagged as the words permeated the aura of fear she'd trapped herself in.

"Maiya." Edmund gestured to Dell.

The healer knelt and lifted the bottom of Dell's shirt to press her palms against his skin. She closed her eyes and threw her head back, lost in some unseen force.

As Maiya worked, Tyson nudged Helena out of the way and used his knife to cut the strips of fabric binding his wound.

Helena's mind protested—he couldn't afford to lose more blood—but as she caught sight of the wound, the words died in her throat. Dell's skin tugged and pulled, closing the gap where the knife had sliced through soft flesh.

Dell's breathing—a struggle only moments before—evened until he appeared to be only sleeping. The hard lines of his face softened into a peaceful mask, and Maiya pulled her hands away.

Helena choked back a sob. "He's..."

Maiya reached for her hand. "He's going to be okay."

"But he's still..." Helena gestured to where Dell remained unconscious.

"His wounds were deep. Any longer and I wouldn't have

been able to save him. It took a great deal of his remaining energy to heal." She lifted her eyes to Cameron, giving him a signal. "We'll bring him to a room and make him comfortable. It could be a day or so before you're able to speak with him."

Helena sniffed and nodded before rising to her feet. Cameron and one of his fellow guards lifted Dell and carried him toward the enormous stone entryway of the great house. Helena made to follow them, but Edmund gripped her arm.

"We could all do with a bite to eat, a hot bath, and some sleep."

Helena pulled her arm free and ran a hand over the top of her head. He was right. Her oily hair was proof of the need for a wash. Her stomach growled. But she couldn't.

"I won't leave him." She took off through the mahogany front doors. This time, Edmund didn't stop her.

The guards carried Dell through dark halls lit only by a few candles that burned through the night. They didn't see a single other person before reaching a simple room with a large bed sitting against the far wall covered in furs. Dim light spilled in through an open window, illuminating the green draperies.

Helena made to pull her cloak tighter about her, forgetting she hadn't had it all day. The air's chill hadn't touched her on their ride as Edmund used his magic to keep the winds at bay. Yet a sliver of ice had still worked its way into her heart.

The guards laid Dell on the bed before turning to her.

"I'll send someone to get a fire started." Cameron looked to the barren fireplace. Two chairs sat before it. A long table rested against the wall near the bed.

Helena only nodded as they left. She went to the window, pulling the two glass panes shut to block out the night. She turned to Dell who had yet to move. Pushing out a breath, she crossed to the bed and tugged at the laces of his boots. As soon as she had the shoes off his feet, she shifted him to free the fur covers and pull them over his body to trap him in warmth.

A knock came from the door, and she answered it to find a handful of servants who looked as if they'd been roused from their beds.

"Miss," one of the said with a bow. "We are here to ready the room."

Helena stepped aside for them to enter. A young man went straight to the fireplace while two women carrying trays of food moved to set them on the table. Her mouth watered as she smelled the meat pastries and wine.

How long had it been since she'd eaten a proper meal? At the Gaulean palace, she'd been too worried about their upcoming battle for Quinn. On the road, none of them had wanted to waste time stopping when Dell's life hung in the balance.

She muttered a 'thank you' as the servants retreated from the room, leaving her alone once again with Dell. Walking to the fledgling fire, she stood closer than her mother would have approved to thaw her frozen limbs.

When she was warm, she used every ounce of strength she possessed to push one of the high-backed maroon chairs to the side of the bed.

She then stood in front of the table, examining the trays. A bowl of water sat on one with a rag inside. She lifted it and sat on the edge of the bed.

When Dell woke, he would want the grime cleaned off his face. She wiped the dirt that had been kicked up onto his skin as he'd rested across a horse all day.

Each stroke of the cloth brought his handsome face further from the darkness. She set the rag in the now muddy water and ran her thumb down his soft cheek to the firm jaw covered in short blonde hairs.

She closed her eyes, imagining him as he'd been in Madra the day she saw him bathing in the river. Cocky. Confident. So darn charming. And infuriating. She'd hated him and been completely fascinated by him. He was the reason she continued to risk going into the city without her mask.

Where had she lost that feeling? She was still risking herself for many reasons, but for months, she'd only felt this crushing defeat that led to a burning need for revenge. Against her brother of all people. A man she'd once loved with her entire heart—just like the rest of her family who were now gone.

She pulled her hand away from Dell's face and stood to put the bowl aside. Her stomach pleaded for food, but nausea rose up in her when she thought of eating. Instead, she settled in the chair by the bed, pulling her legs in beneath her.

The movement of Dell's chest mesmerized her until all she saw was him.

Eleven

Dell didn't know where he was as his eyes slid open. Heavy furs weighed him down on the unfamiliar bed. Was he back in Bela? How did he get here?

His eyes roamed the sparse room until settling on the girl sleeping next to the bed. Helena. If she was there, he knew he had to be somewhere good. He was okay.

Early morning light streamed through a window, casting a glow along the floor.

An ache began in his head, stretching down through his entire body. He tried to push the covers aside, but his arms lacked the strength.

"Len," he whispered, trying to force strength into his voice.

She didn't stir.

"Len." Louder that time.

Helena shifted in the chair that couldn't have been comfortable, her lids peeling back slowly. She took a moment to find his gaze, but her entire body jolted when she did.

"Dell." She stood to get a closer look. "You're awake." A

sad smile slid across her lips. "I should wake Maiya to check on you."

As she turned, he finally forced his arm to move enough to catch hold of her wrist. She froze, breathing deeply for a moment before turning back to him.

"Tell me what happened," he pleaded.

She shook her head, unshed tears hanging in her lashes.

"Please."

Sucking in a shuddering breath, she squared her shoulders. "There was a fight at the cove and someone stabbed you. We rode a long way to bring you to the only known Draconian healer in Gaule."

Something sparked in his memory. He'd heard them talking. Maiya. Yeah, that was her name. But that wasn't what mattered in that moment.

"Quinn?" He asked, fearing the answer.

Her gaze hardened. "On his way to Madra."

Dell slid his hand from Helena's wrist to lace his fingers through hers. "Come here."

Surprising him, she didn't object as he pulled her into the bed, lifting the covers for her to slide underneath.

The warmth of her body burned into his memory as he pulled her into his arms. She melted against him, burying her face in his chest.

"How long have I been out?"

His shirt muffled her voice. "The fight was more than a day ago."

"Did you spend the night in here?" He settled his accusing glare on the chair as if it was the offender.

"I couldn't leave you."

Dell had known how he felt about Len from the moment he saw Ian with her at the Madran games—before he knew who she truly was.

For him, nothing had changed.

But she'd given no hint of how she felt... until now.

Neither said anything for a long moment as he stroked her back.

She pulled back to look at him. "I'm gross. I'm sorry. Edmund tried to get me to bathe and eat, but I—"

"Len," he cut her off. "You could appear covered in Vérité's droppings and I wouldn't care."

A laugh shook her. "Yes, you would."

"Okay, bad example. Please don't cover yourself in horse dung."

"I don't know. Now that I know you enjoy the smell of barns, I may have to try it."

He brought his lips to her ear. "It won't change the simple facts."

"And what simple facts are these?" She lifted her face to gaze at him.

"I don't think I annoy you as much as you pretend." He smirked. "I even think you might like me."

She raised an eyebrow. "I tolerate you."

"Yeah?" He dropped his voice. "Then why do you feel so good in my arms?"

"I'm only here because I was cold."

"Okay, Princess." He rested his chin on the top of her head, his words dropping off at the thoughts her title provoked. Princess. And she'd just lost another brother.

He ran a hand the length of her back before inching it along her side. "I'm sorry about Quinn."

She didn't respond for a long moment. "You don't know Cole and Quinn. Those two... they were as close as siblings could be. I always envied them. But Quinn... he's good. And Cole will try to take that from him. What if he turns Quinn against me and Kass?"

Dell shifted down to press his forehead against hers. "I'm not sure goodness is something that can be stripped away. Have faith in your brother, Len."

She nodded, swallowing heavily. "I'm going to help him." Her eyes darkened. "It's time, Dell. No more waiting. I need to return to Bela and find a way back to Madra. It's time to go home."

He didn't respond. He'd seen it coming, her decision. Helena had wanted to go back to Madra since she woke aboard a ship bound for Bela. It was her kingdom. He couldn't blame her, could he?

But he feared if she set foot on Madran soil, he'd never see her again, that she wouldn't make it out alive. His arms tightened around her.

He released a sigh into her hair. "Len, I don't want to lose you."

He didn't realize he'd said the words out loud until she lifted her head to look at him. She didn't make false promises, but the determination in her eyes softened. She'd do what she needed. He had no doubt of that.

Her fingers dug into the fabric of his shirt and she pulled him closer, her lips finding his.

When they'd kissed at the ball in Madra, Dell had seen every possibility before them. It had been powerful and all-consuming, but it ended too quickly.

Now, they took their time to pour everything into that moment. Len's lips moved over his as she opened for him, pressing harder against his body.

Dell ran his fingers over her cheeks, her shoulders, down her sides before wrapping his arms around her waist, wanting every part of her and terrified he'd end up with nothing.

The coming trials held a darkness neither of them was

prepared for. He only knew he'd do anything to keep the vengeance from shattering his princess.

HELENA HADN'T REALIZED she'd fallen asleep until a pounding on the door woke her. Before she could rise, the door opened, and Edmund walked in.

She scrambled from the bed but not before Edmund saw her and raised an eyebrow. He didn't mention it. Instead, he gestured to Dell's still sleeping form. "How is he?"

"Getting better," she answered. "He woke early this morning."

Edmund nodded. "Good. Then we can leave him alone. Lady Amalie returned late last night and has requested our presence at breakfast. First, you need to bathe." He wrinkled his nose, and she swatted at him.

A young maid entered behind him and curtsied. "Miss, I can take you to your room."

Helena glanced toward Dell once more before following the girl into the hall. In the light of day, the estate house held a cheerier air. Brightly colored fabric decorated the walls, yet its appeal was in the simplicity. They used no great amount of money on the house, and Helena appreciated the modesty.

The room she arrived at was identical to Dell's save for a washroom attached. The maid showed her where a fresh set of clothing lay and a copper tub sat, filled with steaming water.

As soon as she was alone, Helena removed her clothes and sank into the tub, allowing the water to relax every muscle.

She closed her eyes, leaning her head back. Had it only been a day since they fought on that beach? It seemed as if a lifetime had passed. She scrubbed the dirt and road dust that was caked on her skin, feeling like a girl for the first time in a while. Her fingers worked lye soap into the tangled strands of her once beautiful hair.

Her mother and Sophia used to spend hours washing the dark tresses, brushing them, and pinning them so she always looked as proper as a princess should. What would Sophia think of her now? The old maid hadn't approved of the things the queen taught her daughter, considering knife skills too manly.

But her mother never cared what anyone else thought. She made sure Helena always appeared the perfect and obedient princess around her father or his priests. But then she also gave Helena the means to be her own person.

The throne hadn't been everything to Chloe Rhodipus, and it wouldn't be everything to her daughter.

Helena dipped her head beneath the water before emerging fresh and new with a different thought. She didn't want the crown from Cole. She had no desire to issue commands or collect taxes. That wasn't why she needed to return to Madra. Even if Helena couldn't be the queen, Cole didn't deserve the title of king. He didn't deserve the respect and obedience when he'd had none.

She stood in the tub, letting the water drip down her body before stepping out. Someone knocked on the door.

"Len?"

Dell? What was he doing out of bed? She dried herself as best she could and pulled her clothes on, jumping to secure the snug pants. There was no doubt in her mind how much Dell meant to her. She'd seen him fall and her heart stopped. But she didn't have the luxury of being an infatuated girl. She had to be hard, cold, and calculated. She could no longer be the pretty princess behind the mask. It was time to be a warrior.

Feet still bare, she padded across the cold stone floor to let Dell into the room. He practically fell in as she opened the door.

"Hey." She caught him around the waist. "You shouldn't be standing."

"You were gone when I woke. One of the servants told me where I'd find you."

A smile tried to break free, but she held it back. "Lady Amalie wants to see us."

"I'm coming."

"Dell..."

"I can't stay in bed anymore. I'm okay."

She studied him for a moment and narrowed her eyes. "Fine. Wait here for a second." She shifted him so he could use the doorframe for support and went to retrieve her boots. Dry mud still covered them, but they'd have to do.

After pulling them on, she ducked under Dell's arm and let him lean on her to walk down the hall. As a few servants eyed them, Dell leaned in to whisper. "Does this place give you the creeps?"

"A bit," she admitted. It was as if ghosts of a brutal past roamed the halls. Lord Leroy and his eldest daughter were long dead, but their influence must have lived on.

"I heard a few maids talking when they thought I was asleep. Lady Amalie fought to recover this estate after the queen seized it."

"She fought the queen?"

"Her father was a traitor, and the crown has rights to a traitor's lands, but..."

"But Amalie was no traitor," she finished for him. How

could the queen take everything from the woman her son loved? "Do you think she knew about Tyson and Amalie?"

Dell shook his head. "I hope she didn't. If she did... that's just wrong." He was quiet for a moment. "They say Amalie's hard. She disappears for days at a time and no one other than a few trusted people know where she goes."

Helena swallowed, not relishing the thought of meeting the woman. Then she thought of Tyson. The man with a boyish charm and infectious joy. How could he love someone with ice in their heart?

The same way Dell could have feelings for Helena, she supposed.

They reached the dining hall where Edmund and Tyson sat at a long table. Tyson jumped up when he saw them and ran forward to help Dell.

"I told him he should have stayed in bed." Helena shook her head as Dell stumbled and latched on to Tyson's arm.

Tyson didn't respond as he'd gone still. Helena followed his line of sight to a woman standing in the doorway. An elegant deep green gown hung from her slim frame. Golden laces ran the length of her sides from bodice to skirt.

Chestnut hair spread around her shoulders in ringlets, framing a heart-shaped face. Wide dark eyes sat in contrast to her pale skin. Her chest rose as if she prepared herself for something difficult before stepping farther into the room.

"Edmund." Her pink lips pulled into a tentative smile as she walked past Tyson without so much as a glance.

Edmund rose and stepped around the table to hold his arms out. "Amalie." He grinned. "Beautiful as ever."

She stepped into his hug. "It's been too long."

He chuckled. "I don't make a habit of entering Gaule if I don't have to and seeing as you no longer visit us in Bela..."

She pulled away and flattened her palms against her

stomach. The smile that had been there before was no longer visible. "I have too much to do here. I can't just leave."

Tyson grunted as he helped Dell down into a chair. "If you don't leave, where were you when we arrived?"

Amalie turned a scowl on him. "That is none of your concern, *Prince*." She said the title as if it were a weapon before facing Dell. "Is this the man Maiya healed? He shouldn't be out of bed."

"That's what I said," Helena muttered. She thought no one had heard her until Amalie fixed her with a suspicious glare. "Edmund, Tyson, what trouble have you brought to my door? Cameron said something about a princess."

Edmund rubbed the back of his neck. "Amalie, meet Helena of Madra."

Amalie only raised an eyebrow at that. "The dead princess? She looks very much alive to me." Amalie crossed her arms, moving on from Helena and scanning the rest of the faces there. "I know you have only come to my door because you had no other choice, but while you are here, I have rules."

"Rules." Tyson scoffed.

She narrowed her eyes. "First, this is no longer my father's house. The people here will be treated with respect, even the ones who served my father or sister. I have worked very hard to cultivate loyalty. I come from a family of traitors, but that is in the past."

Edmund nodded. "We wouldn't dream of pissing you off."

Amalie almost cracked a smile. Almost. "Elegant, Edmund, as ever."

"That was only one rule." Helena sat beside Dell.

"You're a smart one, aren't you, Princess?"

Dell tried to sit up straighter before slumping back. "You ask for respect and then give none."

Amalie pushed her hair over one shoulder, regarding him. "Rule number two, you stay out of my way. I don't want to see anything from you or hear anything. My people will take care of you, but I have sensitive goings on at this estate, and I will not have you butting your heads in where you're not wanted."

"What has happened to you, Amalie?" Edmund shook his head, sadness in his gaze.

Amalie pinched her lips together as she considered him. "What has happened to me? In the three years since I rode to fight La Dame, I have seen Gaule descend into a pit of hunger and despair. I returned to my family estate, only to find it seized by the crown. It took events I will not speak of to win it back. My only goal in this life is to see all those who live on my land fed. As the nobles sit in their estates feasting, the people starve. And what does the queen do about it? She allows these same nobles to control every food shipment, every trading route. She never even leaves her palace. I'm sorry Edmund, but I have long since lost faith in queens or nobles." She glanced sideways at Tyson. "Or princes."

With that final word, she turned on her heel and left them all staring after her.

Tyson collapsed into a chair.

Edmund's jaw opened and closed as if he had something to say but couldn't quite find the words. He settled for, "Well, I'd say she's changed."

"I don't know." Dell leaned forward against the table. "I always felt the same way. I saw hunger in Madra every day. Yet the king did nothing but levy more taxes and take more food for his armies."

Tyson buried his head in his hands. "Amalie resents that

I stayed in Bela away from the problems of Gaule even though she told me to go. The last time I saw her, she called me a coward. Maybe I am."

"Ty." Edmund's hand landed on his shoulder. "You fought your war. Everyone in Bela did. Peace is their reward for generations of abuse."

Two servants entered the hall, both carrying trays. They set a bowl and a plate before each person present before leaving as silently as they'd come.

Helena regarded the food before her. Thin broth, a bread roll, and a piece of salted fish. Respect grew within her. Amalie wasn't only a woman with high ideals, she actually walked the walk. This meal couldn't have been any better than what the people in the village were eating.

She dipped her spoon into the bowl and brought the tasteless broth to her lips. They ate in silence.

When they were finished, Edmund helped Dell back to his room. Tyson disappeared. Helena wandered the halls of the barren estate, her mind wondering about the traitorous acts carried out within those walls.

She skimmed her hand along a wooden banister as she ascended a staircase into the upper levels of the house. She came to a crossing of hallways. Looking down one, it seemed only to be the servants' quarters. But the other... the glow of a lantern seeped through a doorway.

Helena couldn't stop her feet from moving that way.

Voices drifted into the hall.

"Did you find them?" Cameron. At least she thought it was the guard.

"I tried." Amalie's voice was much softer than it had been before. "We're going to need to search farther out. Tuck is already out looking. We came upon a string of wagons headed for Duke Ingold's estate. I have the boys out distributing the food right now."

"That was lucky." Cameron paused. "Did you have to..." He stopped as if cut off.

"No one died. We knocked out the wagoneers and left them far enough back from the road that bandits wouldn't have found them before waking."

Helena couldn't wrap her mind around what she was hearing. Amalie was... stealing? For her people, but still... they could hang her for the offense.

She inched back along the wall and down the stairs. Her breathing didn't even out until she was back in her room. She settled in a chair by the fire and stared into the glowing flames until a knock at the door startled her from her thoughts.

She sighed. What did they want now? Edmund and Dell both had nasty habits of barging in without knocking so it must have been Tyson, and she didn't think she could take his morose attitude for one moment longer.

Opening the door, she reeled back as Amalie's face came into view.

"I know it's late." Amalie spoke with none of the confidence she'd had before. "But may I come in?"

Helena nodded and stepped back to allow the young woman entrance.

Amalie shut the door and took no time in dropping into a chair, exhaustion tugging at the features on her face.

"I—" Helena started, but Amalie shook her head.

"I must apologize for the way I spoke earlier. Whenever Tyson shows up, I see only anger."

Helena sat in the chair opposite her. "It's okay."

"No." She shook her head. "It's not. But many... things are hard right now, and he only makes them more difficult."

Helena couldn't look at Amalie without a chorus of *thief* running through her mind, but her mother raised her to hide her own thoughts, so she smiled in sympathy.

"I'm sorry we had to come here."

Amalie waved her words away. "I'm glad Maiya could help. I know she misses using her magic regularly, although my people give her plenty of opportunities. Look, I wanted to talk to you because I obviously know who you are. Not only that, I understand. Ty would like to think I'm this hard, unbreakable person now, but I still know who I am and where I've come from. My father and sister betrayed the king. I know it's different for you because your father *was* the king when your brother betrayed him."

Helena let the girl ramble.

"I'm sorry, you don't need me dredging this up. What I really wanted to ask is what you plan to do about it?"

"Do?"

"I got my revenge on my father when I fought him in battle and I continue to live my vengeance every day as I run his estate while he's buried deep in an unmarked traitor's grave."

Vengeance. The thing Helena had pledged to enact on Cole but had made no move to do so.

She shifted in her seat. "I'm going back to Madra."

A grim smile slithered across Amalie's face. "Do Edmund and Tyson know this? They've been raised around an army. Plan. Plan. Plan. I much prefer to let spontaneity be my weapon."

Helena shook her head. "They won't come. Well, at least Tyson won't." As she said it, she knew it was true. But Edmund? It was one thing speaking the words in the woods of Gaule, but actually bringing Edmund back to Madra was another matter. Why should Edmund and Tyson leave the safety of Bela? Edmund may have lived in Madra, but it wasn't his kingdom. Without Estevan there, it held nothing for him. No, Cole was her responsibility. None of this would stop until she faced him.

"I have someone you need to meet." Amalie shot to her feet. "Come."

Helena followed Amalie through the halls until they reached the courtyard. Instead of turning toward the gate, she veered around the corner to where a set of barracks stood at the back of the estate. Their walls leaned in on each other as if they might fall and pieces of thatching littered the ground.

"We haven't had the funds to repair the barracks, but my people don't care. They don't spend much time here, anyway."

Helena glanced from side to side nervously as they ducked inside. Rows of bunks lined each wall, but most stood empty. Only a few people lingered about. Amalie nodded to each. In the back, she stopped in front of an occupied bunk. A monster of a man slept with his legs dangling over the end.

Amalie kicked the bed. "Will. Oy, wake up."

The big man stirred but didn't wake. "Will."

He cracked one eye open. "Shove off, Ames."

"Get your hairy butt out of this bed right now, or I will stick an arrow right through your thick skull."

He groaned and rolled over.

Helena sucked in a breath as she caught sight of the line of tattoos snaking down his neck and disappearing under the collar of his shirt. A Madran Mercenary.

"I'm counting, Will." Amalie tapped her foot. "One. Two..."

"I'm getting up." He sat and rubbed a hand across his angular jaw before pushing his long, dark hair away from his face. "I was up late because someone knocked out a couple of traders who obviously hadn't been starving by the weight of them."

Amalie's eyes widened as they flicked to Helena. Will, seeing her for the first time, scrunched his brow.

"Who is she?" He jabbed his thumb toward Helena but kept his eyes on Amalie.

Helena's heart seized as he turned his gaze on her and slid it down her body. She'd never been face to face with a mercenary before.

Amalie ignored the question. "Do you remember the story you told me of how Quinn Rhodipus saved your life when the Madran army captured you in Cana?"

He nodded, hesitation in his eyes.

"Who did he save you from?"

Helena got the impression Amalie already knew the answer, and the question was only for her benefit.

"His own priest darned brother," Will spat. "I'll never forget that. When Cole Rhodipus controlled the army, he viewed mercenaries as traitors. I can't believe that blasted bastard is king now."

Helena understood now. Why Amalie had brought her to this man. She had allies.

Amalie bit her lip for a moment before turning to face Helena. "Will has contacts in Bela. Traders. It's how we... let's just say he's an asset to me. He can get you to Madra."

Will scowled. "Ames, I work for you. I'm not helping some blasted..." His eyes scanned her again. "Noble get across the sea unless you give me a priest darned good reason."

Summoning every ounce of courage she could muster, Helena stuck out her hand. "Helena Rhodipus, rightful heir to the Madran throne. How do you feel about a little vengeance?"

Will stood, taking his time to examine the truth in her eyes. "You are her, aren't you? The masked princess?" He grasped her hand. "I'm a mercenary, doll. We're always prepared to fight." He considered her for a moment longer. "I won't set foot in that kingdom again, but if finding you a way across aids in taking down that bastard king, I will do it."

That was it.

The plans formed in her mind. No more waiting. She was going to Madra.

Twelve

Helena gripped the horn of her saddle, every muscle eager to begin the journey back to Madra. Will's words the night before ran through her mind. He knew more about the current situation in Madra than he should have, but each time mercenaries passed through, they stopped to try to convince him to join them. His family was well-respected within their ranks.

A ship. That was the first part of the plan. Then a place to stay once she reached Madra. He'd told her the mercenaries were staying out of the city but that there were rebels hidden throughout. A bakery held their secrets and she'd find them there. They would help her get into the palace.

No one knew of her meeting the night before, and now Will was nowhere to be found. He'd travel into Bela by a different route. Madran mercenaries weren't welcome in the kingdom they'd fought to destroy only a few years ago.

Deep-seated resentment ran through every bit of Bela, and it would probably never go away. It didn't matter that the mercenaries were only doing a job they were paid handsomely to do. They'd had no loyalty to La Dame. Loyalty was a foreign concept to them altogether.

Helena's eyes slid over Tyson, Edmund, and Landon. What would they think if they knew she planned to put her trust in someone they'd consider an enemy?

What would Dell think? He didn't have the same hatred inside him, but she hadn't told him, and she didn't know why.

Beside her, Vérité lifted his head as if giving his approval. The horse was right. They'd wasted enough time waiting for Dell to recover from the healing. But it hadn't been wasted if he recovered, had it? Her anxiousness to return home overrode all sense.

Dell's exhaustion would last a while longer. Helena had enough experience with healing to know that. She observed him for any sign of struggle. He showed none.

After meeting Will, she'd slipped into Dell's room to find him thrashing on the bed. He only calmed when she crawled in beside him and wrapped her body around his.

He hadn't woken, but his heart had slowed, and his breathing had evened. His body may recover but his mind... that would take longer. She could still remember the moment before a knife sliced into her as she fought during the rebellion. The second she thought it was the end.

It wasn't something she'd ever forget and now Dell had a similar memory. The bite of metal sliding into his flesh would be forever burned into his brain. He'd been a street fighter in Madra, but his weapon had only been his fists.

She tore her eyes away from him to find Tyson standing in front of Vérité feeding him an apple.

Edmund mounted his horse. "Is Amalie coming to wish us well?"

Maiya appeared at his words, walking down the steps

But should you have need of us we will come to your aid. The past counts toward something."

Tyson clenched his fists but bowed his head. "Yes, lady Maiya. I will do well to remember your words."

Unlike Amalie the night before, the young man couldn't hide the pain in his eyes.

He kicked his heels and took off through the open gate.

Helena spared one final glance for the fortress at her back before following him. Soon, she'd return to Bela, but that was only the beginning.

Thirteen

Helena glanced over her shoulder at her companions as they crested the rise in the valley before riding down into the village.

Relief washed through her when she spotted the shack at the top of the hill. Aron would have seen them by now from his spot in the watch tower—if they could call it that.

As if to prove how right she was, four horses cantered toward them bearing Belaen guards. Etta and Alex's version of city guards wore no armor. Helena suspected they didn't need it when they could rely on magic.

Riding in the center of the guards was none other than the king himself.

Alex shouted a greeting.

"Oi, King." Edmund smiled, more in exhaustion than from any sense of joy.

Helena had long since stopped being shocked by the informality in Bela. She reminded herself Edmund wasn't disrespecting Alex. They were friends. She suspected her father had never had any friends. Stev hadn't either... until Edmund.

Such was the price of power. But here in Bela, those rules didn't seem to apply. Etta and Alex had surrounded themselves with people who loved them despite their crowns, not because of them.

Helena's cheeks warmed as she caught Dell studying her, but she glanced away and nudged her horse forward.

Alex stopped in front of them, the guards hanging back. "You've returned."

"Good observation, Alex." Tyson turned away from him. With that, he snapped his heels against the horse's sides and took off toward the village.

Alex raised an eyebrow.

Edmund's gaze followed Tyson until he disappeared among the trees. "We had to stop at the Leroy Estate for a few days."

Understanding dawned in his eyes. "Which one of you was hurt? Ty would only go to Amalie if he had need of Maiya."

Dell raised a hand. "That would be me."

Alex nodded. "You okay now?"

"Yeah, I'm fine."

"Good. Now tell me what the bloody hell happened to you in Gaule. We've had no word and you all look as if you've been..."

"In Gaule?" Edmund finished for him.

Alex rubbed his eyes. Helena struggled to see the man before her as Queen Catrine's son. He'd grown up as a prince of Gaule before the kingdom fell apart and became a haven for civil war and the bandits picking over the carcass of a troubled land.

"Yeah." He blew out a breath. "My mother?"

"Can rot in that kingdom of hers." Helena directed a challenging gaze to him. At the mention of the woman who had handed Quinn to Madra, rage slammed under her skin, twisting around her heart.

Edmund sighed. "Can we talk about this once I have an ale in me… or three?"

"Priest, that sounds like heaven." Dell tried to sit straighter in his saddle, but Helena saw the struggle.

Alex glanced to the guards at his sides. "Fine. Etta will want to know you've returned. I swear, she loses her mind with worry every time someone she cares for steps across the border."

Helena's anger simmered, lessening with each passing moment. She couldn't resent Bela for what Gaule had done despite their connections. The world still wasn't safe for magic wielders. They'd fought for every bit of freedom they had.

But hadn't everyone?

She touched her cheek out of habit, half expecting to feel the confining lace of a mask. Instead, her fingertips brushed soft skin that didn't feel like hers. She wasn't this beautiful princess. Not anymore.

Her hand slid into the dark tangles atop her head, unkempt from days on the road.

Alex took them down the path that circled the village and led to the bridge across the narrow river.

Once on the other side, they dismounted outside the palace stables.

Etta ran out to greet them, passing each person until she reached Vérité. She threw her arms around his neck. "You're back."

Vérité rubbed his nose against the side of her head.

Edmund snorted. "I survived Gaule as well, but no… nobody cares about Edmund."

Etta released Vérité and grinned before stepping to

Edmund and rubbing his nose. "You're a good boy too, Edmund."

He swatted her hand away and pulled her into a hug.

"Looks like the journey was good for you." She pulled back and reached up to touch the edges of his smile.

He shook his head. "This journey wasn't good for anyone. I'm just glad to be back in Bela."

Etta turned to Helena. "Tyson arrived a few moments before you. He explained the basic events. I'm sorry about your brother but relieved you have returned safe." Her gaze flitted to Dell. "And that you survived your wounds."

Dell dipped his head in thanks.

Etta met Helena's gaze once more. "We must talk. Alone." She began walking. "Edmund, see to the horses."

"Yes, my liege." A mocking note rang in his voice but also affection.

Where was Etta leading her? They rounded the side of the small house and Helena sucked in a breath. She hadn't seen the gardens before.

Laid out before her were rows of the most vibrant flowers she'd ever seen. Living in the city, the only flowers most people saw were in small window boxes or on dying stems in the markets. The palace of Madra had gardens, but even those didn't compare to this.

Yellows, pinks, and blues stretched across the landscape, winding around paths of pale stone. Large trees hung their flowering vines over the paths.

A white stone bench sat in the center.

Helena imagined she was seeing things, but it was as if the flowers woke to Etta's presence and an excited buzz filled the air, tingling along Helena's arms.

She'd heard of the queen's power of growth, but this was beyond anything she'd imagined. "Did you..." She shook her head. No, even after all the magic she'd witnessed, it still felt impossible to her.

But Etta confirmed her first thought. "I created this place to think." She closed her eyes, inhaling the floral scented air. "When I was younger, I lived in a forest and my world was so dark, I made a field of flowers just to add light to my life. Some beauty. It was the first time I realized being surrounded by my magic allowed my mind to clear. When we built this home, the first thing I knew I needed was a place like that."

"It's beautiful."

"Thank you." Etta lowered herself onto the bench. "You must be exhausted from the journey. I know a lot has happened since I saw you last, but we're short on time. First, I am so very sorry about your brother."

Helena lowered her gaze to hide the sadness in her eyes.

Etta patted the seat beside her. "Sit, please." When Helena obeyed, she continued. "I know you're disappointed in how little help you have received from foreign kingdoms. In your eyes, we should all act against a usurper. I'm not going to defend what Queen Catrine allowed to happen, because I don't agree with her decision. But I do understand it. Gaule is not what it once was, and Camille is the heir. It does sound as though she offered small aid in letting you try to capture Quinn. She couldn't have known Reed would betray Dell."

Etta fixed her eyes on a flowering yellow bush. "I want to help you, but I can't ask any of my people to fight in a foreign land. Not again."

Helena stopped her. "I understand your decision. If Bela gets involved in Foreign affairs, you become the peacekeepers of the six kingdoms. I don't want magic used in my kingdom any more than you want it used outside yours."

A smile lit Etta's face, and she brushed her blonde braid

over her shoulder before growing serious once again. "There is news out of Madra. The port has been closed to all foreign trade. We had already ceased trading with them, but now they've cut off the rest of the six kingdoms."

Helena snapped her eyes to Etta's. "But that's..." She had no words to describe exactly what it was, but Etta seemed to understand.

Etta tapped her fingers against her leg. "Your brother has also pulled all troops from the Draconian border."

Helena's brow scrunched. "I thought the war was over years ago." She suddenly hated her father for refusing to allow Helena to learn of the other five kingdoms.

"It was, but when we signed the peace accords, Madra promised a significant force for five years to ensure Dracon rebuilt their towns, but not their army. I have a sizable force there as well and this morning I received word from one of my generals that our allies have abandoned them."

Helena's mind refused to quiet. What was Cole doing? Isolating Madra from the rest of the six kingdoms? There'd long been a sentiment within Madra that the struggles of the kingdom resulted from foreign involvement. They weren't wrong. Her father's wars kept the people from thriving. But to shut the borders entirely?

"Will you be able to hold off Dracon without the Madran units?" Helena asked.

Etta didn't hesitate. "Oh yes. Without La Dame, Dracon is no real threat. I'm more concerned with our supposed allies abandoning us."

"Then don't let them." Helena turned her body to angle toward Etta. "Let's go to Madra. Let's remove Cole from the throne."

Before Helena finished speaking, Etta was shaking her head. "I'm sorry. When I said I can't do that, I meant it." She scrubbed a hand across her face. "I've only been a queen for a few short years. I only know what I can't do. I'm not sure how to fix this."

It was on the tip of Helena's tongue—to reveal the man who promised to help her. But would Etta allow a mercenary into her kingdom?

Helena sat up straighter, thinking of something Etta had said. The port was closed to foreign vessels. How was she supposed to return home? She refused to believe her plan had failed before she even started.

What plan, though? So far, all she had was "Get to Madra." She hadn't seen Will on the roads into Bela and didn't even know if he'd made it.

Etta's eyes stayed transfixed on the flowers before them. Was she thinking of everything to come as Helena was? This would only get worse before it got better, and they both knew it.

"I respect you, Helena." Her words were so sudden, they made Helena jump. "You would make a wonderful queen."

Queen? Helena couldn't think that far ahead. She'd never wanted the role. All she could see was the fight ahead.

Etta hadn't finished. "But I need to ask you a question, and I want you to be honest with me."

"Okay." She could try, at least.

"If you go to Madra, what is your purpose?"

Helena clenched her hands together. "I don't know what you mean."

"Our sources tell us Cole Rhodipus has not made sweeping changes that will hurt the Madran people. He hasn't raised taxes—in fact, he lowered them. Madran trade will suffer, but it will drive prices down for the average city-dweller. He may not do right by the rest of us, but he could be good for Madra. You can stay here in Bela where you're safe and set up a life for yourself. Why fight this fight?"

"Cole has Quinn. I have to do it for my brother."

"Quinn can take care of himself from all accounts. That isn't your true reason."

"It's the only one I have."

Etta gave her head a sad shake. "Now you aren't even being honest with yourself." She stood. "Just... be careful, Helena. I've been down the vengeance road before. All it does is break you apart until the only thing left is a shattered girl. You don't want to be the person with nothing left to lose."

Those words stuck in Helena's mind, rattling around until they latched on and refused to let go.

As Etta walked back to the house, another face appeared, breaking into a wide smile as soon as he saw Helena.

"Kass." She scrambled from the bench and sprinted toward him, ignoring her tired muscles.

He jumped into her arms, nearly knocking her over. "Len. You came back."

She pulled away to look at him and wiped a tear from his damp cheek. "Kassander, did you think I wouldn't return?"

He shrugged, and it broke her heart. "Quinn isn't with you."

She smoothed down his unruly curls.

"No. He's in Madra now." Bending down, she peered into his glassy eyes. "But we'll get him back. I promise."

He nodded. "I know you'll try."

When did her kid brother lose the hope he'd always had inside him?

"Come here." She pulled him back into her arms. "If nothing else, you and I still have each other, right?"

"Lenny, please don't leave me behind again. I know you're going back to Madra, and I want to come."

She closed her eyes, resting her chin on his head. No. It was too dangerous. *You never want to be the person with nothing left to lose.*

As long as Kass was safe, some small part of her would remain whole.

Fourteen

Helena felt eyes on her with every movement as she slid into the bench at the village tavern. A young woman with bright eyes and auburn hair twisted into a bun appeared at their table.

Her eyes fell on Edmund and Tyson. "Rumor is you two were across the border."

She gestured to a small man darting between tables, and he appeared carrying a tray laden with mugs of ale.

As soon as he set them in front of the boys, the tension surrounding them snapped.

Edmund sighed as he lifted the cup to his lips. Dell and Landon drank half of theirs in one gulp. Tyson, moving more slowly, eyed the young woman.

Helena didn't touch the cup in front of her.

"Lana." Tyson seemed to be the only one still focused on her question. "Crossing the border isn't anything new for me."

Lana leaned down, the bodice of her simple dress bunching at the waist. "Is it as dangerous as everyone says?"

Roaming bands of Madran thieves. Gaulean bandits. A

Queen who lacked control over her own nobles.

"No." Sarcasm dripped from Helena's words. "It was just like a stroll on the beach."

What was this girl thinking? Of course, it was dangerous. But not everyone had the luxury of sitting in Bela where none of that danger could reach them. And just like that, she resented everything in this kingdom.

Lana couldn't hide the shock on her face, but Helena didn't care if she was being rude. Those who considered the truth rude weren't worth her time.

Before she said anything else, a movement caught her eyes in the corner of the room. A large man sat in the shadows with a cloak covering every inch of skin save his face. A face she recognized.

Will.

He'd come.

"I need air." Helena shot to her feet.

"But we just got here." Dell reached for her arm, and she stepped away.

Her eyes scanned the noisy tavern, crowded with people laughing and joking as if the world wasn't breaking apart. Maybe only her world was.

She walked with purposeful steps to the door and yanked it open. Moonlight cast the ground outside in an ethereal glow. She shut the heavy door behind her, cutting off the laughter from other patrons.

Only a moment later, the door opened again.

"Not here." Will walked past her as if he didn't know her at all.

She followed him into an alley connecting the main road to the docks. Living in Madra, she'd grown up used to the constant smell of fish, but in Bela it seemed to permeate everything, as if the sea was a part of the kingdom.

Only a few sailors lingered this late at night. Will came to a stop and turned to face her. He didn't push back his hood, but she could make out the edges of black ink on his neck.

"I want to get something straight right now," Will said in a low voice. "I'm here because Amalie asked it of me. I don't give a lick what happens to Madra. It is no longer my home. I fight for more than gold now, and that means I am no more mercenary than you."

Everything Helena had learned of Amalie came to mind. She still hadn't told anyone of the conversation she'd overheard. She cocked her head to the side. "Then what is it you fight for?"

His lip curled up. "The first thing you're going to learn about me, Princess, is not to ask questions."

"Noted." Helena crossed her arms. "Tell me how you plan to get me to Madra."

Will blew out a breath. "You should be going to the Belaen Queen for help."

"This isn't Bela's problem." She grabbed his arm, regretting it as he sent her a cutting look. But she didn't let go. "You may claim Madra isn't your home, but it's mine."

"How do you plan to even get close enough to the king, let alone take the crown from his bastard fingers? The people I'm sending you to can keep you safe for a time, but they can't work miracles."

Helena released him. "You don't get to ask questions any more than I do."

"Fair enough." He lifted his eyes to the darkened sky where ominous clouds gathered, threatening to cut off the village from its silver spotlight. "There's a mercenary ship here in Bela."

Helena sucked in a breath. "Etta would never allow it."

He lowered his face to pierce her with a stern gaze. "The

queen assumes she knows everything happening in her land, but we're good at what we do. A mercenary knows how to mask themselves. Something you have experience with."

She touched her face before even realizing she was doing it. His eyes followed her hands, but he didn't say another word about it.

Swallowing thickly, Helena peered around Will to make sure they were still alone. She had to get back to the tavern before Dell came looking for her. Was she really considering boarding a mercenary ship? The only thing she knew about the mysterious Madran warriors was the danger they represented.

"This... ship..." She pushed out a puff of air. "When does it leave?"

"The third day of every week at dawn."

"That's only hours from now."

He dipped his head to speak. "Unless you want to wait a week."

No. She bit her lip nervously. Would she have the courage to face Cole a week from now? What would happen to Quinn in that time? She could use a week to gather help.

She shook her head. "I have to get to my brother."

He nodded as if he had known that would be her answer all along. "It'll be the only ship preparing to leave before the morning tide. Be there before the sun rises. It won't wait for you." He turned to leave.

"Wait," she called after him. "You're not coming with me?"

He didn't face her, but his words rang in her ears. "Like I said before, Princess, Madra is no longer my home. My loyalty lies elsewhere. I will not see you again."

He left before she could utter the words "thank you."

until she stood in front of them. "Mistress Amalie had to take care of something. She wishes you well on your travels."

"Bloody brilliant," Tyson grumbled under his breath. Was he upset she didn't bother to say goodbye or that they'd come there in the first place?

Helena hadn't missed his many glances toward Amalie when he thought no one was looking. His eyes held a longing that sent a crack right through the center of her heart. He still loved her, but something in Helena told her Tyson didn't know the girl who ran this house. Not anymore. She had her own secrets now, just as they all did.

Helena's eyes drifted back to Dell. Were her secrets going to break them? She wanted to tell him to come with her. To stand by her side. But Cole would kill Dell without a second thought. She didn't believe Cole wanted to kill her. It was maybe a foolish hope, but if true, his hesitation would be her opening. Cole never loved Estevan or their parents... but she'd thought he'd loved her, despite how hard he tried not to.

Tyson patted Vérité's neck before climbing on. "I just want to be back on the road home."

Home. Helena envied him. But soon she'd be returning to hers as well.

Edmund nodded in agreement. "The quicker we're away from the Leroy estate, the better."

"Prince Tyson." Maiya's small voice made them all pause. "Mistress Amalie wishes you could have parted as friends."

Tyson turned the horse away from her. "Yeah? Well, she sure showed it, didn't she?"

Helena didn't like the sarcasm in his voice. It was so very different from the kind prince she knew.

Maiya fixed Tyson with a soft stare. "She wishes me to ask you..." She sucked in a breath. "Please do not return here.

Fifteen

"Helena's been gone a while." Dell glanced over his shoulder toward the door. "Should we go look for her?"

Tyson only grunted, his mood no better than when they'd been at the Leroy estate. Landon watched the door, suspicion clouding his face.

Edmund didn't look worried. "Lenny sometimes just needs to be alone. She's been like this as long as I've known her." He reached over to slap Dell's back. "Relax, Dell. The village is as safe as any place."

He didn't understand. Dell wasn't worried for her safety. Helena hadn't been the same since they left Gaule.

It was as if she was pulling away from him, refusing to let him near. He'd thought she'd finally let him in. The cold princess had warmed.

But now the ice was back, and he didn't know what to do.

When the door opened, and she slipped inside, relief spread through his chest. Just the sight of her calmed him. And then she looked at him and all calm faded away. The light he'd seen in her eyes when he first met her was gone, replaced by a dullness that didn't fit the princess.

He stood when she walked toward the table, her dark curls pulled over one shoulder.

"I was getting worried," he said, fully aware of the eyes on them.

Helena gave him a tight smile. "I'm okay, just tired. I think I'm going to go back to Etta's. I could sleep for a week."

His heart sank, but he let out a soft "okay."

Without saying goodbye to anyone else, she turned and left the way she'd come.

Dell dropped back onto the bench and lifted his mug, swallowing the contents before slamming it onto the wooden table.

Tyson jumped with a curse.

Edmund shook his head. "Dell..." He laughed but there was no joy in it. "You just had to fall for the princess, didn't you?" He drained his own mug seconds before the thin man appeared to refill it. Edmund wasted no time in drinking the fresh ale.

Dell watched him, noticing his drawn face. The Edmund he'd known in Madra had walked with the kind of confidence few possessed. He'd moved with grace and had a deadly charm.

Now, his shoulders slumped forward as he hunched over the table. Remnants of stress lined his skin. His hands, once made to wield a sword with power and skill, now shook as he wrapped them around the mug.

Landon rose, breaking Dell from his examination. "I'm done for the night."

Dell nodded a goodbye, but no one else acknowledged him as he left.

Edmund lifted one hand to run it through his hair, tugging on the ends. He raised his eyes and for the first time,

Dell saw how closely they resembled the desperation he'd seen in Helena's.

They sat in silence for a few minutes, the heady scent of ale swirling in the air. The drink buzzed through Dell's veins as he lost count of how many he'd had. In Madra, ale wasn't a common drink. They stuck to cut wine—nothing as strong as in Bela or Gaule.

Edmund leaned his forehead against the table, his words muffled by the cracked wood. "Why did you let yourself do that, Dell?" He turned his head so his cheek rested against the surface and his eyes found Dell. "She can't give you everything you want, and you're going to end up like the rest of us. Empty."

Edmunds words were like salt in the wound of Dell's life, but he knew the Belaen wasn't truly speaking of Helena.

"They all leave you empty, princess or not," Tyson grumbled.

Edmund closed his eyes. "I just... I wanted to do something. He didn't let me save him. I thought if I helped Quinn it would feel like he was still with me. Some part of him."

How much had Edmund had to drink already? He traced unseen shapes on the table with a finger. No tears stained his cheeks, but his voice broke. "I miss him."

Dell put a hand on his friend's back. He owed so much to Edmund and yet couldn't do a thing to help him. "He's with you as long as Helena and Kassander are. As long as you keep them safe for him."

Dell had only met Estevan Rhodipus on two occasions. When he'd thought Helena was the prince's mistress, he'd fought to keep him from controlling her, even brandishing his carving knife knowing full well the consequences of threatening a royal.

The second time, he'd also been fighting for Helena, but

this time the prince had been on his side. He'd thought Estevan to be cold, ruthless. But Edmund saw something else.

He squeezed Edmund's shaking shoulder.

While they had a purpose, a mission, they could all push the events in Madra from their minds. Now they were back in Bela with no path forward. Were they supposed to forget? Was it even possible?

All Dell knew was with each passing day, Helena drifted further and further away. Yet, she was still there with him. Edmund didn't even have that.

He needed to see her. To touch her. To help her forget. Bela was their life now. They couldn't return to Madra where they'd be arrested on sight. There was nowhere else for them to go.

He stood and gripped the table as the world tilted around him, and his stomach lurched.

Tyson laughed. "Looks like Dell had a bit too much."

Dell swatted at him, but missed and almost toppled over. All he wanted was his bed, but he wasn't sure he could leave Edmund in his state. "You going to be okay?"

Edmund lifted his head, but no answer left his lips. Instead, a new voice intruded on their night. "I've got him."

Dell turned and tried to place the man behind him. His uniform spoke of importance... "Mathew?"

"Matteo." Tyson corrected. "My cousin."

The man hadn't removed his eyes from Edmund. "We met when you first arrived in Bela."

Dell remembered then, but it was hazy.

"You going to make it back okay?" Matteo finally glanced at him.

There was an intensity to the man Dell had only ever seen in one person. Estevan.

"I'm going with him." Tyson stood and stepped around the table, the drink seemingly not having as much effect on him. He eyed his cousin. "Take care of him. He isn't himself tonight."

"Always."

Tyson patted Matteo's arm before issuing a quick "coming, Dell?"

Dell hadn't been in Bela long enough to understand the relationships between the people there. They'd fought together, bled together, and that was sure to bond, but it was more than that. Even through Tyson's dark mood, he watched out for Edmund as if they were family.

Dell hadn't ever had that until Edmund came into his life. Not even his family would have fought for him.

Neither man talked as they began the short walk among the deserted village streets, both stumbling occasionally.

Finally, Dell couldn't hold his questions in anymore. "Matteo... he loves Edmund?"

Tyson nodded. "Yes." Dell didn't think he would elaborate until he heaved a sigh. "They' were together for two years when Edmund asked Etta for the open ambassador position. None of us wanted him to take it, but he was searching for something. Nothing had ever been easy for him growing up. The war with Dracon only made Edmund want to do something grander with his life than play the day to day political game."

"And Matteo didn't want to go with him?"

Tyson rubbed the back of his neck. "Edmund didn't ask him to."

Dell glanced back at the road they'd just walked down to where the tavern stood. When he'd first met Edmund, he'd known the stories of the battle with La Dame and the Belaen ambassador with magic. But he'd never truly considered his past. That while he was risking himself playing a dangerous spy game in a kingdom that wasn't even his, he'd had people in Bela who would have mourned him if it all went wrong.

Who would mourn Dell?

They stumbled into Etta's "palace", finding the king and queen sitting together near the fire. They both looked up.

"I didn't want to go back to my empty home in the village." Tyson looked to the ground as if afraid they'd tell him to leave.

Instead, Etta rose and crossed the room to wrap her arms around Tyson. "You smell like an alehouse."

Her shirt muffled Tyson's laugh as he buried his face in her neck.

Dell walked toward the back hall to give them some privacy. He stopped outside Helena's door, preparing to knock, needing to see her. Raising a fist to the wood, he paused. If she'd managed to escape their realities for a few hours of sleep, didn't she deserve the peace? Besides, Kassander shared her bed.

With a resigned sigh, he turned to push into his own room, freezing as he caught sight of the wild dark strands splayed across his pillow, illuminated by a single candle on a table nearby.

Helena shifted and turned to face him.

He wanted more than anything to bring the light back to her eyes.

"You're in my room," he breathed.

"Dell." Her voice cracked. "I don't know what's going to happen tomorrow, but I need you tonight."

He toed off his boots, almost stumbling, and sat on the edge of the bed. "I'm right here. I'm not going anywhere."

She bunched his shirt in her hands and pulled him down beside her, scooting over to give him room. His fingers skimmed from her face down to her shoulder. He thought of Edmund and the words he'd said. *You just had to fall for the princess.*

"Like I had any other choice," he whispered as he pressed his lips to hers.

They came from different worlds. He'd spent much of his life swabbing decks, mucking stalls, and avoiding beatings from his brothers. No one to love him. No one to care.

She'd grown up in a beautiful palace, but hidden from the kingdom. Loved by her brothers and betrayed by one as well.

How could a man with nothing to give deserve a woman like her?

He couldn't. And yet he'd show her they weren't the people they were raised to be. He wrapped his arms around her back and pulled her flush against him.

Helena opened, allowing his tongue to dance with hers, sending sparks through his blood. Digging her fingers into his hips, she kissed a line across his cheek and down his neck.

"Dell," she breathed.

He pulled her shirt free of the trousers and pushed it up to run his hands across the soft skin of her stomach. She shivered under his touch.

"Tonight I'm yours." She'd broken the kiss to speak. "All of me. I've never... I know you've done this before."

Dell smiled and pressed a kiss to her forehead. "I've never been in love before."

She closed her eyes, a brief smile flickering across her lips before it disappeared. "I can't promise you anything... just right now. I really need you to hold me together."

Dell inched his hands up, tracing every curve, memorizing the way she felt in his hands. She hadn't told him she loved him, but he didn't need her to. Not yet. They had time.

Sixteen

Helena watched the slow rise and fall of Dell's bronze chest. Only hours ago, she'd run her hands over every ridge, every muscle. And Dell had plenty. His body resulted from years of hard labor. He hadn't had a choice in how he spent his days.

"Just like I don't have a choice now," she whispered into the dark. Would he forgive her? She lifted one finger to her lips. A part of her knew this decision would change everything. She just hoped he'd understand.

Confronting Cole wasn't something she could run from. Even if it weren't for the people he now ruled, she'd have to do it for herself. Dell wanted to have a peaceful life. He thought they could start fresh in Bela. But there'd be no peace within her until she dealt with the past and the person who took it from her.

Bending down, she brushed her lips across Dell's. "I'm sorry." As she slid from the bed, she glanced back, wishing she could take him with her. He'd go if she asked. She knew that.

But he'd never make it out of there alive.

Would she? She wanted to not care, to not feel anything.

Risking her life to get vengeance for her family should have been simple.

But nothing was ever simple.

She stepped into her clothing, pulling the trousers up her legs and tying them at the waist. After dragging on a tunic and tucking it in, she paused.

Sitting on the table beside the short candle was a tiny wooden sword. Of all the things Dell could have carved... She'd seen him create angels and elegant shoes, but this... maybe it was an omen of what was to come. Making a quick decision, she slipped it into her pocket and peered down at the sleeping man once more.

The first time she'd met him, he'd had blood running down his face from a fight. And still, he'd been beautiful. Even after years of hardship, there was no darkness inside him. Unlike her.

She closed her eyes, her hand hovering over the top of his head. She could wake him. Decide it had all been a mistake and beg him to come. Her fingers curled into a fist as she retracted her arm. This wasn't his fight.

A tear slid down her cheek. "I love you, Dell. For what it's worth."

Wiping the back of her hand across her face, she slipped into the dim hall before returning to her own room. Kassander curled in on himself in the center of the bed.

She walked forward and leaned down to kiss his forehead. His eyes fluttered open.

"Len." Sleep coated his words.

"It's okay." She brushed his hair out of his eyes. "Go back to sleep."

He rolled away from her, a soft snore echoing through the room. Trying to be as silent as she could, Helena pulled on her boots and then slipped one of her knives into the sheathe. She wrapped a scabbard around her waist.

Unable to look at her brother again, she left, shutting the door behind her and leaning back against it.

She'd promised not to leave him again. His voice entered her mind and tears pricked her vision. There was no time for sentiment. She wiped her eyes and walked into the living space. A leg was draped over the back of the couch. She rounded it to find Edmund sprawled face first on the velvet cushions.

"Matteo dropped him off."

Helena jumped at Etta's voice. Etta walked around her to sit on the arm of the couch, a mug of tea clutched between her hands. She gave Helena a sheepish smile. "I couldn't get him into a bed and didn't want to wake anyone."

"When did he get home?"

"Oh, that was hours ago. I just couldn't sleep after seeing him like that." She peered into her tea as if it was the most interesting thing she'd ever seen. "He's struggling, and I don't know how to help him."

Helena glanced at the door. She didn't have time for this. But it was Edmund. "I don't think anyone can help him right now."

He rolled over with a groan and peeked one eye open. "Why are you two here in the dark?"

Etta, as if noticing the early hour for the first time, gave Helena a questioning look. "I know why I'm awake. But what are you doing?"

Helena shrugged, nerves fluttering in her stomach. "Couldn't sleep either."

Etta didn't look as if she believed her. She scanned Helena's outfit, taking note of the visible knife at her waist. "You're leaving."

Edmund groaned. "She isn't leaving, Etta. Where would she go?"

Helena clasped and unclasped her hands, but the queen only studied her. "How do you plan to get there?"

Silence hung between them for a long moment. Edmund glanced between the women, eyes wide, before sitting up. He grabbed his head. "Remind me never to drink again." He closed his eyes.

Finally, Helena relented. "There's a ship leaving at sunrise."

"The mercenary ship." Etta nodded.

"How...?"

Etta waved away the question. Helena guessed she truly knew everything that happened in her kingdom.

"You can't stop me." She crossed her arms.

Etta sighed. "I know. You have to do this. I've been in your shoes before."

Edmund snapped his eyes open. "I don't understand what's going on."

"You need not understand, Edmund." Helena put a hand on his bare shoulder and squeezed once before walking past them.

Etta's voice stopped her at the door. "I'm not going to you do the disservice and assume you don't have a plan. You're a smart girl, Helena. Remember what I said though. Make sure this is about more than revenge."

"It is." It was about family. She stepped into the predawn darkness, letting the beginnings of light guide her way. Sleep still hung over the quiet village as she made her way through the streets and turned into an alleyway.

Footsteps sounded behind her and she turned but saw no one. Was someone following her?

She tugged in the edges of her cloak and removed the

knife from her belt. As she reached the docks, she breathed out a sigh of relief. One small ship sat amid commotion on its decks as sailors readied it to set out. Men and women loaded crates across a ramp.

A sense of familiarity hit her as she took in the Madran vessel. High Cherrywood walls circled a wide deck, dipping and rising in an intricately carve design. Whoever owned the ship had wealth. She could tell that just by looking. At the bow, a golden statue of a serpent hung out over the water, protecting the seafarers from anything lurking below.

She walked closer, her heart pounding in her throat.

Dawn light stretched out over the water and she focused on it for a moment of hesitation before turning her gaze on the sailors who'd paused their work to stare at the approaching girl.

Three large men stood on deck. One set down the crate he was carrying, his thick muscles stretching. The other two continued to wrap ropes, clearing the deck of all debris. Tattoos stretched down each of their necks in the same way Will had worn them. Thick black scrawl that gave them a darker appearance. She didn't know what the symbols meant, only what it signaled. These men were mercenaries.

The man closest to the rail jumped over, landing with a heavy thud on the dock. Helena's limbs froze in place as he approached. "And who might you be?"

She swallowed thickly, unable to form a single word. How many times had her father warned her of mercenaries? They weren't allowed in the city and for good reason. His voice rang in her mind. "They're dangerous, Helena. They do not obey their king."

She worked her throat, trying to breathe as he stopped only feet in front of her. Now that he was near, she could see he was younger than he'd appeared, probably even younger than herself. Wavy chocolate hair framed a boyish face that didn't fit a man of his size.

He grinned as if taking pleasure in making her squirm. "You can speak. I don't bite." He leaned in. "Much."

"Leave her alone, Ez."

Helena's closed her eyes briefly. She knew that voice. Forgetting the boy in front of her, she sighed. "You followed me."

Edmund stepped up beside her. "Of course I did."

Helena wanted to be mad, but instead, she was just so relieved Edmund was there.

He turned to the mercenary whose grin had widened. "Since when do you transport more than just goods, Ezio?"

Ezio's eyes widened. "You're the one uncle Will sent?" He smacked his own forehead. "Of course you are."

Uncle?

Edmund seemed to sense her confusion. "Len, this is Ezio. His mother captains this ship."

Len... that was a signal. No real name? She nodded, understanding his meaning. He didn't trust them enough to reveal her identity.

A woman appeared on deck, hands on her hips. "Ezio. There's work to do."

He shot Helena a wink before running back to the ship.

Edmund raised a hand in greeting.

"Edmund." She leaped from the ship and walked forward. "Are you delivering our passenger?"

Helena studied the woman, seeing the resemblance to Will in the confident set of her shoulders, the tilt of her head. Not her looks though. He'd been larger, looming. This woman had a slight build and delicate features. From the way she walked, Helena guessed she was anything but delicate.

Edmund leaned close. "This is Damara," he whispered. "Be careful around her."

She still didn't understand why Edmund was there or how he knew these people, but she trusted him.

"Damara." Edmund met her gaze, hardness entering his eyes. "When the queen told me Len had left, I knew you were behind it."

Damara raised one arched brow. "I'm not behind anything, boyo. My brother came pleading for her passage. He knows I will give aid to anyone trying to escape Bela."

Escape Bela? Who'd ever want to do that?

Edmund's jaw clenched. "Queen Persinette allows you to move your trade through Bela despite my advice to turn you away. The least you can do is respect her."

Damara turned to Helena, ignoring Edmund's words. "Do you wish me to get you out of this kingdom or not?"

Despite Edmund's tension beside her, Helena couldn't deny that was what she wanted. Even if this woman couldn't be trusted, she was the only way back to Madra.

Slowly, Helena nodded.

"Speak, girl!"

"Yes." She sucked in a breath. "I need passage to Madra."

Damara clapped her hands together, making Helena jump. "Good. Will already paid me, a gift from his mistress he said. I knew there was a reason he refused to return to Madra."

She was wrong. Helena had seen it. It wasn't money keeping Will with Amalie. It was loyalty.

Edmund gripped Helena's arm, preventing her from moving forward. "I'm coming as well." He released Helena and strode past Damara. "Consider my payment your continued ability to enter Bela." He didn't turn back. "Len, come."

She ran after him, not wanting to spend another moment in the harsh woman's presence. "You can't be serious, Edmund." Fear overcame the relief she'd felt that he was there.

He didn't respond.

"You can't come with me."

He stopped before boarding the ship as she grabbed his arm, holding him back.

"Edmund..."

He turned so suddenly she took a step back.

"Why, Len? Why can't I come?"

Her voice dropped as if she didn't want to hear her own words. "He'll kill you."

A strangled sound escaped Edmund's throat, but he held back a sob. "Does it matter anymore?" One last flash of pain flickered across his face.

Ezio held out a hand to help her across the wooden walkway. The ship bobbed in the waves crashing against the docks.

Edmund spoke to no one, and Helena didn't know what else she could say to convince him to stay behind. She'd never recover if something happened to him. But at the same time, his presence made her feel as if maybe this mission wasn't as stupid as she'd thought.

Oars dipped into the water in syncopated rhythm as the ship began its journey. Colors streaked across the horizon, welcoming a new day, but in Helena's world, everything remained dark.

Seventeen

He was alone. Dell reached an arm out, feeling for the warm comfort he'd had through most of the night. Images from only hours ago rolled through his mind. Helena had given him everything in one night. He'd never been more sure of anything in his life. She loved him. Her scarred, broken heart hadn't frozen him out completely.

Maybe there was happiness to be found among the heartache after all. But where was she? For the first time, they didn't have some journey to start out on or some mission to accomplish.

Why wasn't she here?

Dell rubbed his tired eyes, blocking out the light streaming through the window. Did last night mean Helena was finally telling him she was giving up her vendetta? That she knew there was still a future for her? Quinn would be okay. He could stay by his twin's side as long as Helena let him.

No one had to risk their lives.

He didn't have to lose her.

He rolled over, groaning as his muscles ached from days

in the saddle. He sat up, pushing the blanket from his lap and swinging his legs over the edge of the bed. Food. He needed food. As if in agreement, his stomach growled. Maybe that was where Helena had gone. Alex usually cooked breakfast. It was his thing. Etta said he'd only learned to cook once he lived in Bela without people to do it for them. She'd refused to hire servants, so he did it and fell in love.

And he was good at it.

Dell's mouth watered as he pulled on a fresh shirt and trousers, not bothering with shoes. The weather turned colder each day as they inched toward winter, but Etta's home was never cold.

He reached for the carving he always carried, never leaving without his current work in progress. But it was gone.

Maybe Kassander took the small sword replica. Even as he thought it, he knew Kass wouldn't have even come in here.

Only one person had entered this room besides him.

Panic coursed through him as he ran to the living space. Alex and Etta were awake and talking in murmured voices in the kitchen.

No one else was there.

"Where's Helena?" Dell's eyes searched every corner of the room before he sprinted out the front door to the stables. Vérité greeted him with a snort. Alex's horse only lifted its head.

Landon lay passed out in the loft above.

No Helena.

He turned to search the yard and found Etta standing on the front porch with her arms crossed in front of her.

Her lips drew down in sympathy. She knew something.

Dell crossed the yard, stopping in front of her. His chest heaved with a single word. "Why?"

Not where. He had a sinking feeling he already knew the answer to that.

Not how. That wasn't important at the moment.

He should have known. On some level, he did. She'd never give up. But... "Why did she leave me behind?"

His shoulders sagged. He'd have gone. Without question. He didn't care what the risks were. He wouldn't have left her side. And she'd known that.

"Dell." Etta rushed forward and wrapped her arms around him.

In that moment, he understood how their family worked. How Etta had so many people who would follow her to their deaths. She took care of them. Not in a motherly fashion, that wasn't her. But when they fell apart—as they all seemed to do frequently—she could hold them up.

But he couldn't take it. Her arms weren't Len's. He shrugged out of her hold as Kassander appeared in the doorway. "Where's Len?"

Suddenly, Dell hated Helena. She'd left him to tell her brother he too wasn't needed. That the fight belonging to both Rhodipus children would only be fought by one.

He put a hand on Kassander's shoulder, resentment curling in his gut. "She left, buddy. And I don't think she plans on coming back." He walked into the house and dropped onto the couch. Putting his head in his hands, he let anger overwhelm him. Around him, people spoke. Etta comforted Kass. Alex welcomed Mari and Corban when they showed up at the door.

It all blurred together in Dell's mind until Kassander sat beside him. "Are we going after her?"

Those words were like a bucket of ice being dumped over his head, waking him from the nightmare he was living in.

There was something he could do. He didn't have to just sit in Bela and wait for news of her fate.

Helena may not have wanted him there with her, but it was time she realized she didn't make decisions for him.

He lifted his eyes, seeing the prince as he truly was for the first time. They'd treated Kass as a child, too innocent and too young to be part of this fight.

But he'd lost his innocence the day they murdered his family. Youth was a luxury he no longer had. And he looked... ready? Dell shook his head, not knowing if that was the right word. He had a stubborn bravery Dell admired.

"Yeah, Kass. We're going after her."

All chatter in the room stopped as his words wrapped around them. Mari came to sit beside him, the closest thing to a mother he'd had in years. Along with Corban, she'd tended Dell's physical wounds for years. Now, she tried to soothe his emotional ones as well. She squeezed his hand as if comforting a child. "Dell... you can't return to Madra. Helena has made her choice and I wish it were different, but I don't want that danger for you."

"You don't understand." He shook his head. "I have to... I..." He leaned in to Mari, letting her wrap an arm around his shoulders. "I would walk through fire for that girl... I'd face La Dame herself. The only risk that matters is losing her."

Alex broke the tension with a chuckle, surprising all of them. "Well, being that I did ride to face La Dame because I was in love... I'm probably the only one here who understands."

Tyson's tired voice came from the doorway. "Please, Alex. You didn't even have to enter Dracon until the fighting was done. Etta was the only one of us who faced La Dame."

Alex took a plate of fresh fruit from the kitchen and set it on the table. "But I still gathered an army and rode to Dracon ready to fight. I could say it was some noble reason like wanting to help the people of Bela. But Etta was there, and I'd have done anything to protect her."

Etta grunted. "You boys need to realize we don't need you to protect us, only fight beside us." She snagged a piece of bacon from the tray Alex had grabbed. After taking a bite, she pinned Dell with a look. "Okay, everyone. Family meeting. Right now."

Tyson grumbled something under his breath as he plopped down into a chair near the fire.

Mari moved to get up, but Etta held out a hand. "Stay. You're family now. Someone wake Landon."

Mari gave Corban a push, and the boy ran out to the barn, returning a few minutes later with a half-awake Madran general.

Someone was missing. "Where's Edmund?" Dell met Etta's gaze. Her eyes gave him the answer he needed.

She'd taken Edmund and left Dell behind. Perfect.

"Dell." His name was a sigh on her lips. She didn't know what to say to him.

Tyson drummed his fingers on the arm of the chair. "I don't understand. Where is he? Where's Edmund?"

"He's on a ship headed to Bela with Helena." Alex was the only one who seemed to be able to voice the words.

Tyson shot up to his feet. "What the hell? Why was Helena allowed to leave for Madra? Why wasn't I asked to go? I know I told her I couldn't... but that was before we lost her brother."

Dell had those same questions.

Alex scratched his jaw in confusion. "Why would she ask you when she didn't even let Dell go?"

Tyson crossed his arms. "Not Helena. Edmund. I go where he goes. He already left for Madra once over a year ago and you just let him go again? What if this time he doesn't return?"

"Ty..." Etta said it like he was a child.

But Dell knew Tyson had a point.

"He's my best friend, Etta." He sank back into his chair.

Dell looked to each of them, realizing he wasn't the only one with something to lose.

Etta slammed a fist into the table behind them, the crack echoing around the room. "Everyone sit."

Alex and Landon had been the only people still standing, so they pulled chairs over from the table and obeyed.

Etta crossed the room to stand in front of them, the flames from the fireplace at her back. "This isn't easy on any of us, and we won't get anywhere if we're arguing at every turn." She faced her brother. "Tyson, your behavior has been unacceptable. I won't let Amalie Leroy turn you into a simpering fool. So, get it together or you won't be a part of this at all. I know you love Edmund. I love him too. Alex loves him. Hell, everyone who has ever met that blasted idiot loves him. But he loves Helena." Matteo interrupted her by walking through the door. He took in her expression and hurried to pull over a chair.

Breathing out slowly, she spared a glance for her cousin. "And Edmund loved Estevan Rhodipus. He had to go. They both did. I wasn't going to stop them. We can worry about them, but we can't let it tear us apart."

"How are they getting to Madra?" Dell asked. "I thought they'd closed their port to all foreign ships."

"They aren't on a foreign ship."

Dell scrunched his brow. They all knew official Madran vessels had stopped coming to Bela over the past few weeks.

Etta straightened her posture as if preparing herself. "They're on a mercenary ship."

Protests erupted throughout the room. The mercenaries had fought for La Dame. No one was more hated in Bela. Not even Draconians for they had been forced to do her bidding. The mercenaries did it for gold.

Etta held up a hand, and to their credit, everyone quieted. "It is done. There's nothing more we can do but wait for news."

Dell couldn't believe her. Or any of the rest of them for that matter. The anger he'd felt toward Helena simmered over, finding a new direction. She really hadn't had a choice. If she'd asked the Belaens, they'd have said no. Unlike him.

His anger was just about to spill from his mouth, but before he had a chance to speak, Kassander jumped to his feet. "We can't just sit here." Tears dampened his face, and he didn't bother to wipe them away. The boy wasn't ashamed of his emotions. "Lenny is going to Madra where Cole..." A sob shook his chest, but he tightened his jaw and lifted his chin. "We should be with her."

"Kassander." Etta reached to draw him to her, but he twisted out of her grasp.

"No!" His scream stunned them all into silence. "No." The look he sent her could have cut glass. "You're a coward, Persinette Basile."

No one spoke as the meaning struck them. Kassander didn't back down. He stared at the magic queen who'd once fought La Dame—and won—as if she were nothing.

Dell looped an arm around Kassander's waist and pulled him back into his lap. The boy's entire body shook.

Breaking the silence, Dell spoke. "This isn't only Helena's problem. Madra is closing itself off, insulating themselves from the rest of the world. With Cole Rhodipus in power, you can no longer draw on them as an ally."

"We survived without them before." Etta's words didn't have the confidence they'd once had.

He could recognize when it was time to stop fighting. He breathed in slowly, tightening his grip on Kass. "You've made your stance on the issue clear. You may not consider Madra your problem, but as long as Helena is there, it is mine and Kassander's, and I intend to go after her."

"So do I," Kassander said.

Dell nodded. "I'm taking the kid. He deserves to be part of this."

Tyson lifted his eyes, but the only person he seemed to see was his brother. "Alex..." Pain threaded through his voice. He scrubbed a hand across his face. "We can't let them have her."

Dell had been wrong. Tyson and Alex had just as much to fight for in Madra as he had. Their sister was trapped within the castle walls, betrothed to the man who'd killed his own family to take the crown.

Alex didn't respond as he busied himself cleaning up from a meal they didn't eat.

"She's our sister."

A clang came from Alex's direction as a heavy cast-iron pot hit the ground. "Dammit," Alex growled. He didn't bother picking it up as he straightened.

Etta had gone pale as she watched her husband.

Tyson stood and closed the distance between him and his brother. He put a hand on each arm and met his dark eyes. "It doesn't matter how we feel about her or what she's done, Alex. Camille is family, and we don't abandon family."

"Edmund is family too," Etta whispered. She closed her eyes, one tear squeezing through. A breath shuddered out of her. "I can't believe I was going to abandon him to his interests in Madra."

Alex rushed to pull her into his arms. "You were thinking of your people."

She clung to him. "Sometimes I get so caught up in being the queen, I forget to be me."

Matteo, who'd been quiet, leaned forward. "Etta."

She pulled away from Alex to face her cousin.

"It's okay."

As if his permission lifted a weight from her shoulders, she straightened and crossed to stand in front of Kassander and Dell. Leaning down to meet the boy's eyes, she smiled. "Thank you for reminding me who I am, young prince. I've been so worried about keeping Bela safe, I've forgotten about the rest of the world."

She straightened and walked to Tyson, wrapping her arms around his shoulders. "I love you, you know that?"

"Even if I'm a simpering fool?" The sound that left his throat was half laugh and half sob.

She pulled back. "Even if you're making me go help Camille." She scrunched up her face in distaste.

Alex laughed, the tension leaving the room. "No one said you had to like your family."

Landon stood. Dell had almost forgotten his silent presence. "We have preparations to make."

"Yes." Etta clapped her hands together, reverting to queen mode. "There aren't any more Madran vessels in port, but I have a few Belaen captains I can question about passage. We'll need horses since they won't allow a Belaen ship into the city. So much to do."

As she issued orders, Dell lifted Kassander off his lap and strode out the front door. Preparing horses would take his mind off the emotions swirling inside him.

He'd go to Madra. He'd fight his brothers and even the

king. But what then? Helena hadn't trusted him. She'd forced circumstances on him when his place was with her.

Dell had grown up in a lonely household, but he'd never experienced true loneliness until that moment. Even surrounded by people who cared for him for the first time in his life, something he hadn't known he needed was missing.

And he didn't know if he'd ever get it back.

But what did it matter to him, anyway? He may not make it through this. But Helena... she would. He knew it.

Eighteen

Helena watched Madra draw near with dread clenching her stomach. She was home.

The noon sun hung above them as sailors took up their oars and the sails lowered. The once busy port of Madra now seemed… abandoned. It wasn't a sight she'd ever thought to see. With no foreign vessels coming in and no Madran trading ships allowed to leave carrying goods, a sad aura sat over the place.

They reached the river bordering the city in the early morning and left the expansive sea behind. Any chance of turning back was gone now.

Who was Helena kidding? It had been gone since she boarded the mercenary ship.

She'd spent a long couple of days among the gruff men and women aboard, their suspicious looks needling her skin everywhere she went. Mercenaries didn't trust foreigners like Edmund, but then, who did? As time marched on, each one of the six kingdoms isolated themselves. Bela refused to help others reach the peace they enjoyed. Gaule was too embroiled in their own civil wars. Dracon no longer had high walls protecting them, but the battle scars didn't go away.

Cana and Andes were both too dangerous for anyone to venture.

What did that leave them with? A broken world.

She didn't hate Etta for her decision. Even Queen Catrine of Gaule she understood. They had done what was necessary for their people. Now it was her turn.

But could she do it? Could she kill her own brother if it came to that?

A hand covered hers on the rail. She didn't turn, but leaned into Edmund. Every time she'd caught sight of him over the last two days, she was thankful he was there. She'd explained everything Will had told her and shouldn't have been surprised that he already knew of the rebel hideout. He knew of many within the network of people wanting to take their kingdom back.

And she'd thought of Dell. Did he hate her for leaving him behind? Probably. Would she do it again? Yes. It didn't matter how he felt about her as long as he was safe from her brother. Cole wouldn't take another person Helena loved.

Edmund rested his chin on Helena's head. "It looks the same."

Helena snorted. Edmund was just trying to make her feel better. This wasn't the same port she'd left behind.

A few ships bobbed in the water, knocking against the wooden planks. A handful of people walked the boardwalk going about their various tasks.

"What happens next, Len?" Edmund's sigh rustled her hair. "Now that we're here. I know you want to follow Will's instructions, but that won't get you close to Cole."

She had a plan, but she still felt lost. She had to get to Quinn as quickly as she could. Whatever happened, she just needed to see he was all right. Will told her to go straight to the safe house, but now, she knew she couldn't risk it. If word of her presence in Madra reached the palace before she did, she'd lose the upper hand.

She didn't have an army to challenge Cole with or even the skill to battle him. But she did have his affections. If anything had been true in her life, it was how each of her brothers had always loved her. Each in their own ways. Stev protected her, shielding her from anything that could hurt her–including their father. Kassander looked up to her as if she were the best part of his life. Quinn respected her, trusted her. He was the one who went along with any crazy idea she'd ever had. But Cole? How had he loved her?

With everything he'd had.

His love had never been easy, but it was always powerful.

And he'd let Edmund and Dell go because of it. Cole already had Estevan in his power. He hadn't needed to bargain with Stev for their lives. But then she'd been hurt. The pain she'd seen in his eyes had been real.

Helena steeled herself for the words she had to say. She slid her arm around Edmund's waist, knowing he wouldn't like the plan forming in her mind. "I'm going to walk up to the palace gates and demand entrance."

Edmund reeled back. "Len..."

"I can't be seen before approaching them. If I am arrested and arrive a prisoner, it's over."

"You'll be a prisoner as soon as you set foot on the property."

She shook her head. "Cole won't hurt me." She lifted her gaze to Edmund, needing to know the thoughts causing his eyes to darken.

"You can't know that. He killed Stev."

She shook her head. "No. Stev died of sickness in his cell.

All indications were that Cole would execute Stev, but he couldn't go through with it. He never had much love for our oldest brother. But me? This might be our only chance to take him down. Even if he won't hurt me... it doesn't mean I won't hurt him."

Edmund's grip on her tightened. "For Estevan."

Helena nodded. "For my parents." Her mother's face flashed in her mind. "And Edmund..." She sucked in a breath. "I have to do this alone."

He opened his mouth to speak, but she clapped her free hand against it. "Don't argue. Cole might not kill me, but you don't have a chance with him."

Edmund sighed, brushing a hand over her hair. "Okay, but I won't sit idly by while you save Madra. That's not why I came. You need a backup plan. I still have my network in the city. I'll reach out to my people. You have two days. If I don't receive a message that you're okay, we're coming for you."

She nodded, some of the tension leaving her. "I was hoping you'd say something like that." She closed her eyes, leaning against him for support. "I'm scared." The words were only a whisper, but when she opened her eyes, it was clear Edmund had heard them.

He lifted his gaze to the nearing city. "Me too."

Ezio skidded to a halt as he found them, intruding on their last moments of peace. He ran a hand through his shaggy hair before rubbing his tattooed neck. "Captain wants you two below deck."

Helena released Edmund and turned to scan her eyes over the young man. He'd been one of the few mercenaries to talk to them on the journey to Madra. Maybe it was his youth or just some sense of innocence, but Helena had grown to like him... despite everything screaming at her not to trust the fighters for hire.

When you fight for nothing, you're bound to no ideals, no kingdom. They may have lived in the mountains of Madra, but they were not Madrans.

Ezio shifted from foot to foot. When neither Helena nor Edmund responded to him, he flicked his eyes to the galley door behind him. "Ummm... I need you to come. Please? Captain doesn't want you seen until nightfall."

Helena sighed, eager to get off the ship and into the city. Ezio was right, though. If the docks were being watched, they needed to wait until darkness hid their homecoming.

Without a word to Ezio, Helena walked past him and yanked open the door before descending the narrow staircase into the dimly lit galley.

Edmund followed her down, and the door shut behind him. All the sailors were on deck preparing to dock, so Helena and Edmund were the only ones in the small space.

Helena picked up a roll from a platter on the table in the center of the room and slid onto the wooden bench, propping one leg up underneath her.

Edmund dropped into a chair with a heavy breath and scrubbed a hand across his face.

Waiting was the worst part. Neither of them knew what the night would bring. Helena took a bite of the bread before setting it aside as her stomach protested.

She drummed her fingers on the table, her mind escaping back to Bela as she closed her eyes. Rolling hills. Flowering gardens. It was no wonder Etta ignored the rest of the world's problems. She had everything. It was her people's reward for generations of struggle.

She fixed a stare on Edmund. What was his reward? He should have lived his life in Bela, never having to face another hardship.

Instead, here he was, hurting. The man he loved was dead. And now what did he have? Revenge?

Some days, it felt as if that was all she had left as well. If she didn't take it, hold on to it, she'd truly lose.

But she'd already lost. This mission would have no winner.

She didn't know how long they'd been sitting in that room. Hours? Finally, Edmund hunched forward, his elbows on his knees. "Lenny?"

She retreated from the chaos of her thoughts. "Yeah?"

"Did Ezio seem nervous to you?"

Helena shrugged. "He's always a bit hyper."

Edmund thought for a moment. "I've known that kid a while now. And his mother. Something's wrong." He stood, glancing over his shoulder at the stairs. Straightening his spine, he crossed the room and bounded up the steps. As soon as he reached the top, a litany of curses rained down.

Helena shot to her feet as he reappeared.

Edmund's jaw clenched as he tried to contain the fury beneath his skin. "Locked."

"Locked?" She didn't understand. Taking the steps two at a time, she ran up and gripped the handle, giving the door a shove. Nothing. She did it again, this time, slamming her shoulder against the wood.

"You won't get it open that way." His eyes drew down, defeated.

Helena wouldn't stop. She crashed into the door again, ignoring the pain slicing through her shoulder. She prepared to strike again when Edmund gripped her shoulder, holding her in place.

"Edmund. Let me go."

His grip tightened. "You're only going to hurt yourself."

She turned on her heel and shot a hand out to grab the

railing. The step wasn't big enough for both of them. But Edmund wasn't going anywhere. Pushing past him, she stormed down the stairs.

"Why would they lock it?" She twisted her dark hair over one shoulder and sucked her bottom lip into her mouth. "It doesn't make sense."

Edmund didn't respond. As Helena took in his resigned expression, she finally understood. Mercenaries were loyal to whomever paid them. Damara had no great love for Etta or Edmund. Ezio's nervousness...

"They didn't bring us here so I could face my brother." The thought sent a wave of fury rushing through her. "We've been prisoners since leaving Bela."

Edmund cursed. "I should have known. They might not know who you are, but I'm still a wanted man in Madra."

Heavy footsteps sounded above them. A lot of heavy footsteps.

Edmund pulled Helena away from the stairs, and the door flew open, letting in the little remaining light from the day.

A shadow appeared at the top, tall and lean. As he descended into the room, Helena took in the crisp Madran uniform, glowing red in the candlelight. Her eyes skimmed up over the straight lines and pressed folds to the angular jaw and sparkling eyes she knew so well.

"Quinn." His name was only a breath on her lips. Her heart leapt, and she wanted to go to him, to have him tell her everything would be okay, to comfort her as he'd done most of her life.

But he wasn't alone.

Three more Madran soldiers followed him.

Quinn's eyes held no recognition for his sister. They were

darker somehow. And that was when she knew. The uniform. The stiff reception.

Quinn hadn't returned to Madra as a prisoner. He'd joined Cole's side as an ally.

Edmund stepped in front of Helena as if he could protect her from the crushing realization the brother she'd come to save may not want to be saved.

"Stay back," Edmund ordered.

Quinn showed no emotion as he gestured to the men behind him. "They come with us. Pay the mercenary and tell them to get out of our city." He turned without another glance and marched up the stairs.

Helena collapsed in on herself. Tears clogged in her throat, making it hard for her to breathe. As she gasped for air, a strong grip yanked her arm forward.

She cried out as Edmund fought back and received a heavy punch to the gut. He would have fallen if not for the men holding him up. With one final hit to the head, Edmund's chin fell against his chest and his body sagged.

Helena didn't fight after that. Up on deck, her eyes burned into Quinn's back, but he didn't turn.

She'd thought Cole couldn't hurt her any worse than he already had.

She was wrong.

Nineteen

The cart rumbled beneath her, and Helena focused on each bump of the road. They had bound both her and Edmund with ropes tethered to the side of the wooden wagon. Two speckled mares pulled them through the city streets.

Beside the cart, Quinn and his soldiers rode large steeds.

In the waning light, Madra looked unchanged. In Helena's heart, everything had changed.

As they approached the city center, Helena saw shops boarded up and the streets of the once busy marketplace were now empty. At this time of night, the shopkeepers should be closing up their stalls for the day and going home to their families. They were the backbone of the kingdom. The citizens who were neither merchant nor pauper.

And yet, where were they?

Quinn's low voice seemed to come from everywhere and nowhere as he spoke to his guards. "We will ride through the front gates. My brother will want to see the prisoners immediately, but he will also want the rest of the palace to see them."

One of the guards nodded. "Sir, can I ask who the girl is?

I recognize Edmund of Bela. When the mercenary's messenger said she brought him to us, we expected him to be alone. Why did we take her?"

Another guard spoke up. "We aren't in the habit of kidnapping young ladies."

"No," Helena growled under her breath. "Only killing their families and following a man who didn't deserve to be king."

The guards didn't seem to have heard her, but Quinn snapped his gaze to hers. He was still watching her as he answered the guards. "It is not up to us to question the king. But you can trust him not to harm her. Not while I'm there."

She got the distinct impression his words were meant for her instead of her guards. Was Quinn saying he wouldn't let anything happen to her?

It should have made her feel better, but instead, it only reminded her that the last brother she thought would protect her had chosen Cole instead.

The guards continued to chatter, but Helena tuned them out, focusing on Edmund's unconscious form beside her.

Their party turned onto a side street that would take them to the palace road. Someone shouted from the road ahead of them, and the lead guard's horse reared up as an arrow soared past, striking the ground at the beast's feet.

Quinn yelled orders as a volley of arrows sailed into the alley amid shouts. Helena ducked low in the wagon, shielding Edmund's prone form, and scanned the rooftops, finally making out shadowed figures.

"Fire," the shout came from up high. More arrows rained down, striking two of the guards next to the wagon. "Don't hit the prisoners!"

"Edmund." Helena shook him. "Wake up. Please." She

tried to free her wrists, but the rope only tightened. They were under attack, and all she could do was watch.

Quinn.

She searched frantically for her brother. An arrow struck his horse, and he jumped to the ground, aiming his own bow toward the rooftops. Firing rapidly, he didn't even pause when a few people fell from the roofs, his arrows embedded deep.

People swarmed the street, crude weapons in hand, surrounding Quinn. His guards lay dead in the road. Quinn paused, taking in the tightening circle of fighters. He lowered his bow and straightened.

A man popped up at the back of the wagon, a grin stretching his brutish face. It dropped when he took in the sight of Edmund.

"He..."

"Alive," Helena said quickly. She didn't know the man, but by the worry in his gaze, he must have known Edmund.

She relaxed. Edmund hadn't needed to find his people. They'd found him.

Panic struck her, and she whipped her head around to find Quinn once more. Two men pushed him to his knees. A woman stood above him, her sword drawn.

Before she knew what she was doing, Helena screamed. "No!" She turned back to the man nearby and held out her wrists. "Get me out of here!"

He pulled a knife and made quick work of the ropes. Helena scrambled from the wagon and pushed through the people in her way until she reached Quinn. Looking into his eyes was like looking into Cole's. And that... she couldn't take. She hardened her gaze. He didn't look to her in apology, only resignation, and that angered her more.

But this wasn't Cole. It was Quinn. She couldn't kill him.

She lifted her eyes to the tall woman. "Knock him out. He comes with us."

Amusement lit in the woman's eyes. "Darlin', you don't issue orders. We came for Edmund. Who are you?"

She met Quinn's warning gaze. He shook his head, but she was past the point of listening to those who betrayed her.

Not releasing her brother from the intense stare, she sucked in a breath. "My name is Helena Rhodipus. I am the rightful heir to the Madran throne."

Quinn seemed to sag at the words.

Helena turned away from him. "Can I give orders now?" She walked back toward the wagon without another glance. "We can't be in the street. I assume you all have somewhere safe to take me. Let's go."

The wagon's driver lay dead in his seat, so Helena climbed onto the bench and pushed him off. He hit the ground with a thud as she took the reins.

A man strode forward, jamming the hilt of his sword into Quinn's head before lifting his now unconscious body into the back of the wagon beside Edmund.

Helena sighed. News that she was alive and back on Madran soil would travel fast. Tonight, she'd follow Edmund's people. Tomorrow, she'd return to her home.

HELENA'S EYES widened in shock when she realized Edmund's people were taking her to his home on ambassador row. But with Madra forcing all foreigners out, it was an unused part of town.

She hopped down from the wagon and waited as someone removed Edmund and then Quinn, carrying them through the back gate.

The man who'd appeared at the wagon stepped up beside her. "Someone will take care of the horses. We need to get inside."

"Bemus," someone snapped. "Bring the princess."

A wide hand landed on Helena's back, urging her past the swinging gate and up the steps into the house she'd only been to once before. She remembered thinking there was nothing distinctly Edmund about his house. He left no trace of himself, but that was before she'd truly known him.

Now, as she walked down a long sparse hall, she could see him there. He was a simple man. She stopped, her feet freezing as she saw a row of floorboards they'd pried up to reveal a hidden compartment. Empty.

What had Edmund kept there?

Had she known him at all? Here she was, surrounded by people who were loyal to Edmund instead of the Rhodipus name. They followed him, spied for him, fought for him. He'd been creating a network of people to protect her family while she'd been sneaking out of the palace in search of freedom.

Suddenly, she felt like nothing more than a silly girl playing at rebellion.

Bemus led her into a sitting room where stiff furniture surrounded a crackling fireplace. As she stepped closer, the warmth licked her skin and she unclenched her frozen fists.

Rebels dropped into chairs without ceremony. Others scrambled to make space near the fire for Edmund. Two men set him on the ground, his face awash in an orange glow.

They didn't give Quinn the same consideration. Bemus tied the prince's wrists the same way Quinn had tied Helena's that very night.

Helena could only go to one of them. Only one of them

hadn't betrayed her. Tearing her eyes from Quinn's olive-toned face, she knelt at Edmund's side.

He mumbled something and his eyelids shifted but didn't open. She bent down. "I need you to wake up, Edmund. Please. I don't know these people."

The rebels watched her with wary fascination. They hadn't exactly said they didn't believe she was the princess, but she felt their skepticism in every glance. Judging by the raggedy state of their clothing, these weren't the type to attend balls at the palace so they hadn't gotten the brief glimpse of her face on her name day—before Cole had spirited her away.

She rubbed her eyes to hold back the tears as she thought of that night. But she wasn't the only person to have suffered. Many people died in the fight, and the group surrounding her had fought. They may have lost ones they loved as well. For her. For her family.

Because Edmund asked them to.

What was it about him that brought out such loyalty?

She brushed a hand over his forehead, pushing hair out of his face. He'd have made a good partner on the throne for Stev.

Edmund's eyes fluttered open, and a groan rumbled through his chest. "My head."

Helena released a relieved laugh. "You'll survive."

"What happened?" His eyes cleared, and he finally took in their surroundings. "What... Helena... we're not in the palace?"

Bemus crossed the room and leaned over with a grin on his face. "Welcome home, Edmund."

Edmund closed his eyes and inhaled deeply before opening them once again. "Help me up and then tell me what the hell happened."

Bemus reached a hand down and hauled Edmund to his feet. The blonde Belaen put a hand to his head with a wince as he took in the room.

His eyes landed on the woman sitting on the arm of the couch, her arms crossed over her chest and one eyebrow raised. "Catsja?" His eyes scanned the group, settling on the man who'd carried him in from the wagon. "And Orlo. You two..."

"A lot has changed in Madra, Edmund." Bemus clapped him on the back. "But we've been waiting for our chance, watching the docks for all ships entering and leaving. We even have our people within the new palace guard. We lost the battle, but we're still waging this war."

Edmund rubbed the back of his neck.

Catsja set her feet on the ground and stood, matching Edmund's height. "They took our tavern, Edmund. Our livelihood. It's now a business run by the crown for the crown's soldiers. Most shopkeepers can't keep their doors open with no foreign trade coming in. The king has turned both merchants and the poor against him. Do you know how rare it is they agree on anything?"

Orlo broke his silence with a grunt.

Helena didn't know what her brother was thinking. Many Madrans had long since blamed foreigners for the kingdom's problems. But it hadn't been their fault at all. The constant wars in foreign kingdoms caused famine and poverty. But Cole wasn't bred to be king. He wasn't taught the intricacies of keeping one's crown... or one's head. Their father had spared no time to teach his bastard sons.

Only Stev and Helena received formal educations. Only they attended meetings of the crown. Estevan was meant to be king, but Helena would be his right hand as head of the merchant council.

But what happens when the merchants no longer bring trade into the kingdom? She jerked her head up, eyes snapping to Catsja.

"Has the king disbanded the merchant council?"

Catsja peered at her as if she didn't want to answer, but she did anyway. "Yes. Ian Tenyson is the sole head merchant now."

"The spiral," she whispered. Everything Madran society was built on. Merchants worked their entire lives to near the tip of the spiral, the peak of status and power. "What are the priests saying about this?"

The rebels exchanged glances, none of them wanting to speak. Edmund gripped Helena's elbow. "Len... Dell and Bemus went to the monastery as the rebellion began. The priesthood had been..." He closed his eyes. "Massacred."

"Gone?" The breath rushed out of her.

Edmund nodded. "Gone."

She stumbled back, pushing away from him. Everything she'd known, everything they had taught her... The spiral... the priesthood...

Cole hadn't just taken the crown, he'd changed Madra forever.

In the corner, Quinn stirred. Catsja wasted no time in going to him. Before he even opened his eyes, her fist flashed and crashed into his head. He sagged against the wall once again.

Helena winced and forced herself to turn away. Quinn was not her main concern.

"Edmund," Orlo demanded. "This girl says she is the princess. Tell us she lies."

Edmund fixed Helena with a stare, and she didn't know what it meant. These were his people. Surely it was time for them to know. She met his gaze, refusing to back down.

Finally, he scrubbed a hand across his face. "It's her."

Silence followed his statement.

Catsja laughed, bending forward to slap her leg. "Of course she is. This is just bloody perfect." When she smiled, Helena stood mesmerized. The woman had an unusual beauty. Her laugh cut off, and she straightened, all humor gone from her face. "Here's how it is, Princess. We fight to keep the little we have from being taken, to keep our kingdom safe. We do not fight for the Rhodipus name. As far as we're concerned, your father was no better than this new king. We owe you nothing. We do not follow you." She stepped closer. "Try not to get in our way."

She bumped Helena's shoulder on her way into the adjoining room.

Bemus shook his head. "Welcome to Madra's rebellion, Princess."

HELENA TRIED to get some rest in a corner far from prying rebel eyes, but also far from her unconscious brother. Thoughts of better times blocked her sleep. Times when it had been her and her brothers against the world. Back when her mother could hold her and tell her it would be okay.

She wiped at a tear as Bemus sat beside her. He held out a mug of tea, and she took it gratefully. Not waiting for it to cool, she sipped the scalding drink, letting it burn through her, enjoying the pain.

It seemed pain was all she knew anymore. Not for the first time, she wished Dell was there with her.

Bemus sat silently for a moment before speaking. "I knew who you were tonight when I first saw you."

She pulled herself into a sitting position and waited for him to continue.

"I fought alongside Estevan and Dell in the rebellion."

She lowered her gaze to the cup in her hands.

"I was sorry to hear about Estevan's death."

Her hands shook and Bemus took the cup from her. "Stev was... he didn't deserve to die like that."

Bemus set her cup aside on the floor. "No. He did not."

"I know you rebels hate my entire family. My father... was not a good king. But Stev would have been. Maybe if more people had fought for him, he'd be sitting on that throne right now."

And there was the truth Helena had been scared to voice before. She was bitter. Angry. Not only at Cole. No. Some of the blame lay with the Madran people who hid in their homes while their ruling family was slaughtered.

"Maybe so," Bemus said. "But we're here now. Our numbers have grown rapidly since Cole Rhodipus became king."

Helena shook her head. "And you all think we need more blood staining the palace walls?" She pulled her knees in and rested her chin on top. "My father told me never to trust a rebel. That they always had another motive and did nothing for the good of the kingdom."

Bemus didn't respond right away, but his eyes drifted to Edmund. "Princess, I hate to tell you, but you've been trusting a rebel this entire time."

She shook her head. "Edmund only wanted to keep my family safe."

"He wanted to keep you safe and the princes Kassander and Estevan. But he has never been beholden to the bastard princes."

Helena let her eyes rest on Quinn's still unconscious form and Bemus' final words took a moment to register.

"He was never loyal to the king."

She peered sideways at the monstrous man. She wouldn't have admitted it, but she didn't need Edmund to be loyal to her parents. He hadn't risked everything to keep the Rhodipus line ruling Madra, and she'd known that. He only wanted to keep her and Estevan alive.

Even now, he hadn't returned with her to take the throne. Only to take his revenge. And maybe help the people he'd left behind. His place was among them, and Helena wished more than anything hers was too.

But the time for indecision had passed. She rose to her feet.

"Where are you going?" Bemus asked.

Steeling herself, she took a step. "To do what I came here to do."

He didn't move to stop her as she reached the door. Out in the hall, Edmund spoke to Catsja in a low murmur as they bent over a table laden with various weapons. He lifted his head as Helena approached.

She studied the blades and axes. The mercenaries had taken her knives, and she felt naked without them. Yet, she pulled her hand back without picking one up. They wouldn't let her into the palace without first taking her weapons, so there was no point.

Edmund opened his mouth as if to say something, but Helena shook her head.

Edmund nodded, understanding shining in his gaze.

She held up two fingers. If she didn't send word within two days, the rebels would launch an attack on the palace.

Edmund must have told Catsja of her plan because the woman looked on in sympathy. "If you have need of aid, look for our top rebel contact inside the palace. His name is Reed."

Helena's blood froze.

Reed.

Edmund had gone pale. "Reed Tenyson?"

Catsja nodded, flicking her eyes between them. "He came to us the day after you two left Madra. His information has been invaluable."

Helena clenched her jaw. "If I find myself in danger, the last person I will seek out is Reed Tenyson."

She turned to stride past them without another word. Reed was the reason they had been unable to save Quinn in Gaule. If it hadn't been for the youngest Tenyson, she might have had her brother by her side now. Instead, he sat as a prisoner inside a rebel base.

Instead, he was a traitor.

As she stepped into the courtyard, she tried to control her breathing. Dell. She'd been trying so hard not to think of him. A fresh wave of pain washed over her. Reed's men almost killed him that day on the beach. There would be no forgiveness for that. The panic from that day returned, and a tear rushed down her cheek. She wiped it away with the back of her hand as the door opened behind her.

A hand wrapped around her upper arm and turned her into a solid chest. Edmund wrapped his arms around her.

"Promise me again he won't hurt you."

Could she? She was starting to think she didn't know Cole at all. Edmund's arms tightened at her silence.

Finally, she lifted her face to peer up at him. "I'm going to be okay."

He swallowed thickly, pressing his lips to her forehead. "You're my family now, Lenny. If something happens to you..."

She squeezed his arm. "Nothing will happen to me."

She wished she could be as confident as her words. Edmund released her as an older man led a horse from a stall.

Edmund helped her into the saddle. Helena swallowed back the tears threatening to choke her. "Edmund... if something happens... tell Dell..." She closed her eyes for a moment, picturing his face. "Tell him I'm sorry."

And that I love him, she wanted to say. But she held back those words as Edmund squeezed her leg and stepped back.

With nothing else to be done, Helena nudged the horse forward.

Ambassador row sat on a stretch of now abandoned streets. The sound of the horse's hooves striking stone was like a drum beat to her ride to battle.

As she'd always worried, Helena was now utterly alone. But the knowledge didn't weigh her down as it once had. Now, there was no one else at risk. No one to keep safe.

As she turned onto another empty street—this one with shops and homes crowded on each side—she let the moon bathe her in its silver glow. These streets, this kingdom was worth any sacrifice. She knew that now.

Her father hadn't ever known, but her mother had. Rule without sacrifice was only tyranny. War without hope was only death. A fight without reason was only murder.

She loved them all. The merchants climbing the spiral. The poor struggling for food. The priests who'd once thought they were doing good and lost their way.

Her family. Madrans. Foreigners. Magic-folk. Non-Magic-folk.

They were her reason.

She rode through town until she could see the high walls of the palace she'd once called home. They'd fixed the parts of the wall blown to bits by explosions, but black still streaked much of the surface, a reminder of what took place here only months ago.

Guards lined the top of the wall, shadows in the night. Their torches lit up the sky, casting orange across the vast expanse.

Shouting erupted as Helena neared.

"Oi, you there! Stop!" Heavy footsteps pounded down the steps behind the wall.

Helena held her breath, reminding herself this was what she'd come for. She slid down from the horse, setting her feet on solid ground.

The door at the base of the gates opened, spilling guards onto the street. They jogged out, their armored boots crashing against the ground as they surrounded her, weapons drawn.

Lifting her chin, Helena found the guard with the general's stripes on his uniform.

"I am here to see the king."

None of the guards moved. Their faces were impassive masks. The door opened once more, and a man Helena would recognize anywhere stepped through.

A grin slid across Ian's face. "Helena." He gestured to the guards to drop their weapons. "Your brother will be happy to see you alive." He held out a hand to her. "Come."

She didn't take it. After a moment, his smile dropped, and he grabbed her elbow, jerking her forward. The guards followed them closely.

Was this how they treated everyone who came to the palace or had they known she'd come to them?

One of the guards broke off from the group, leading her horse away. Helena barely noticed as she walked up the familiar steps, knowing her parents or oldest brother wouldn't be there to greet her on the other side of the tall doors.

But she wouldn't allow herself to cry for them. Not now.

Not here. They'd be better served by how she'd deal with Cole.

At the door, one of the guards patted her down, looking for weapons. Once he was satisfied, Ian gestured inside. He hadn't touched her again, but his eyes slid over her, making her skin crawl.

Inside, the palace sat unchanged. If she didn't know better, she'd think the crown hadn't changed hands at all. Her father's tapestries and maps adorned the walls, the opulence grander than anything she'd seen in Bela or Gaule.

But the warm cherry walls and plush carpets didn't soothe her as they once had. Now she saw them for what they'd been. Unnecessary. Paid for by taxes the people couldn't afford.

Servants watched her pass with curious eyes. She looked for faces she knew but found none. Her heart pounded against her ribs, the pulse throbbing in her ears until it was all she heard. There was no turning back now. No getting out. She either took care of Cole or spent her life trapped within these walls.

As she'd spent her entire youth.

Ian turned the corner, and she followed him wordlessly. He burst through a door to a stairwell, and Helena's feet stopped moving. She knew where they were going.

No.

It was destroyed.

The place her family had been happy. Where she'd enjoyed life with her brothers by her side.

The royal residence.

A guard prodded her forward, and she climbed the stairs. At the top, Ian unlocked a door and held it open for her. The hall leading to the residence remained the same, untouched by the fire she'd started to free herself from Cole.

After the ball that had forever changed her life, they had locked her in her mother's rooms. Her mother—being trained as a Canan assassin—picked the lock. Once in the main corridor, Helena had set flame to the tapestry hanging nearby. She hadn't known it would spread so rapidly.

Ian procured a second key at the end of the hall and pushed Helena through the door. The living space that greeted her had new furniture, and she suspected the old was too damaged. But there was no other sign of destruction.

A doorway opened and Helena sucked in a breath.

Cole stood stock still on the threshold, his face displaying no emotion other than shock. "Lenny?" He shook his head as if not quite believing his own eyes.

Helena took in his haggard appearance. Shaggy, uncut hair. A scruffy face. Wrinkled uniform.

This wasn't the man she'd expected.

She pushed away any sympathy she might have once had for her brother and straightened her spine. "My name is Helena." Her eyes narrowed. "Lenny is a family name."

The unspoken meaning behind her words hung between them. He was no longer family.

He nodded as if believing he deserved everything she said to him. "I just..." His eyes found Ian and hardened. "Leave us."

"Your Majesty..."

All weariness faded from Cole as the coldness she recognized from the night of the rebellion set in. "Ian, not now."

Ian bowed stiffly and turned on his heel. The guards followed him, leaving Helena with only her brother.

She crossed her arms over her chest, suddenly unsure of what she should say to him. She'd come to pledge her support —however fake it was. But now the words wouldn't come.

He took a tentative step toward her.

She stepped back.

Pain flashed across his face, quickly replaced by something she couldn't interpret. "I thought you were dead."

"I almost was."

Interesting. Reed hadn't told him she lived. That still wasn't proof of his loyalty to the rebels.

Cole swallowed heavily and rubbed the back of his neck. "I'm glad you came home."

She scanned the room and its unfamiliar furnishings that stood as a symbol of what happened here. "Home." She shook her head. "This isn't my home." In her mind, she saw the vast fields of Bela, but that didn't feel like home either. Not without her family.

Uncertainty shone in Cole's eyes. That had never been like him. He was confident. Sure. He shifted his weight to his other foot, never taking his eyes from her.

"I don't expect you to understand, Helena." He brushed a hand through his unkempt hair. "I don't expect you to forgive me."

"Good."

"Can I..." He rushed forward before she could stop him and wrapped his arms around her shoulders.

She stiffened, and a sob escaped her throat. The comfort felt as it always had. Growing up, Cole had been her companion, her protector.

And now he was the one breaking her apart.

He buried his face in her neck. "You're alive," he breathed. "I never thought I'd see you again."

After a moment, she put her hands on his chest to push him away. "Cole, I'm here, okay. I came back. But it wasn't for you." She had to mix pieces of truth in with her lie. "You killed my mother. That isn't something I can..." She sucked in a breath, stepping farther away from him. The words came to her. Quinn wouldn't be able to refute them while the rebels held him. "Quinn sent for me."

Cole straightened in alarm. "Quinn. I sent him to the docks. A mercenary captain claimed to have Edmund being held prisoner." He looked to the door. "He should have returned hours ago."

Tears swam in Helena's gaze. "I was with them, Cole. I didn't know Edmund was a rebel. I swear. He told me he'd escort me home, and I let him. When Quinn arrived, I was so relieved. But Edmund's people came for him. And..." Her lip shook as she met Cole's eyes. "They took Quinn. That's why I told your guards I needed to see you as soon as I got here."

Cole stumbled back. "We need to find him."

She nodded, wanting Cole to go out searching himself. It was his twin after all. Getting him away from the protection of the palace would allow the rebels to help her.

Cole pulled her back into his arms and this time, she let him. "We will. We'll get our brother back. Then we'll kill every last rebel." He spoke into her hair. "I want us to be a family again, Helena. Now that I know you're alive..." He pulled back. "I need to tell you something."

"What is it?"

"I've had no word of Kassander. Many people died in the fight, including some who were burned beyond recognition. I'm afraid he might have been one of them."

Tears spilled from Helena's eyes but not for the younger brother she knew was alive and safe. No, they were for the one she was sure was gone forever.

Her shoulders dropped. "Word reached me of Estevan as well. It seems you, Quinn, and I are all we have left."

A smile split Cole's face, and Helena wanted to wipe it off with the blade of a knife. He'd always hated Stev, but the obvious joy on his face cut straight through her.

He strode across the room and threw open the door to speak to the guards and Ian waiting outside. "Scour the city. The rebels have Quinn. The order is to kill all you find."

Ian nodded. "They won't have him for long. I'll call in the regiment that just returned home."

Cole shut the door once more and turned the lock.

"You aren't going with them?" Helena asked, her stomach dropping in disappointment.

Cole shook his head as he faced her. "They'll find him. As for you... there's something you need to see."

He reached the door he'd first come out of and pushed it open before grabbing a candle from the table near the couch and entering the room.

Stale air struck Helena as she followed Cole inside. The room once belonged to Stev. Someone had erased all smoke and fire damage. A large four-poster bed sat against the far wall with the shape of a sleeping man under the blankets.

Cole reached him and as the light from the candle hit his face, Helena gasped.

The man's chest rose and fell with a steady rhythm. Sweat soaked hair clung to his face as he turned his head. Pale skin stood in contrast to the dark circles under his closed eyes.

Helena's legs weakened beneath her, and she fell. As her knees crashed into the cold stone, one word escaped her lips.

"Estevan."

Twenty

Dell stared out at the dark water, letting the first morning light wash over his face. In the cabins below deck, people slept. Only a few sailors managed the sail as the rest of them finished morning preparations. They'd reach Madra soon. He could see it getting closer, a sleeping city on the edge of the river.

Sometime in the night, they'd left the sea behind to sail into the delta and upstream. A failing wind made the journey slower than Dell would have liked.

He wanted to reach Helena.

Before it was too late.

He closed his eyes, feeling as if she stood next to him, dreaming she slipped her hand into his. If he'd had any doubt in his mind, their last night together washed it away. He loved Helena like he'd never loved anyone in his life.

He only wished she loved him the same. He tried to be angry, to feel betrayed, but it only ended in a crushing realization he wasn't enough for the Princess of Madra. He never had been. She did what she thought was right in fighting for her kingdom. He was only a man who had nowhere else to go. No one to return to in Madra.

Except her.

He opened his eyes as Kassander leaned up against the rail beside him.

"I couldn't sleep any longer," the boy admitted.

Dell sighed. How could he feel sorry for himself when the young prince had lost so much? Was it better to have never had a family or to lose the one you had?

"Is everyone else still sleeping?" Dell rested a hand on the kid's shoulder.

Kass shook his head. "They were talking when I left, but I couldn't take the quiet whispers any longer."

Dell knew what he meant. Alex, Etta, and Tyson's anxieties were getting to the rest of them. They still didn't know if they'd made the right decision. Could the queen and king of Bela involve themselves without involving their kingdom? If they failed and Cole Rhodipus kept his throne, would it throw them into war?

Kassander shuddered under Dell's grip. "What do you think it'll be like to see Cole again?" When Dell didn't respond, he answered his own question. "I think it's going to hurt." His eyes scanned the city they approached. "But then, it already does."

Dell wrapped an arm around Kassander. The boy was almost as tall as Helena and had the same dark hair and olive skin. There was a common look to the Rhodipus children that was both enchanting and disarming. Innocent. Beautiful. But also wild.

He pulled Kass away from the rail and directed him to a crate near the wall. They sat side by side. Dell leaned back and pulled his newest work in progress from his pocket. Helena had taken his unfinished sword, but now his hand closed around a crown. He worked his carving knife along the various dips and curves of the wood as Kassander watched in fascination.

He'd whittled so much over the years, he didn't need to keep his mind on the work. Instead, he thought of every possible scenario that could occur once they reached Madra.

Morning mist hung low on the water, shrouding the ship in a haze.

"What's going to happen once we reach Madra?" Kass asked.

A new voice joined their conversation. "We're going to find your sister." Etta stepped in front of them, bending to look Kass in the eye. "Do you believe me?"

Kassander nodded.

She smiled. "Good. Now, run down to the galley. You're going to want food in your belly. Alex and Tyson are down there. By the time you're finished, we'll have reached Madra."

Kassander's eyes lit up, and he jumped from the crate.

When he was gone, Etta took his seat.

Dell dug harder into the wood, cursing as the knife got stuck in a rut he hadn't meant to carve. With a sigh, he set the wood aside.

"Landon is preparing the horses." Etta pulled her legs up under her. "Captain Smith will set us ashore west of the city. From there, we'll ride in."

Dell nodded. A Belaen ship wouldn't be allowed to dock in the city. It was the only plan that made sense.

"You know Helena more than any of us. What's the first thing she'd do when she reached Madra?"

Dell scratched the side of his face. "Well, that depends."

"On?"

"If she's calling the shots or if she's listening to Edmund."

"Why would they want different things?"

Dell peered sideways at Etta. She claimed Edmund was her best friend. She'd given him the ambassador position, but even she hadn't known what her ambassador had been up to. That he'd become more ingrained in Madran life than he was supposed to. So, Dell explained. He told Etta of the network of spies reporting to Edmund. Of the rebels who were more loyal to a foreign ambassador than their own king.

And then it came time to tell him of his own role in Edmund's world. "Edmund came to me because my brothers were integral in Cole Rhodipus' plans to take the crown."

Through it all, Etta remained silent. Finally, she lifted a hand to her mouth. "He did all of this to protect Estevan?"

"And Helena and Kass, but yes."

She shook her head as if not quite believing it. Tears hung in her lashes. "When I was first told of Edmund's feelings for the dead prince, I didn't know what to think. Edmund's infatuations have always changed with the wind. At one point, he even fancied himself in love with Alex, but I truly think it was only because it would never become more. They love each other, but as brothers now. Then Matteo... My cousin lost himself to Edmund the first time they fought." She smiled. "Then it grew serious, and Edmund begged me to send him to Madra."

A tear slid down her cheek. "But he risked everything for Estevan... and then he lost him. I didn't understand before now. I even resented his new loyalty to Helena because there was a time I was the most important woman in his life." She buried her face in her hands. "I can't believe I almost didn't come for him. He has never once let me down, and I almost failed him."

Dell didn't know how to comfort a crying queen. He patted her back, deciding to answer her original question.

"Both Helena and Edmund are strong willed. I think they'd split up."

She lifted her head. "He wouldn't leave her."

"No." The words hurt to say, but he felt every one of them. "But Helena would leave him if she thought it would save him."

She'd done the same thing to Dell.

Dell watched the sailors prepare to head below deck and man their oars. Their movements were like a choreographed dance. Everyone knew their place, their job.

Helena knew hers as well.

Dell leaned his head back against the wall. He suddenly knew exactly why Helena had left him behind. "She's going to face her brother. Alone."

Etta opened her mouth as if she wanted to argue, but then shut it. She couldn't refute the truth in his words.

Fear engulfed him because he knew if Helena had gone to speak to the king, they were already too late.

Twenty - One

Cole left Helena alone with Estevan and hadn't returned. She didn't know how long it had been, but she sat beside her oldest brother, staring at him as if he'd disappear again.

She stroked the damp hair away from his face.

Helena held back the tears threatening to break free. Estevan needed her strength, not her weakness. If she'd ever had doubts coming to the palace, they vanished the moment she set eyes on Stev.

"You're supposed to be dead," she whispered. "We mourned you."

Edmund. His name popped into her mind so suddenly, she pulled her hand away. If Helena and Edmund had known Stev still lived, would they have come for him sooner?

Helena thought Stev was still sick with fever, but though his skin was damp, it wasn't warm. He didn't shiver, yet there was an alarming pallor to his skin.

His eyelids twitched. "No," he murmured. "No more. Don't touch me." He flipped onto his side and the blanket slipped down to reveal his naked chest. Helena gasped, jumping off the edge of the bed.

Fresh red lines crisscrossed his torso. The long deep cuts crusted with dried blood, flaking and falling onto the bed..

Anger welled up in Helena as she saw the truth right before her. Estevan wasn't sick. His weakness was from blood loss.

Cole. His name burned through her mind, and she turned on her heel, determined to march from the room. To find the brother who caused her family so much pain.

But a voice called her back.

"Helena?"

She froze, thinking she'd imagined it. Turning slowly, she swallowed back a sob. Estevan's eyes slid open, and his clear gaze found her.

Helena ran to him, dropping to her knees beside the bed. "Stev." She took his hand, the tears finally pouring forth. "Stev." She rested her forehead against their joined hands, not wanting to let him go.

He took a shuddering breath. "They told me you were dead."

She made a sound that was half laugh and half sob. "They told me you were dead."

His free hand rose to her hair, arching over the crown of her head. His chest shook, and she lifted her eyes to his tear-stained face.

She'd never seen Estevan cry before. Reaching up, she wiped a tear from his cheek. "What has Cole done to you?"

He shook his head. "Not Cole." His eyes slid shut for a moment. "Our brother--"

"He's not our brother."

Estevan shuddered at the words, and when he fixed his eyes on Helena once more, the force of his pain seared into her. To those who didn't know him, Stev had seemed cold and calculating.

But Helena knew differently. Her oldest brother had been the best of all of them. He'd felt everything on a level she couldn't imagine, but had always seemed ashamed of those emotions. So, he internalized them, hardening himself in the presence of others, especially their father.

But right then, when it was just two Rhodipus children mourning the death of everything good inside another, he finally let her see him.

She leaned forward, running her fingertips down the side of his face. He was really there.

"Kass?" He whispered, fear edging into his voice.

Helena pushed out a breath. "Safe." At least she could give him that. She may have abandoned Stev to Cole's control, but she'd kept the youngest brother alive. Stev's eyes held more questions, but the words didn't leave his mouth as a breath rasped through his chest.

"Edmund is here," she whispered.

Estevan jerked his head from side to side. "No. He can't be. He was supposed to leave with you and never look back. I never wanted..." He coughed, blood dripping down his chin.

Helena didn't have time to say anything more because Camille appeared in the doorway. Jumping from the bed, Helena sprinted across the distance, throwing herself at the other princess.

Camille caught her, her arms stiff. "Helena." She pushed her away, smoothing a hand down the front of her sapphire blue dress. She fixed her ebony curls over her shoulder, not sparing a glance at Stev.

Helena scanned her for any sign of poor treatment. Camille leaned on the same cane she'd had since the day she arrived. Her attire was smoothed to perfection almost as if she wasn't a prisoner at all.

"I was so worried about you," Helena finally admitted.

Camille's stern stare cut through her. "Helena, you're to come with me."

And then she did the last thing Helena had ever expected. Camille raised one hand that held something Helena hadn't noticed before. Something she never thought to see again.

A mask.

She shook her head, hair splaying about her shoulders wildly.

"Put it on."

"Camille." Helena stumbled back. "Why are you doing this?"

In that moment, the Gaulean princess looked very much like her mother—the woman who'd sold Quinn to the Madrans.

And Helena hated her for it. "No."

Camille narrowed her eyes. "It'll be much easier for you if you just obey."

Helena's eyes flicked to the mask. Not again. She'd spent most of her life imprisoned by such fabric. She wasn't that girl anymore.

Two guards appeared in the doorway.

Helena glanced back over her shoulder at Stev who was trying to climb from the bed to help her. He fell back, his body jerking as his eyes rolled up into his head.

"Stev!" Helena tried to turn and run back to him, but one of the guards grabbed her to hold her in place. "Let me go, you bloody bastard." A meaty arm wrapped around her waist, hauling her off her feet as she kicked and screamed.

Camille's words barely registered in her mind. "Get the healer. If Estevan dies, the king will be very aggravated."

No, Helena thought. *Cole wouldn't care what happened to any of them.*

Her own words came back to her. *He's not our brother.*

Only he was. And that made the pain all too real.

"Stev," she cried once more before a fist flashed in front of her face, and the darkness beckoned to her with its peace.

VOICES SURROUNDED HELENA, but she struggled to open her eyes. Heavy footsteps crossed in front of her. The jangle of many armored boots came and went.

Where was she?

As she took in the surrounding room, it all came back to her. Coming to the palace. Cole. *Estevan.* How could her brother be alive after all this time?

Her father's council room took shape around her. No, not her father's. Not anymore. Sound echoed off arched ceilings, only slightly muffled by plush carpets.

Helena lifted her aching head off the soft white fibers of a pillow. She lifted a hand to her face as another piece of herself broke apart. The mask clung to her skin, a cage she had never really escaped. She wanted to cry, to scream, to tear the place down, but she wouldn't give Cole that satisfaction. She refused to fall apart. Not again.

The mask strengthened her, bolstering her need for vengeance. She'd felt the anger slipping through her fingers after Cole brought her to Estevan, but now as she scanned the faces of those loyal to the new king, she wanted them all to pay.

Two boots stopped in front of her before a stocky man crouched down, balancing on the balls of his feet.

Helena lifted her eyes to Reed's and all she could see was the man who took Quinn, who let his people almost kill Dell.

Sympathy entered his gaze, and he held out a cup of water.

When Helena didn't move to take it, Reed sighed. "I'm not going to hurt you, Princess."

A hand landed on Reed's shoulder, jerked him backward. He landed heavily on his butt, water spilling over his shirt. "Dammit, Ian."

Ian ignored Reed's exasperation. "The princess is needed."

Without waiting for a response, he gripped Helena's arm and jerked her up, pulling her toward the table in the center of the room.

Cole stood ramrod straight, newly shaven. His hair was slicked back in the same style he'd always worn it. Only now, he seemed... older. His cold eyes found hers, none of the emotion from earlier appearing in the dark globes.

"We have had great fortune," he said, his eyes scanning the faces around the table. Helena recognized a few generals and merchants, but some were strangers. Camille stood to Cole's right. "Princess Helena has returned to help lead Madra to greatness."

Helena choked on a breath.

Cole continued. "But Prince Quinn has gone missing. We believe rebels have taken him. The palace guard has been scouring the city, but I've brought my sister here to shed some light on his whereabouts."

Helena froze. Did Cole know about her connection to the rebels?

He rounded the table, stopping at her side and peering down at her. False affection rang in his voice. "Dear sister, tell me where Edmund is."

"I-I don't know."

Cole struck her before she even knew what was happening. His palm left a biting pain burning her cheek.. She lifted a hand to her stinging cheek, stumbling back.

"Here in this palace, we do not abide lies." Cole's low voice rumbled through her.

Danger lurked behind his gaze, and Helena swallowed heavily. Did he want her to fear him?

She stood straighter, lifting her chin to meet his gaze. "Even if I knew, I wouldn't tell you."

Cole gestured to one of his guards who struck Helena in the stomach. She doubled over, gasping for breath as pain shot through her abdomen.

She bit back a scream and stood tall once again.

Not a single person at the table made a move to stop Cole.

"Where is my brother?" Cole screamed, the veins in his neck pulsing with his irritation.

Helena narrowed her eyes. "I could take him from you in an instant. You stole everything from me. Why shouldn't I do the same?"

Cole smashed his fist against the side of her head, knocking her sideways. She stumbled, falling to her knees when he kicked the back of her shin. The beating continued with Cole unleashing every bit of his fury on her until all Helena could focus on was the pain.

She held onto consciousness like a falling man holds on to the edge of a cliff. The strikes eased as Cole let out a roar and covered her body with his.

"I had to," he murmured. "Helena, I had to." His tears dripped onto her skin.

The mask hid her ashen face, and Cole's weight on top of her crushed her into the floor. She felt as if she no longer existed.

She'd told Edmund Cole wouldn't hurt her. That had

been the one thought holding her together. As evil as her brother was, he loved her. She'd wanted it to be true. It would have made the mission possible, but it also would have healed some small part of her.

Her bruised body may not have completely broken, but she lay there as if she'd been nothing more than a glass princess.

And now, finally, she'd shattered leaving only razor sharp shards that would slice through anything they touched.

For the second time that day, darkness pulled her under its swift current.

Twenty-Two

The midday sun hung in the sky by the time Dell rode through the city streets of Madra. Beggars sat on each corner, more common than they'd once been. The few shops that had opened had long lines stretching out of the doorways as people tried to get their share of food brought in from the Madran farms.

"We need to ditch the horses," Dell said, coming to a stop and sliding down. He glanced each way down the busy street, pressing back into an alleyway as a cart rambled by.

"It'll take us too long on foot." Etta scanned their surroundings, always watchful.

Dell shook his head. "It won't matter how far we have to walk if we never make it there. This is not Bela. The average Madran doesn't have a horse because they can't afford one. We're marking ourselves with wealth and I'm getting the distinct impression that's an even worse thing now than it was before."

A man walked by, scowling as he caught sight of them, but he didn't pause.

No one else argued as they dismounted and led their horses down the narrow alley.

"We're close to the ambassador's sector. Edmund's house is there." Dell peered around the side of a shop, scanning the road. A troop of palace guards rode through town. People scrambled out of their way, and Dell grabbed a young boy by the front of the shirt.

"Why is the guard in the city?" Before, the king had been careful not to impose his warriors on the people. Force didn't work in Madra. Only money did. They claimed the mercenaries had evil inside them with their only loyalty being to the gold in their pockets, but it wasn't only their way of life. Madra had been built on the concept.

The boy's lip shook. "The prince be missing, sir."

"The prince?"

The boy nodded. "They be saying them rebels got Prince Quinn."

Dell released the boy. "You want to earn a bit of gold, kid?" He gestured to the purse on Etta's belt.

The boy's eyes lit up. "How, sir?"

"You're going to help my friend here." He put a hand on a confused Landon's shoulder before turning to the others. "Change of plans. We can't go to Edmund's when the city is crawling with guards. Landon will take the horses to the public stables since he knows the city as well as I do."

The last time Dell had been at the public stables was when he spirited Helena away from her own tournament. He refused to let the memories cloud his mind this time.

Etta leaned into Vérité, whispering words none of the rest of them could hear. When she backed away, she looked to Landon. "Worry about the others. Vérité will follow you or he won't. That's his choice."

Landon scrunched his brow, issuing a short nod. "Stay safe."

"You too." Dell thought for a moment. "If you make it before dark, there's a bakery in the market square. It's run by a woman named Agathe. Search for us there."

Dell wasted no time strolling out onto the street as if he had every right to be there. This kingdom and this city had once held such familiarity for him… and also a lot of pain. It'd shaped him into the man he was. Allowed him to form his own convictions.

When he'd first helped Edmund, he hadn't known which side of the fight he wanted to be on. He hadn't thought the Rhodipus line deserved to keep their rule.

Now, he knew. He fought to take back what had been stolen. This wasn't just out of loyalty to Edmund any longer. He'd have joined the fight, eventually. Madra was his home.

He led them past Catsja's tavern and images from another life assaulted him. He'd chased the woman only after her husband called Dell's mother a whore.

The boy he'd been thrived on rage, fighting illegal street matches and enjoying every hit. He'd been foolish and desperate for anything to give his life meaning.

The sign no longer read *The Cooked Goose.* Instead, it had been changed to *The King's Tavern.*

With a sigh, he turned away. Etta, Alex, and Tyson asked no questions about Madra as they took in the crowded city. In Bela, everything smelled fresh and new. Madra's air hung stale between the buildings; a combination of fish and urine.

A troop of palace guards in gleaming black armor rode down the street.

"Come on." Dell ran around the corner, barreling through a familiar door. The others skidded in behind him, ducking below a table so they couldn't be seen through the window.

The smell of fresh bread replaced the putrid Madran air. Dell had spent as much time in Agathe's bakery as anywhere else growing up. She'd helped raise him when his stepmother refused.

The counter near the back wall sat barren, no longer filled with pastries and sweet treats she was so known for. Then why did it smell as if she'd recently baked a new batch?

"Stay here," he said. Something didn't feel right. Where was Agathe? Why was her store open if she wasn't there?

Along the walls, candles burned, signaling someone's recent presence.

"Latch the door," he hissed back to Tyson. Alex and Etta watched guards walk past the window as Dell crouched low.

He ducked behind the counter, almost crashing into a bucket of dishwater, and pulled his sword free as he nudged the door leading to the back rooms open. Agathe lived behind her bakery in a one room home. Darkness greeted him, but he sniffed the air, smelling the remnants of burning candles.

Someone was still there.

Agathe's bed sat across the room, a blanket folded over the surface. The only other furniture was a table pushed against the wall and a high-backed chair with ripping seams sitting in front of a still burning fire.

Dell froze.

Still burning.

Dell felt a presence at his back and turned, ready to strike. Tyson raised an eyebrow, his face aglow in the light of the candle he carried.

"I told you to stay back," Dell growled. Back in Bela and Gaule, he'd listened to them, followed them. But now they were in his kingdom, around his people.

He was in charge.

In true Tyson fashion, he shrugged as if the nerves weren't getting to him at all. "Thought you'd want to know about the staircase Alex found in the ceiling."

Staircase? Of course.

A thud sounded from above and Dell moved without thinking. He'd only ever been in Agathe's large attic once when she needed help carrying storage containers. The stairs folded up into the ceiling, but Dell had seen her pull them down enough he knew exactly where the string wrapped around the top corner of the larger oven, out of sight.

Reaching up, he pulled it free.

Please let Agathe be okay. His plea went up to the heavens while at the same time, never leaving his mind.

He couldn't take losing anyone else.

The steps descended from the ceiling, and Dell began the climb. Wood groaned under his feet as the stairs swayed with his weight.

He held on with one hand while keeping the other gripped around the hilt of his sword. At the top, a thin board covered the opening into the attic. Dell slammed his palm into it, shifting it out of the way and pulled himself through. Before he could brandish his sword, a length of steel flashed in front of his face.

His heart pounded against his ribs, threatening to burst through his chest. He sucked in a breath, reaching a hand down to tell those below him to wait.

A flame appeared with a familiar face behind it. Dell lunged, knocking Orlo onto his back. "What have you done with Agathe, you bloody bastard?"

Hands grabbed him, hauling him from a grinning Orlo.

"Should have known you'd show up." A low chuckle drew Dell's gaze to the man still holding him back.

"Edmund." He shook his head and sat back on his heels. "You can come up now," he yelled down to the others. "It's safe." He didn't know what Orlo was doing here, but at the moment, he didn't care because he caught sight of a weathered face smiling at him.

Crawling forward on his knees, he wrapped Agathe in a tight hug.

She gripped him with surprising strength. "Wasn't sure I'd ever see you again, boyo."

"You know me, Agathe. I can't seem to stay away from trouble."

She barked out a laugh and released him.

Tyson, Alex, and Etta crawled into the small space. Edmund's eyes widened when he saw them.

Tyson shrugged. "I couldn't let you have all the fun without me."

It had been a given that Tyson would want to help Edmund. But the blonde man stared at Etta and Alex as if he was seeing them for the first time.

"You and Camille are family," Alex said.

Edmund nodded. "I'm glad you guys are here."

"What have we stumbled into, Edmund?" Etta pinned him with a stare.

"How did you find me?"

Dell was the one who answered. "I had a hunch Agathe would know where you were." As his eyes adjusted to the darkness, he took in the cramped space. Empty platters were scattered over the floor next to overturned cups. How many people had been here? A shadowy figure sat hunched in the corner. Dell studied him for a moment before recognition set in.

"Quinn Rhodipus."

The man's head jerked up, and it was only then Dell noticed the ties around his wrists.

"Do I know you?" Quinn's glare was so much like Helena's, Dell looked away.

"I'm just the man who almost died trying to save you back in Gaule." He faced Edmund. "Why is he tied up? What's happening around here? We came to help, but we can't do that until we know the full story."

Edmund rubbed his tired eyes. "When the king sent the guard out searching for Quinn, it forced the rebels to split up and abandon the post they'd set up at my old house. We have rotating scouts out picking up information and others searching for any sign that Helena may send us a message."

Dell's blood surged. "I knew it. That's why she..." He couldn't say the words *left me behind.* "She knew I'd never let her do something so foolish."

"Finally someone who sees how stupid it was." Quinn scowled and shifted where he sat. "You were supposed to protect her, Edmund. Isn't that what Stev asked you to do?"

Edmund lunged toward Quinn, stopping just short of pummeling him. "You don't know what Stev wanted. Every breath you take betrays him. You work for the man who killed him."

A look Dell couldn't discern flashed across Quinn's face, but Edmund didn't notice it.

"You think he won't hurt her?" Quinn said lowly. "You don't know him at all."

"Is that a threat?" Edmund pulled a knife free from his belt. "I should kill you for everything you've done."

Quinn focused his eyes on the blade. Dell wondered if he should stop Edmund, but he didn't dare intercede.

"I did it for her." His voice was so quiet it took a moment

for the words to sink in. Quinn hunched forward, burying his face in his hands.

Edmund sat back, tucking the knife away. There'd been a time when Edmund had been friends with most of the princes.

"What do you mean you did it for her?" Danger lurked behind Dell's words.

Quinn lifted his eyes, allowing Dell a glimpse into the pain he tried to keep hidden. His family was tearing him apart. "I knew she'd come back." His eyes flicked to Edmund. "I knew you both would, and I'd be no use to you locked in a cell at the ghostly monastery."

Edmund pushed out a breath and rubbed his eyes. "I've known you since the day I set foot in Madra, Quinn. Yet, I'm not sure if I should believe you. You showed up at the docks to arrest me. Cole wouldn't have known she would be there too, but you would have."

"I had to. If I didn't go, Cole would have sent someone else. I'm not going to lie to you, Edmund. I wouldn't have been able to protect you. But Helena... you don't know what has been going on at the palace in the months you've been gone. We have people there—more than you know—who have been working on returning Stev..." He stopped speaking as if he'd said something he hadn't meant to.

It took Edmund a moment to react. He jerked forward, pulling his knife free once again and holding it to Quinn's throat. "What about Stev?"

Quinn didn't flinch away from the blade as he held Edmund's gaze.

Dell and the others watched with bated breath.

Quinn lifted his chin. "We want to put Estevan back on the throne."

Edmund's knife clattered to the ground, and he fell back,

his head shaking as if not believing a single word spoken. "He's... He's..."

"Alive."

It was strange. How one word could change the entire outlook of a mission. Dell barely knew the oldest Rhodipus, and even his heart leapt. They'd come to Madra to take down a king, never thinking of what came after. Helena could have taken the throne, but Dell knew all she wanted was her family returned to her.

But Estevan?

If Helena was at the palace, had she seen him?

Edmund sucked in air like a man who never thought he'd take another breath. He ran a shaking hand through his hair.

Etta sat beside him and pulled his other hand away from where it scratched at the skin on his face. She laced her fingers through his.

"He's alive, Edmund," she whispered.

As if her words snapped something inside him, he folded in on himself, his back shuddering.

Dell knew he should look away, but he couldn't. He'd only seen Edmund look so... breakable twice before. Once when he'd been forced to leave Estevan in Madra. And again when he'd learned of the prince's supposed death.

For most of his life, Dell hid behind charm and a false ego, letting no one get close enough to have the kind of power over him that Estevan had over Edmund. He'd thought strength was being unbreakable.

He'd been wrong.

If he didn't get to Helena in time, he'd never recover, but he loved her anyway.

Edmund had never stopped loving Estevan even when he thought he was dead, and it was the bravest thing Dell had ever seen. He let himself feel it all.

Edmund wiped his face. "I have to get to him." He crawled toward the stairs. "We can't sit here waiting any longer."

Quinn, who'd silently let Edmund process this world-changing information, called Edmund back. "And what do you think you're going to do?"

Edmund paused. "Whatever I have to."

"If you go to the palace with nothing but vengeance on your mind, you won't make it out. Cole has no ties to you like he does Helena." At least he hoped Cole wouldn't hurt his sister. If Stev was still alive, there had to be hope, right?

"I don't care if I survive as long as Estevan does."

Dell reached forward to grab Edmund's arm. "You know what you went through after you thought he died. Do you wish that for him?" Dell had to make him see reason.

The door slamming down below made them all freeze.

"It's probably just Landon." Dell wished he was as confident in that as he sounded.

"Landon?" Quinn's gaze snapped to his. "My cousin?"

"He's the one who brought us to Gaule to try to save you. Then he decided to accompany us here."

Quinn's eyes widened.

"I'm going to see if it's him," Edmund said.

"Wait!" Quinn tried to move forward, but the ropes holding his wrists hindered him. "You can't trust him."

"He's the only reason we knew you were being held prisoner in Gaule." Alarm bells rang in Dell's mind.

"Because he gave me to them." He hardened his jaw. "Landon works for Cole."

And he knew exactly where they were. Dell cursed. Should they have seen it? "We have to leave this place."

Footsteps sounded below. Without thinking, Dell lowered himself through the opening in the floor, not bothering with the stairs. He hung for only a second before dropping on top of the intruder.

A string of curses flew from the woman's mouth. A mouth Dell knew too well. They landed in a heap on the floor. He rolled off her with a grunt. "Catsja?"

She grimaced in pain as she sat up. "Dell Tenyson, you bloody fool. What was that for?"

He shocked her by pulling her into a hug. "It's good to see you."

The others descended the stairs, and Orlo's thick hand gripped the back of Dell's neck, hauling him away from Catsja.

He shook his head, surprised both Orlo and Catsja had joined the rebels. He shouldn't have been. They hated the Madran army like none other.

"Another rebel?" Etta asked, checking her weapons.

Dell didn't get a chance to answer because voices sounded out front as the door opened.

"Get down," Edmund hissed, pulling Agathe behind a crate with him.

"They're here," a familiar voice said. "Find them."

Landon. Fire raged through Dell's veins. They couldn't just wait to be found. He met Tyson's gaze, knowing at least the impulsive young prince would agree with him.

Tyson nodded, gesturing to Etta. Without waiting to make sure the rest of them followed, Dell pulled his sword and charged into the front of the bakery.

The guards still pouring through the front door looked up, startled for only a moment before arming themselves to meet the charge.

Dell didn't stop moving until he barreled right into one of the guards, swinging his sword in a wide arc.

Beside him, Tyson sprang forward, crashing his sword against Landon's.

The rest of their group jumped into the fight, bumping into each other in the tight space. Tyson jumped away from Landon, letting Etta take over. The queen muttered under her breath. Dell knew little of her history with the general. Only that they fought La Dame together.

Tyson ran behind the counter, finding a bucket of water. He threw it into the air, holding his hands high and expanding the substance with his water magic, before sending spears of water crashing against each guard with enough force to drive them through the glass windows.

Shards rained down, but before hitting them, a gale of wind pushed the sharp pieces through the now open windows.

Out on the street, a crowd formed to watch the sopping guards pick themselves up. Quinn appeared and held out his wrists to Edmund. It was now or never. Trust him or don't.

Edmund glanced sideways at him before slicing through his ropes and then extending the knife hilt first.

Quinn took it. "I need to return to the palace."

Edmund, seeming to understand his meaning, nodded and faced him. "Do it."

In a flash, Quinn's fist connected with Edmund's cheek, and he took off running toward the guards who were preparing for another fight.

"We have to get out of here." Edmund glanced at Agathe, and the old woman smiled in understanding. "Catsja, get the powder."

The powder. Dell knew instantly what kind of powder it was. He'd seen kegs of it in his family's cellar while trapped there.

"Dell, Alex, Tyson." Edmund looked to each of them. "You get Agathe out and far from here. We'll hold them off."

Etta shot him a grin, tossing her sword between her hands. "It's been too long since you and I have fought together, Edmund."

"Go!" Edmund ordered to the rest of them.

Dell didn't want to leave Edmund to the fight, but he couldn't have Agathe in danger. And he knew he wouldn't be the kind of help Etta would.

Everyone did as they were told. Dell let the others out the back door, only looking behind him once as the sounds of the renewed fight filled the air.

They ran down the back alley until they reached a crossroads and turned into a seedier part of town. Agathe seemed to know the way, so they followed her.

Before they got too far, an explosion rent the air. Dell froze, glancing behind him. They were okay. They had to be.

"Edmund and Etta know what they're doing," Alex said as if reading his mind.

How did he have such faith in them? Dell wished he had that kind of confidence in anyone other than himself. He still felt the need to protect the people in his life rather than let them protect themselves.

A thought struck him as they paused. "Kassander." He froze in the doorway. "We sent Kassander with Landon." They'd thought it was the safer option. Going to the stables had to be safer than meeting the rebels.

Only it wasn't. They'd given the young prince over to his brother.

Once again, Dell failed Helena.

His horror was mirrored on the faces around him.

Agathe ushered them down another familiar road, not

stopping until they reached the gates Dell never wanted to see again.

"Agathe." He froze, staring up at the ominous structure. "What are we doing here?"

"This is another rebel base." She pushed past him and pounded her fist against the gates.

How could the home he'd grown up in have become a base for the rebels when Ian and Reed stood by the king's side? Was it further proof of Reed's disloyalty to Cole?

The gates swung open slowly, and a weathered face greeted them, showing no surprise at the site of Dell.

He blew out a breath. "Stepmother."

She ignored him, instead settling her eyes on Agathe. "I heard the explosion from here. I'm glad you found a use for the powder I supplied. Come in. Let's get you out of sight."

Agathe smiled. "Thank you, dear." She led them in, leaving the gates open slightly for the others.

Tyson leaned in to Dell as he eyed the grand Tenyson house. "You grew up here?"

"No." Dell's eyes fell on the familiar building out back. "I lived in the stables." The young prince looked like he wanted to ask more questions, but Dell sped up to prevent the conversation. His mind whirled with the possibility of his stepmother fighting against the king. A king her sons supported.

The last time Dell had been there, his brothers trapped him in the cellar. Now, he walked through a front entrance they had never allowed him to use. The once grand house, seemed sparser than before.

Agathe, as if reading the questions in his mind, spoke in a low tone. "Your stepmother has been forced to sell many things to get by with the port closing. She released all of her staff and now lives here alone since both your brothers live in the palace. Ian hasn't been home since the rebellion. Reed comes often on rebel business."

"How did she become a rebel?" he asked. The woman he'd known only ever looked out for herself. She wouldn't care what a king did to the kingdom.

"With the spiral gone, she has lost her place in society. Everyone has something to fight for in this."

Dell nodded. It made sense. She was still looking out for herself.

His step-mother led them to the stables he'd spent most of his life in.

"I can't have rebels in the main house," she said. "I'm sorry. I hope you understand."

Dell hadn't ever heard her apologize for anything.

Agathe put a hand on her arm. "Of course. When the others arrive, please show them to us. We won't bring you any trouble. I promise. We'll be gone in the morning."

She hesitated for a moment, her eyes finding Dell as if she had more to say. Instead, she only nodded and walked out.

Dell inhaled, his heart pounding against his ribs as the inadequate feeling of his youth came back to him. No matter what she said, she'd always had that effect on him.

A horse neighed, and he breathed out a sigh as he caught sight of horse-Ian. The familiar sight of the beast in his stall calmed him. He was no longer the boy with no family who mucked stalls and let that woman push him around.

No, now he had more purpose. A family. She could no longer control his life or his mind. He let Agathe have the bunk he'd spent most nights in and sat down with his back against horse-Ian's stall.

Wiping at his face, his fingers came away red.

He felt for a cut but found none. The blood wasn't his.

Silence choked the room for what seemed like an eternity until Edmund burst through the door. His shoulders sagged in relief. "You're here."

Alex pushed past him to wrap Etta in his arms.

"Why did you come here?" Edmund scanned the sparse room.

"It's a rebel safe house." Catsja elbowed him out of the way. "I told you, Edmund, the movement has grown since you left."

"But Lady Tenyson?"

Dell studied Agathe. She'd led them there. How involved in the rebellion was she? They'd just destroyed everything the woman had. Her shop was nothing but rubble. Her livelihood gone.

And yet, there was life in her eyes like he'd never seen before.

Dell met Edmund's gaze. "What's next?"

Catsja sat with an exaggerated grunt. "That's why I came to find you all in the shop. I have news." A smile slid across her face. "It seems like the princess' return is what we needed. Our sources inside the palace indicate the king will make his first public appearance. He wants to show Madra that the Rhodipus line is intact and supportive of his reign. His advisors seem to think it's the only way to quell the rebel movement."

Dell took in each word, turning it over and considering it. He needed to see Len, so he asked the one question that would bring her closer to him.

"When?"

Twenty-Three

A warm hand pressed against Helena's forehead as someone coaxed her back to the waking world. Soft blankets tangled around her legs and she tried to roll onto her side, confusion clouding her mind. Where was she?

"Dell?" she murmured.

"Sister."

The voice had her jolting awake and flinching away from his touch. Her eyes snapped open to find Cole's face staring down at her, a concerned frown tilting his lips.

Pain pulsed in her temples and radiated down her torso as images flooded her mind. Cole's fist. A foot to the stomach.

A tear leaked from the corner of her eye. She'd been so sure he wouldn't hurt her. So sure the brother she'd known was still in there somewhere.

Because she saw him. As he sat on the edge of her bed, his hand hovering over her hair, he looked like the man she'd known.

"Don't touch me." She pulled the blanket up to her chin, wincing at the pain the movement caused.

Cole's brow creased. "You know I wanted nothing to happen to you, Lenny. I love you."

"You don't love me, Cole. Maybe you never did." She knew she needed to be careful with him. He'd proven to be unpredictable, volatile. Had he really changed so much? Or had he hidden this part of himself from them all? Even his twin.

The thought of Quinn and his loyalty to Cole burned within her. At least Kass was safe and...

"Estevan," she whispered. Had that been a dream or did he truly live?

"Helena." Cole sighed. "My people need to see my strength. If I do not instill fear in them, what do I have?"

"Father didn't rule by fear." As soon as the words left her mouth, she wished she could have them back. Lies. That's all they were.

Cole moved to stroke her hair again and then thought better of it and curled his fingers into a fist. "You aren't that naïve. All father had was fear. His armies spread across the six kingdoms under the guise of keeping peace. His priests arrested and imprisoned people. Even you, Sister, had to wear a mask your entire life for fear of what they'd do to you."

Helena touched the bridge of her nose. Someone had removed the mask. A thought came to her. "You forced me to hide behind a mask as well."

True sadness crossed his face. "It was how my council would instantly recognize you as the princess. The people do not know Helena Rhodipus, only the image father allowed them to have. I'm sorry I have to use that image as well."

A harsh laugh pushed past her lips. "You aren't sorry for anything."

"That's where you're wrong, sister. I'm sorry for everything."

He stood, smoothing down the jacket of his uniform.

"But if you had to do it over again, you wouldn't change anything."

He didn't turn to face her as he answered. "No. I wouldn't."

His footsteps echoed across the high ceilings long after he'd left. Helena buried her face in the pillow, letting it dampen with her tears until the door opened yet again.

She lifted her head, trying to ignore the pounding in her skull. Camille stood on the threshold.

"I think I'm quite done speaking with traitors today," Helena ground out, letting her head fall back. She needed to pull herself from the bed and find out where she was. She still had a job to do—find a way to take down her brother before the rebels stormed the palace and got a lot of other people killed.

Someone else pushed past Camille, pulled her inside the room, and shut the door.

"Quinn." Helena's eyes widened. What was he doing in the palace when he was supposed to be missing?

He rushed to the bed and dropped to his knees. "Len." His fingertips whispered over her bruised cheek. "I'm so sorry."

She finally pushed herself up to sit and let the blanket drop. Dried blood speckled the side of her shirt.

Quinn uttered a curse and reached for the hem to push it up, revealing a small gash in her abdomen. Purple bruising spiraled out from the wound. Crusted blood sealed it.

Across her stomach, yellow and purple discoloration marked each place they had beaten her.

Quinn closed his eyes. "I'm so sorry."

Anger surged into Helena and she pushed his hands

away. "Leave me alone, Quinn. You don't get to act like you care."

Camille crossed the room to stand at the window. Sunlight lit her pale features as she crossed her arms over her chest. "Tell her, Quinn."

"Tell me what?" Helena flicked her eyes from Quinn to Camille.

"I spent the night as Edmund's prisoner, but he released me."

Her jaw fell open. "Is he okay?"

He covered her hand with his. "He's fine. He's still with the rebels." His mouth twisted. "I just wish he hadn't brought a foreign kingdom into this."

"Foreign kingdom?" This time it was Camille's turn to be surprised. She turned from the window, letting her arms fall to her sides. "Bela is here?"

Helena couldn't ignore the fact she didn't suspect it was Gaule. She knew well her mother wouldn't send help.

Alarm rang in Helena's mind. "Etta? She's here?" That meant... Dell. She shook her head, praying Quinn would tell her it wasn't true, but also hoping he'd confirm her fears. Dell had come for her even after she'd left him behind.

Quinn scratched the back of his neck. "Yeah, along with the king and prince of Bela."

A smile warmed Camille's face. "They came."

Helena clenched her hands around a fistful of blanket. "Well, run along then. You two should go tell Cole. It's what you want to do."

Camille's smile turned into a sneer. "What I want to do is put a sword straight through his heart."

Quinn glanced at the door as if they'd be overheard. "I'm sorry, Len. That I ever made you doubt me. That I ever doubted myself. Cole is... he used to be everything to me.

Before we came to the palace, we were the only family either of us had. That changed for me. It didn't for him. I saw the signs over the years. His hatred of father and your mother. His friendship with Ian Tenyson. Ian always wanted more power than a merchant could have. He didn't want to reach the top of the spiral. He wanted to be the spiral, to be everything Madra needed, the only merchant supplying the kingdom with goods. An empire worthy of a king."

"So..." She glanced from Quinn to Camille. "You're not on Cole's side in this?"

When they both shook their heads, a wave of relief washed over her. She had more allies than she'd thought.

"I can't stay much longer." Quinn stood. "Cole has people watching me. I'm only supposed to be delivering Camille to you." He bent to kiss her forehead. "We'll get through this, Len."

She swallowed back a sob as he left.

Camille walked to the bed. "Come on, Helena. They sent me to help you wash and dress for the ceremony tonight."

"Ceremony?"

Camille nodded. "Cole has invited the city-dwellers to watch him speak. It's to show them that the Rhodipus family is intact and loyal to their king. He hopes it will quell the rebel movement especially after last night."

"Last night?"

"Explosions rang across the city. Many of them. I only saw the dust clouds from my window, but they shrouded the entire city.

Edmund? She'd worried about him every second since she arrived at the palace. And now it wasn't only him. Dell, Etta, Alex, Tyson. All of them were in danger.

As if reading her thoughts, Camille spoke in a reverent tone. "I can't believe my brothers are here."

Helena let her legs hang over the side of the bed before setting her feet on the floor. "Why should it surprise you that they came for you?"

Camille pinned her with a stare. "You don't know our history. I'm not sure why they're here, but it isn't for me."

For the first time, Helena saw a loneliness in the Gaulean princess that matched her own.

Camille gripped her arm and helped her to her feet. Helena stumbled, but the other girl kept her upright, wedging her shoulder under Helena's.

With the help of her cane, Camille aided her into the attached washroom where a tub of steaming water sat waiting.

Camille helped Helena perch on the edge of the copper tub. "Cole won't allow any servants near you. He trusts very few people."

"Why does he trust you?"

Camille frowned. "That's not important."

"It is to me."

A sigh pushed past her lips. "I'll just say Quinn has convinced him and leave it at that. Come on, Helena. We don't have all day."

It took every bit of strength Helena possessed to remove her clothing without crying out in pain. She stepped into the water and sank below the surface, letting out a whimper as if it simultaneously soothed her aching body and stung where the wound opened her skin.

Unable to lift her arms enough to scrub, Camille aided her in removing a days' worth of travel grime.

"Camille," she whispered as the girl scrubbed soap through Helena's dark hair.

"What?"

"I don't understand so many things. Tell me what has happened since I left."

Camille's hands stilled. "That's a heavy task, Princess. Are you sure you want the truth?"

Helena stared at her hands. If she was going to save the people she loved, she may have to do something she'd never thought possible. Remove one of her brothers from this world. She nodded. "I need to know what Cole has done." She needed to know he was truly as evil as she suspected.

Camille lifted a cup above Helena's head. "Tilt your head back." She poured the water to rinse Helena's hair. "The first thing he did as king was have the royal residence repaired. Your fire did a lot of damage. He claimed it would need to be ready when his family returned to live there. Most of us thought it was the ramblings of an insane man. We didn't know Estevan lived. Not at first. He was kept in a far wing of the palace, and Cole had someone questioning him every day."

"Questioning him about what?"

"Secrets of the kingdom. People who were loyal to him and the old king. There were even rumors of hidden tunnels Cole wanted information on."

Hidden tunnels? She sucked in a breath, goosebumps racing along her arms. Other than her, Estevan and Kassander were the only living people who knew about the tunnels. And Edmund, she supposed. He'd helped her get back to them in what seemed like another life.

Camille continued. "Once the royal residence was finished, Cole shocked the entire palace by revealing Estevan and putting him in a room there. Then Quinn returned. Reed Tenyson brought him to the palace in chains. Something Cole still hasn't forgiven Reed for."

Reed. Helena clenched her jaw. He'd been the source of so many of their problems. Yet... the rebels said he could be trusted.

"After that, Cole's mind slipped further into darkness, blaming his own people for the fact you were dead and wouldn't be returning. He had his guards turn over the city in search of Kassander even though he knew he must have left. Ships were no longer allowed in or out of the port in fear that he'd lose another sibling. Everything he's done has been to keep a family around him."

Helena shivered, and Camille helped her stand, wrapping a towel around her body.

Cole had always clung to both Helena and Quinn as if they'd abandon him one day. As if they'd die like his mother had. He'd never had affection for Stev, but it seemed that had changed.

But then... "Why'd he kill my father if he was so set on family?"

Camille sat Helena in a high-backed chair and pulled a comb through her wet hair. "I don't know, but..."

"But what?"

"I don't think the rebellion was entirely Cole's doing. That Tenyson boy is dangerous."

She'd always known Ian was dangerous. How could two boys grow up together and turn out so completely different? Ian and Dell. Cole and Quinn.

Silence descended as Camille braided Helena's hair around the crown of her head. She showed her the dress Cole had chosen for the occasion. A simple midnight blue gown that flared out at the hips. The bust line dipped down low. A sapphire necklace, mask, and the glass slippers she hated so much rested next to the dress.

Camille helped her put it on. "I must go make myself

ready," she said. "Cole will be pleased with your appearance. Tonight is a big night." She gave one final nod and disappeared through the door.

Helena's heart beat solidly in her chest as she laid back on the bed. The dress covered each bruise as if someone had considered it. The silver mask would cover the marks on her face, making it seem like none of it had happened.

But it had. Nothing would erase the scars on her heart or the images in her mind. Her father hitting the ground. The last look of fear on her mother's face. Estevan's wounds.

She'd come looking for revenge, but now it had changed. Vengeance alone would only leave her more shattered than she was before.

She had to protect her family. Nothing else mattered.

HELENA SAT up when the door to her room opened and Ian stepped through. She pulled her knees to her chest as if that could protect her from the hard glint in his eye.

"I've wanted to have you alone for quite some time." He smiled, his eyes flashing.

"Leave me or I'll scream."

Ian laughed. "The only person in this wing right now besides you and me is your dear brother, Estevan, and he's in no condition to move."

"Why are you doing this? Isn't it enough to steal my kingdom? My home? My brother? What else do you want from me?"

"What I've always wanted, Helena." He cocked his head as if it should be obvious. "You and I were always meant to wed. I love you, Lenny."

She shook her head. "Don't call me that. I will never be your wife."

"Oh, but dear, your father promised you to me, and then your brother upheld that promise."

She ground her teeth. "My brother has no power over me."

His smile widened. "I like my women strong. It makes it so much more fun to break them."

Helena hid her wince as she stood. "Get out of my room."

His eyes narrowed in challenge. "Gladly, but you're coming with me." He lunged forward, wrapping an arm around her waist. "Cole sent me to show you something."

She turned her head away from his rancid breath. With a different personality, Ian Tenyson would have been considered a good suitor. Power, money, looks. He had it all. Yet, his touch made her skin crawl.

He pulled her into the main sitting room of the residence and out into the hall. His grip was so tight, she couldn't break free. Holding up the mask he must have snatched, he gestured to her face. "Now."

She complied but only because she wouldn't get anywhere by fighting. Ian led her through the maze of halls and down a stairwell before stopping outside an unadorned door. He didn't release her as he pushed it open.

Helena's heart fell into her stomach. A cot sat across the sparse room and a boy's sleeping form sprawled across it.

Kassander.

She covered her mouth with her hand.

"He'll be moved to the royal residence once he wakes and is questioned." Ian's tone was smug.

Questioned. She swallowed thickly, knowing what that meant. "What kind of information could Kass possibly have?"

"He was brought in with a man claiming loyalty to the

king, and the boy is needed to confirm the information he has given us. Don't worry, he is unharmed at the moment, only drugged."

"What do you want from me?" Helena whispered. "Why did you bring me here?"

"You can help him."

"How?" Her voice was so small she was sure he hadn't heard her until he turned.

"Tell me where the tunnels are."

Her eyes widened. So, Estevan hadn't told them the palace's biggest secret? She released a shaky breath. The tunnels might be her only way out of there after she did what she came to do. It gave her some small comfort that Cole hadn't yet found them. There was one piece of information she could still use.

"I know of no tunnels." She lifted her chin, meeting his gaze.

He slammed his fist into the wall next to her head, and she jumped. "Don't lie to me, Helena."

She narrowed her eyes and clamped her lips shut.

Ian reach down, sliding a knife free from the scabbard at his waist.

I will not flinch. I will not flinch. He doesn't deserve my fear.

He'd thrive on it, bask in it.

He dipped the tip of the knife under the edge of her mask and pushed it up to reveal her face. Trailing the blade down along her cheek, he pressed the tip just hard enough to draw a single bead of blood.

Helena's chest rose and fell rapidly as he traced her jaw with his free hand, letting it wander down over her neck and across her collarbone before stopping at the swell of her breasts. "Where are the tunnels, Helena," he whispered, leaning close.

"Go to hell."

His chuckle vibrated against her skin.

She focused on Kassander's sleeping form over Ian's shoulder, silently praying he didn't wake. She didn't know what Ian would do to her.

Stepping closer so his body was flush with hers, Ian pushed her harder against the wall. "You've always smelled so sweet, Princess." He lowered his face and inhaled. Keeping the knife gripped tightly, he smoothed his hands over her sides, sending a shiver along her spine.

Nausea rose from the pit of her stomach, but she stayed frozen in place. She'd rather Ian try to get the information from her than Kassander.

Tears streamed down her face, but Ian didn't seem to notice as he pressed his lips to her jaw. "Where are the tunnels, Helena?"

She didn't speak.

Ian bit the sensitive skin of her neck sending a shooting pain through her. She let out a tiny whimper, and he smiled against her, enjoying making her suffer. "Today will be the final day of the little rebellion." His hand snaked around to her backside. "I'm going to gut those bastards." His lips moved down to her chest as his hands bunched up her dress to slip underneath.

His clammy fingers latched onto her upper thigh.

"I've been waiting for this for so long." He bit her again, and she held back a yelp.

"My brother will kill you for this," she growled.

Ian laughed. "Cole has already said you're mine to do with as I will."

She didn't say he hadn't been the brother she'd been speaking of.

"I can't wait to show my new woman to my entire family." He lifted his head to meet her gaze. "I've heard my half-brother has returned to Madra. I think he'll like my new bride, don't you?"

Dell. She closed her eyes, willing the tears away. How did Ian know he was in Madra? Her eyes caught on Kassander again. What had he said? Someone had brought him.

Landon. She gasped. There was no other explanation. Another member of her family to pledge loyalty to Cole. And he'd dragged Kassander back here as well. Her entire body shook as Ian continued his attentions.

"Dell is just a boy, Helena. Tell me where the tunnels are, and I'll show you everything he doesn't have."

She shoved at his chest. "Dell is more than you'll ever be."

Her limbs recovered from their frozen state of shock, but his strength overpowered hers, and the knife he held pressed against the hollow of her throat.

"Don't move," he commanded.

"You can't kill me." She wished her confidence was as strong as her words.

"So sure about that?"

Another presence appeared over Ian's shoulder, stopping in the doorway with a finger raised to his lips.

Helena almost couldn't breathe as a trickle of blood slid over her shoulder. "Do it," she breathed. "What are you scared of, Ian? Cole?"

Ian laughed. "Cole doesn't scare me. You really know nothing, do you, little princess? Cole was put onto his throne by us. Me and—"

His words trailed off as a blade pierced through Ian's back. He glanced down in shock, blood gurgling from his mouth, before stumbling back and falling sideways. The carpeted floor muffled the sound of his body crashing into it. Crimson life seeped into the thick fibers. Helena couldn't move. She couldn't look away.

A groan left his mouth, and then Ian Tenyson was dead.

Finally, after what seemed an eternity of silence, Helena found Reed's bewildered gaze. He backed away from the short sword still protruding from his brother's back. His hands shook as he clenched and unclenched them.

"I..." He started, unable to voice what he'd done.

Helena watched him cautiously, sensing the pain in his gaze. Had he felt that pain as he set his men to attack Dell? Or as he'd taken Quinn hostage?

"Reed." She put up a hand to calm him. "It's okay."

"I... Ian. He's dead."

The rebels' words came back to her. "You can trust Reed Tenyson." She didn't know if that was true, but she didn't have the luxury of waiting to find out. If she was going to make it out of this, she had to trust him.

"Reed, we can't stay here."

He shook himself as if waking from a long slumber. "You're right." His gaze slid over her bloodstained gown before settling on Kassander's restless form. "He's waking up. Cole sent me to move him. You must change. Tell Cole there was a tear in your gown and throw this one into your fireplace. I'll have one of my people come here and clean up..." His eyes settled on his brother again, and he swallowed. "Come."

Reed went to the bed and lifted Kassander. "The king was waiting until we could gather information from the boy, but we've run out of time. He'd like his entire family by his side in one hour's time."

Helena followed him into the hall, conscious of the blood on her chest and dress. Her carefully braided hair now lay askew. But none of it mattered. Ian Tenyson was dead. Cole's right-hand man. What would he do?

She couldn't bring herself to care about the consequences as she still felt Ian's touch slithering along her skin like a snake wrapping around her limbs, ready to squeeze the life out of her.

The man who'd spent his life tormenting Dell was gone.

She breathed out heavily, walking in step with Reed. "Are you okay?"

Reed looked sideways at her, a hard glint in his eyes. "Ian had it coming." His jaw tightened. "He has been threatening to kill our mother for being a suspected rebel."

"Your mother isn't loyal to Cole?"

Reed shifted Kass higher in his arms. "My mother can be a horrible woman. But she was loyal to the king who'd given her the power on the merchant's council. She didn't appreciate her son jumping her in station."

"Lenny," Kass mumbled as they passed a gaggle of wide-eyed servants.

"Kass." She reached for his hand. "It's okay. I'm here. We're going to be okay."

"No. We're not."

She squeezed his hand as his words swirled in the recesses of her mind, clouding her thoughts in darkness.

They reached the royal residence and Camille appeared, hands on hips. "What happened?" She directed the question to Reed.

Reed carried Kass to an empty room. "Ian is dead." He said nothing more as he disappeared.

"There's no time to explain." Helena stopped in front of Camille. "I need another dress."

Once Helena bathed and dressed once again, Reed joined her on the couch. "Tonight is Cole's first public appearance. You're going to be at my side the entire time. I won't let anything happen to you, okay?"

"Why would something happen to me?"

He hesitated for a moment before dropping his voice. "There will be a rebel attack. In the chaos we will have our best chance to take Cole down for good." He slipped a tiny knife into her palm. "I'm told you know how to use this."

She quickly slipped the blade down the front of her dress, eying the passing servants. "I can do it."

He nodded. "I know." Considering her for a moment, he spoke again. "This will not be easy. The things you will see tonight..."

"What am I going to see?"

"Cole has a plan to show the people who holds power in Madra. It was Ian's plan. Just... stay on mission. Remember what you have to do."

She nodded. "I can do that." She just didn't know how hard it would be.

Twenty-Four

"Lady Tenyson has had word from inside the palace." Catsja approached Edmund from across the barn.

Dell had watched many rebels come and go throughout the night. Something big was happening and they wouldn't give him any information.

Edmund sat up where he'd been lying. He brushed the hair out of his eyes. "Is it what we've been waiting for?"

Catsja hesitated. "Edmund..." She sighed. "It's not from Helena."

Dell leaned back against the wall, his entire body deflating. He scanned the stables. Bunks sat at one end with a table in the center. In them, men and women caught what little sleep they could. A heavy iron lock hung on the door, keeping people both in and out. The rebels trusted no one.

Beneath Dell, the packed dirt floor made for a poor bed. Morning light fought past the edges of dark window coverings as Dell took stock of each ache and pain in his body. There'd been little time just to consider what it was they tried to do.

Removing a king from the throne wouldn't be easy.

Edmund took his time getting to his feet. He held out his hand for the message Catsja carried. She handed it to him and his eyes scanned the words as he walked to the table where a tray of water pitchers, cups, and simple food sat.

After a few moments of tense silence, Edmund startled them all by slamming the paper on the table. The crack of palm against wood echoed against the stone walls.

Orlo appeared from an adjoining room with others following. They'd all heard the commotion but none dared approach Edmund.

Except Dell. He got to his feet and moved to stand beside his friend. Edmund pushed the paper to Dell.

The king has invited select citizens to the palace to witness a demonstration.

Today. When the sun is high. That is our chance.

Use the tunnels to gain access to the palace.

Dell stopped reading. "Tunnels?"

Edmund closed his eyes. "They lead from one of the rooms in the west wing and come out into the city."

"Those are just a rumor." Catsja crossed her arms over her chest.

Edmund shook his head. "I know where they are." He scratched the back of his neck. "Helena must trust him if she showed him the location."

Dell was about to ask who Helena trusted when his eyes scanned the rest of the message.

The king will not allow Helena, Estevan, and Kassander to leave this palace alive. You must come for them.

R.

R? "Reed."

"I've been telling you he's one of us." Catsja regarded Dell coolly.

His jaw tightened. Reed wasn't Ian, but did that mean he could be trusted? Probably not.

"What does he mean the king won't let them leave alive?" He handed the note back to Edmund.

Edmund read the words again. "I swear I didn't think he'd do it." He lifted tortured eyes. "I would never have let her go if I thought Cole would hurt her. Now he has all three of them."

"Hurt her? We don't even know what Reed's words mean!" Dell searched frantically for any meaning that had Helena returning to him.

Orlo grunted. "Of course we do. The king will end his family to cement his rule." His eyes bore into Dell. "He's going to kill the princes and the princess."

Dell pushed away from the table, turning only to find Edmund behind him. "Get out of my way."

"We can't fall apart now, Dell. I want them back as much as you."

"You read the note. He's going to kill them."

"Not if we stop him." He turned to the other rebels watching him. "Prepare to leave." To Catsja, he gave different orders. "Go to our other safe houses. Warn our rebel brothers and sisters of what we plan. Make sure there is a rebel presence at this demonstration should our plan go wrong."

"And what is your plan?"

Dell finally understood. This was what they'd been waiting for. He didn't wait for Edmund to answer. "We're going to take the palace."

"OUR INTEL SAYS the palace will be mostly empty as everyone is required to attend the king's demonstration." Edmund's voice echoed along the dark tunnel.

Dell traced his hand along the wall. So, this was how Helena had gotten out of the palace dressed as a boy. His feet crashed through a puddle on the stone floor as he pictured the princess creeping along in the darkness. Had she been scared?

If it hadn't been for this tunnel, he might never have met her.

Someone crashed into him from behind, sending him flying forward. His knees slammed into stone and pain radiated up his thighs.

"Sorry," Orlo grumbled.

Dell grunted and pushed himself to his feet.

"Shhh." Edmund held up a hand for them to stop.

Rebels packed the long tunnel, their steps the only sound breaking the silence. Edmund led the way with Alex close behind him. Etta and Tyson would be with the rebels viewing the king's demonstration. Dell wished he was with them, but he trusted them to keep an eye on Helena. He had bigger things to do.

"There's a door ahead," Edmund whispered.

As they neared, Edmund's magic cloaked them in silence. No one on the other side of the door would know what awaited them.

They stopped moving and Dell's pulse throbbed in his temples. Waiting had never been his strength. In a fight, he was an attacker. Quickness and agility had won him many boxing matches. In his experience, hesitancy allowed the opponent to strike.

And without the numbers, the rebels' advantage lay in making the first move.

Edmund ran his hands over the door.

"Did the note say how to open it?" Alex asked.

Edmund shook his head. "Helena never mentioned it either. But..." His hand caught on something, and a piece of the door broke free revealing a hidden latch.

Dell exhaled in relief.

Edmund turned to face the rebels awaiting his orders. "We go in silently and take stock of our location within the palace. Then we move out to our positions and wait for the demonstration to begin in order to strike."

Dell nodded along with the rest. By the end of this evening, he'd have Helena back.

Edmund pushed the door open, leading them into what looked like an unused bedroom. Furniture covered in white linen sat in the center of the room. Near the wall, a crimson pattern stretched across the carpet as if no one had bothered to clean it up. What had happened in this room?

Edmund shut the door after the last person came through, and if Dell hadn't known it was just there, he'd never have seen it. A painting now took the place of the tunnel entrance.

Edmund scanned the wall. "How did I not know this was here?"

Dell shrugged. "Being that the entire plan rests on the king who grew up here not knowing about it, I wouldn't feel too slighted." He eyed each of the rebels as they took up positions along the walls. Scraping steel rang out as blades slid free of their entrapments. Dell pulled his own and positioned himself near the door opposite Alex.

Edmund put his ear to the door, and a rush of wind hit them as he pulled every sound toward that room. Concentration strained his face.

His eyes widened after a moment, and he pulled back. "Into the tunnel. Now!"

No one moved before the door burst inward, rocketing off its hinges as a heavy battering ram crashed into it.

Splinters tore through the air, and Dell shielded his head and neck. When he righted himself again, he came face to face with a man he'd known in his gut he couldn't trust.

One the rebels had been taken by.

Reed.

He grinned. "Hello, brother."

Dell gripped his sword so tightly his knuckles went white. One swing of his sword and he'd take his brother's life. One small movement and he could make up for the years of torment. He glanced behind Reed, expecting to see Ian at his side as always.

As if reading his mind, Reed chuckled. "Our oldest brother was touching something that didn't belong to him, so I'm afraid he's no longer with us."

Ian was dead? The words swirled through Dell's mind but he was unable to comprehend it. Ian couldn't be dead. He was behind everything. The devil moving his puppet of a king.

But Ian had never been the smart one. Reed had seemed incapable of evil, and that was possibly the most genius thing of all.

"You," Dell breathed. "It was all you."

Reed motioned to his men out in the hall, and uniform clad soldiers swarmed into the room.

Edmund waved a hand through the air as if to tell them their fight was over. It was time to give up. But rebels didn't give up.

Reed reached for Dell's sword, and Dell knew to fight

him would be instant death. He'd be no good to Helena from the afterlife.

A satisfied smirk crossed Reed's lips. "We outnumber you, Rebels." He spat the term. "You are traitors to the crown of Madra, and you're under arrest."

The guards disarmed every rebel in the room before pushing them into the hall. Edmund stayed quiet.

"I should have expected another betrayal from you, Reed." Dell still couldn't wrap his head around the fact that this was the brother capable of so much evil. How had he not seen it coming? From Ian, yes. Never Reed.

But that was the brilliance of Reed's plan, wasn't it? His brother didn't answer him with anything more than a satisfied grin. He thought he'd beaten Dell. What he didn't understand, was Dell would never stop fighting as long as Helena was in that palace.

He met Edmund's eye knowing at least one other person would do what had to be done. He wasn't alone in loving a Rhodipus sibling.

Alex walked alongside him, unrecognized by Reed. What would he do if he knew he'd just arrested the king of Bela? Or that the mythical Persinette Basile awaited them?

A smile curved Dell's lips. Reed didn't know the troubles he invited upon himself. Dell only had to stay alive long enough to see retribution come.

Twenty-Five

The sickening sound of a switch hitting flesh rose above the din of the crowd who'd been coerced into watching the king's demonstration.

This was how Cole wanted to solidify his power. Fear. Brutality.

The crowd had murmured in confusion when the royal family marched out side by side. Helena and Estevan were supposed to be dead.

That confusion had quickly turned to horror as their king's plan became clear.

Cole wanted to bring Estevan to his knees.

Helena flinched but refused to look away as a new stripe of red marked Stev's bare back. Two guards had torn his shirt from his body.

Helena glanced over her shoulder, watching for someone to bring Kassander forth. Reed said he'd bring him once the boy woke, but Helena was beginning to wonder if Cole knew of their youngest brother's presence. He'd made no mention of it. Had Ian meant to hold Kassander captive to gain leverage against Cole?

vengeance from the safety of Bela. Now, the thought of what she must do cracked something inside her.

She shook her head, tears coming to her eyes.

"Lenny," a soft voice said behind her. Quinn wore a matching look of desperation in his eyes. He shifted his gaze to Reed, distrust in the dark irises, before turning back to her.

"Quinn." A sob escaped her throat, but he didn't move to touch her. Not in front of the rest of the guard. He had to remain cold. Loyal to his twin.

"You shouldn't watch."

"I have to." She sniffed. "For Stev. For me. I need to see everything Cole does. He has to be the monster, or else..."

"I know." He leaned in, dropping his voice so only she could hear. "There has been a mass arrest inside the palace."

She sucked in a breath. Dell. Edmund. Their entire plan rested on the rebels being there. But how were they found?

Before she could ask Quinn, he'd returned to stand at attention with the rest of the guard. Camille watched nearby, a guard on either side of her. Her face showed no emotion.

The rebels had come in through the tunnels. They should have been able to get into the palace unseen and spread out, melting among the staff. Edmund knew the palace as well as anyone.

Their plan was supposed to be unstoppable.

How had it been stopped?

Her heart sank as realization seeped into her. They'd failed. She would never get herself or her siblings out of the palace now. Unless... She fingered the cold steel of the blade and fixed her eyes on Cole.

How much time would she have? Her gaze flicked to the guards. She only had one chance. If she missed... but Helena never missed.

A blonde head appeared among the crowd as if the face

of the Belaen queen called to Helena. *Etta?* What was she doing there?

Beside her, Tyson stood, taking in every movement. He was ready.

They'd come all the way from Bela to help her, but what if it had all been for nothing? As soon as the knife left her hand, she'd be surrounded by guards who wouldn't hesitate to kill her.

A loud thwack rang out. Blood poured down Estevan's back, staining the ground at his feet. The ropes around his wrists held him in place. Still, he didn't scream.

Cole drew his arm back, a grim expression on his face. He looked as if his actions hurt him as much as they hurt Stev.

The thought sent a bolt of anger through Helena.

When Stev's first scream rent the air, it tore through Helena, driving her to her knees as tears streamed down her face.

REED DISAPPEARED AS SOON as they lined the rebels up against the wall, their wrists tied. An entire unit of guardsmen watched them, weapons at the ready.

Dell glared toward the tip of a sword aimed at his face. "Do you really feel the need to be that close, mate? Don't think you could catch us with just a bit more space?" He smirked. "I get it, you're slow."

In answer, the guard shifted onto one foot and slammed the other into Dell's chest.

Dell let out a grunt of pain. "That's going to bruise."

"Dell," Edmund hissed. "Shut your mouth for a second. I'm trying to concentrate." His brow creased with the effort.

Alex met Dell's confused gaze and mouthed the word

'magic'. For someone who hadn't grown up around the power, it didn't come to mind as a possibility, but now Dell understood. Just as he'd done when they exited the tunnel, Edmund was using air movement to pull sound toward them.

His eyes widened, and he shook his head.

"Edmund." Alex nudged him. "What is it? What did you hear?"

He swallowed thickly. "Estevan... the demonstration. Cole is showing the people who controls the city by weakening Stev. He's..." He shook his head again, unable to continue.

"Do you hear Reed?" Dell leaned forward, careful to avoid the guard's blade.

"He's reached the courtyard."

"Oi," one of the guards shouted. He must have been in charge. "No talking, you dirty rebel bastards."

Edmund's face reddened until he looked as if he'd explode. Alex tried to put a hand on his arm to calm him, but his tied wrists prevented the gesture.

"Edmund," Dell whispered. "You okay?"

Dell had almost forgotten about Orlo's presence until he spoke. "Don't be an idiot, Tenyson. None of us are okay. We're prisoners because your brother..." He didn't finish his sentence as a guard kicked him.

Orlo grabbed the guard's foot midair and yanked with his brute strength. The guard collapsed forward and tried to bring his sword up to fend off Orlo, but the big man knocked it away and pummeled the guard before any of the others could stop him.

The captain shouted to his men to move, but as they lunged for Orlo, a blast of power erupted from Edmund, sending them slamming into the opposite wall. A tunnel of air kept them frozen in place.

"Get his sword, Orlo," Dell yelled.

Orlo held the blade between his knees and sawed through the rope binding his wrists before moving on to help Dell.

Edmund's power held firm as they released the other rebels. Dell cut through the magic man's ropes.

"Go," Edmund ordered, jerking his head toward the corridor.

"Aren't you coming?"

"I have to keep them here until my magic fails." He flicked his eyes to Dell. "Stev and Helena need you."

Dell didn't hesitate any longer. He took off running down the hall, passing stunned servants. None of them moved to stop the thundering rebels. Dell never thought it would be a comfort to have Orlo beside him, but he trusted the man's fighting ability.

"Edmund will be fine." Alex was speaking more to himself than anyone else.

Orlo grunted. Dell kept his mind focused on what was in front of him. He had to trust Edmund to take care of himself.

"Let me go," a cry echoed from the hall leading toward the open entryway. "Please."

Dell's heart clenched as he turned on his heel, searching frantically for the source. The last time he'd seen Kassander, he'd left with Landon, a man they'd trusted.

Landon appeared, dragging the boy behind him. They reached the door before Dell could force his feet to move. They stepped into the columned courtyard.

Dell went after them. The steps leading down to the gates were littered with people. A scream ripped through the air, and Dell tore through the crowd, his sword still drawn. There, at the base of the steps was Estevan Rhodipus. The man who'd once intimidated Dell with a single look. That day in Mari's shop seemed so far away now as blood poured across the prince's back.

A line of guards muttered among themselves, pointing to where Dell stood with Alex and Orlo at his back. Four of them broke off, led by Quinn Rhodipus himself.

Dell's gaze bounced around the scene as his pulse picked up. He twisted sweaty palms around the hilt of his sword. No one would have ever bet on him in a sword fight.

"I hope you know how to use that thing," he said to Alex.

Alex grimaced. "We have to get out of here."

Dell shook his head, his stare returning to Estevan. Would Edmund survive losing him again?

Commotion nearby caught his eye as a masked girl fell to her knees. A mix of emotions swirled in Dell's chest. Elation at seeing her alive. Relief she seemed unharmed. Anguish at the sight she was forced to witness.

He wanted to go to her. To shield her from Cole's cruelty. But she'd proven not to need a shield, only a knife in her hands. He saw the glint of metal slide from her sleeve and shifted his eyes to Cole.

Alex pulled him back from the scene, jerking his head toward the coming guards. Quinn said he was on their side, but his face was that of the king's, and it told him to run.

Before he got a chance, a gasp rose from the crowd and the blood drained from Dell's face.

What had Helena done?

Twenty-Six

When asked about that day, Helena wouldn't remember the thoughts flipping through her mind. She wouldn't recall what caused her to change direction or how the responding chaos ensued.

All she knew was one brother had become a spectacle to keep the people in line and another wielded the whip, leeching strength from the strongest person she knew one lash at a time.

Estevan's single cry echoed in the recesses of her mind, breaking every part of her it touched. But that was the thing about glass. It was more dangerous broken than whole. Sharper. Deadlier.

Movement caught her eye from where she still knelt on the steps. Kassander appeared, his eyes finding hers before settling on Estevan. But he didn't cry.

He made no sound as Landon pushed him forward. His expression didn't change as Reed yanked his arm to pull him to his side.

Fire burned in Helena. She bounced her gaze from Kassander, held prisoner, to Quinn as he detached from his guard. They landed on Cole, standing over Estevan, his chest rising and falling rapidly as he panted from the exertion. Stev lay still.

The fury she'd felt since the day Cole betrayed the family had lain like a line of explosive power, waiting for someone to set it ablaze. It exploded through her, uncontained, out of control.

She slid her knife free, knowing she'd have only one chance to hit her target. The man who'd been behind all of her pain.

He thought he'd shatter a princess, break a kingdom, and avoid the raining shards.

He'd been wrong.

Helena closed her eyes for a moment. Inhale. Exhale. She calmed her heart rate, finding a place of peace in which to concentrate.

Her mother taught her never to expect accuracy while emotions drove her actions.

And they had killed her mother because men wanted to rise above their stations. To grasp even the edges of power they didn't understand and didn't deserve.

Power held in cruelty was only weakness in disguise.

As her eyes slid open, she lifted her face to the warm sun, letting the sound of Cole's whip fade from her mind.

With one final breath, she rose to her feet with the agility of the greatest boxers of Madra, twisting on her heel and snapping her wrist as her fingers released the blade. She didn't watch as it sailed end over end. Closing her eyes once again, she didn't open them until a scream wound through the ranks of guards as they scrambled to catch a fallen superior.

Her knife had found its intended target.

She turned, settling her eyes on her brother who'd frozen, lash in mid-air.

Someone barreled into Helena, sending her rolling down the steps as an arrow sailed through the space she'd been standing.

She pushed at the man on top of her. If they wanted to arrest her, she wouldn't go without a fight.

"Len, stop."

She stilled her hands, finally focusing on the man's face. "Dell." She breathed his name and everything from the past few moments struck her full force. A sob ripped past her lips. "I killed your brother."

Dell rolled off her and pulled her to her feet to avoid getting trampled. A wave of water, pulled from the river, broke over the crowd, and the screams intensified.

Tyson was there.

Her breaths came rapidly until it seemed no air entered her chest. She gasped, trying to suck in oxygen as she saw what she'd done. Kassander lay trapped under Reed's still form. The knife Reed had given her now protruded from its owner's chest.

Blood seeped through his jacket.

Taking in the scrambling crowd, she noticed Cole had disappeared.

Fighting broke out near the gates.

"The rebels are here," Dell said into her ear.

She barely heard him as she ran to where Alex freed Kassander. Her brother sobbed when he saw her.

She squeezed him to her chest. "Stick by me, Kass." She searched the crowd. "I need a weapon."

Alex leaned down, drawing Reed's sword from the scabbard at his waist, handing it to her. She didn't stop to thank him as she pushed through the crowd, running down the steps to where Estevan struggled against the ties binding his wrists and ankles.

She was so relieved to see him moving, she almost threw her arms around him. When he'd screamed and gone still, she thought she'd die right along with him.

At her touch, he flinched. "Stev, it's me."

His body relaxed. "Len."

"Yeah, it's Len. I'm going to get you out of here." She flicked her gaze over her shoulder to where a line of guards approached, weapons ready.

"We must take the prisoner back into the palace for his own safety," one of them said.

Helena knew what they meant. They had to make sure he didn't escape.

She opened her mouth to speak, knowing Dell and Alex wouldn't be a match for all of them.

But another voice cut in. "We can't let you do that." Quinn stepped in front of Helena.

"Sir," the guard in charge narrowed his eyes. "The king's orders..."

"Cole Rhodipus is not the king of Madra," Helena said, her voice ringing loud and clear. "He is a usurper who murdered his own father for power. Reed and Ian Tenyson were his puppet masters, putting ideas into his mind. How many of you have seen the starvation in the streets as the so-called king cut off all foreign trade? How many have had family members apprehended for being suspected rebels when they were nothing of the sort? Has Cole asked you to leave everything you believe in behind?" She paused, examining her audience. No one moved to stop her.

"Tradition has always been important to Madra, but it has been wielded as a weapon by our kings." She lifted a hand to the back of her head, untying the mask and letting it drift to the cobblestones beneath her. "That doesn't mean it should be nothing to us. Have we forgotten what makes Madra great? What has always made Madra great?"

She shook her head. "I have not forgotten because I feel it. And so do you. We're supposed to take care of each other. To take care of anyone needing our aid, whether they are Madran or not. To protect our lands from the acts of those who would do evil." She pointed to Estevan. "Is this not evil? Is this what Madra stands for?"

Helena slipped her sword under the edge of one of Stev's bindings. To her surprise, two of the guards moved to cut the other ties. The rest of their unit, along with a group of Madran citizens who'd heard her every word turned away from her, standing as guards against any who'd take Stev away again.

Quinn cut the final rope, and a groan gurgled in Stev's throat.

Helena examined the open wounds on his back. Reed may have been behind Cole's lust for power, but Cole wasn't innocent in any of it. He'd chosen this.

And now he had to pay.

She lifted her eyes to Dell and Quinn. "Find the man who stole my brother's throne."

QUINN INSISTED on being one of the men to help Stev himself. Careful to avoid the cuts on his back, he helped Dell lift Stev, looping an arm over each of their shoulders. Helena winced when she took in his pale face.

Sounds of battle circulated around them, but the guards who'd flipped to their side provided a barrier as they climbed the steps.

Rebels fought Cole's people while ordinary citizens scrambled for the closed gates, herding themselves against them.

Alex followed Helena's gaze. "Someone needs to get those gates open before those who do not wish to fight are lost." His eyes brightened as he caught sight of the woman Helena now saw.

Persinette Basile, queen of Bela, fought two men at once as if it was what she was meant to do. Helena had seen her in training, but it was nothing like this. The stories about her became more real. Maybe she was as strong as the mythical figure they'd heard about in the minstrels' songs.

As if sensing her husband's gaze, she glanced up, her face brightening. Without breaking the stare, she slammed her knee into one guard while slicing her sword through the back of the other's legs. They both fell.

"The gate," Alex yelled, pointing to the now unmanned gatehouse.

Dodging other fighting pairs, Etta raised her arms over her head. Bright green vines shot up the gates from the ground. Stone broke apart, sending rubble showering down. She yanked her hands back, and the vines tightened.

The parts that Cole repaired after the explosions of the first rebellion hadn't had time to strengthen. They were the first to fall. Tyson stepped up beside Etta, using the force of his magic to pull water from the ground and prevent the rocks from crushing the crowd below.

Helena's jaw fell open when he stopped, and a sea of rocks now stood where the gates had. Dell was the first to speak. "Couldn't she just have fought her way to the gatehouse and opened them?"

Alex laughed, a sound so foreign in that moment. "That would have been easier." He rubbed his face. "Living among the magic folk, I've learned they think with their power before anything else. Believe it or not, that's the third time Etta has destroyed a castle's gates."

Helena shook her head as she turned away from the crowd of people pushing through what was now a hole in the wall around the palace. "Come on."

She took the steps two at a time, knowing the others would catch up. Alex kept stride with her along with another rebel man she didn't know.

The fight hadn't reached inside the palace yet, and the silence slammed into them. Every guard who'd been on duty was now out amidst the battle. Guards. Rebels. They each thought they were fighting for the soul of the kingdom.

Helena was fighting for her family.

Alex glanced down the hall. "We need to get to Edmund." Something akin to fear flashed across his face.

Helena didn't ask why Edmund hadn't come out to the demonstration. Only something of extreme importance would have kept him from Stev.

She followed Alex until they heard the crash of steel on steel.

Unconscious guards littered the hall and up ahead, two figures fought. One of them seemed no match for the other.

"He's exhausted," Alex breathed. "He's used too much magic."

She glanced at the still guards again. Edmund had done all of this?

Alex took off running, and Helena wasn't far behind. Cole had Edmund pinned against the wall as Edmund fought off his attacks.

"You don't belong here," Cole growled.

Edmund lifted his chin in defiance. Blond hair clung to

his forehead and cheeks, sticky with sweat. His eyes blazed. "You don't deserve them."

Cole knocked Edmund's sword away, and it clattered to the ground. He leaned forward. "I deserve anything I take."

Helena was still too far away to stop him as Cole raised his sword.

"He's too weak to use his magic." Alex picked up speed, but they both knew he wouldn't make it.

Blood pumped through her veins, and it was as if she could feel every bit of it drain from her body. Not Edmund. He was too good. Too loyal. Too kind-hearted. Cole couldn't take him. Not like he took everything else. Tears burned her eyes, but she didn't stop moving.

"Cole," a voice cried from behind her. "Cole, don't."

Helena turned so quickly she almost fell. Kassander had followed her inside.

Cole froze, finally seeing all of them. That single moment was all Alex needed to reach them. He dropped his shoulder, slamming into Cole and sending them both sprawling to the ground. He gripped Cole's wrist and slammed it against the stone floor until the sword fell from his grasp.

Edmund slumped against the wall, gasping for air.

Kassander streaked past Helena.

Alex pinned Cole's arms. He might not have won in a sword fight, but his strength overpowered the pretend king's. Helena stopped at Edmund's side, looking into his eyes. "You okay?"

He nodded wordlessly, bending forward to put his hands on his knees.

Cole kneed Alex in the groin and pushed him off before lunging for his sword. He leaped to his feet, facing all of them.

Kass raised a tear-stained face to their brother. "You don't have to do this."

Regret flashed in Cole's eyes, but it was gone so quickly, Helena thought she'd imagined it. "You haven't left me any choice." He straightened. "You are under arrest for treason against the crown."

"Treason." Helena sucked in a breath. "What about your treason, Brother? What about when you betrayed the crown? When will you pay for that?"

Cole tightened his grip on his sword. "Your father had betrayed Madra with his foreign wars. I saved us."

"Our."

"What?"

She raised her voice. "Our father, Cole. You might want to feel better about slaughtering the man, but there's no changing the fact he was your father as well. He wasn't perfect, I know. But what about us, Cole? Does Kassander deserve to be a prisoner in the palace?"

His face tightened in sadness, and he lowered his sword slightly. "I gave you all the option to stand with me. To be allies instead of prisoners... and yet, you chose these foreign monarchs and low-born rebels."

Helena took a step forward against her own judgment. "You killed my mother." She took another step. "Whipped my brother." She stopped when the tip of his sword was only inches away. "And raised fists to me. Are you going to kill me now, Brother?"

A unit of guards entered the hall and relief flooded Cole's eyes. "Guards, arrest them!"

Their long strides quickened as they tried to reach their king. Helena didn't take her eyes from Cole despite the tip of the sword now touching her chest. One movement from him and she'd be dead, unable to save Kassander and Stev. No good to Dell.

But what good was she to them if she didn't fight for them? If she didn't swallow her fear.

"Arrest them!" Cole screamed again, his eyes bouncing wildly.

The stern-faced guards stopped moving and stood still for a moment, staring at their would-be king. The one in front, lifted his chin. "Cole Rhodipus, surrender your weapons."

Cole's jaw clenched, and his eyes slid along the blade for a moment before he took a step back.

Helena released a breath and rubbed her chest in the spot the blade had touched. A tiny dot of blood smeared across her skin, dripping down onto the bodice of her gown.

She saw the signs seconds before Cole made a move. Helena had spent many years watching her brothers at swordplay. His fingers tightened, twisting around the hilt as they always did when he was preparing to lunge. Since he was younger, it had taken his mind a while to catch up with his body.

But it wasn't enough time. All Helena could do as Cole swung his sword was push Alex out of the way.

The blade bit deep into the stomach of the rebel who'd come with them. His big frame stumbled back.

"Orlo," Edmund groaned.

"Stay there, Edmund." Alex ran to Orlo's side as the guards jumped to action.

Edmund tried to push his weakened body off the wall. The stories called him one of the greatest warriors in the Draconian war but now he couldn't fight.

Helena watched as Cole fought two men at once.

Heart thudding in her chest, she dodged a guard as he stumbled back, a gash in his stomach. He dropped to the floor as Helena reached Edmund.

"I need to help them." Edmund tried to step away from

the wall's support again and stumbled back.

Helena gripped his arm. "You'd only get yourself killed, and Stev wouldn't survive that."

He lifted his eyes to hers. "You've seen him?" Thickness choked his words.

Helena rested her forehead against his. "We're all going to get out of this."

Before he could stop her, Helena ducked away from him, and slipped around the guard who was holding Kass back from the fight. Orlo lay unmoving, his blade beside him. Alex had already joined the fight. There was no one left to stop her.

The princess of Madra grabbed the sword, its weight foreign in her hands. She prowled toward Cole, standing with his back to her. His arms struck in fluid motions, never making a mistake.

But he already had made a mistake. He'd killed her parents and let her live. He'd underestimated her. She was no longer the masked princess of Madra, meant to be neither seen nor heard.

She'd traveled foreign kingdoms, consorted with mercenaries. She'd been a prisoner, a warrior and watched too many people she loved fall into danger.

No, in all her time away from Madra, she'd never once been a princess.

The point of her blade dug into Cole's back and she lifted her voice. "Stop this!"

Another thing she'd never been: a killer. At least intentionally. Cole deserved death, but she didn't deserve the bite of vengeance. Not anymore.

Revenge had only left her cold and alone, making her leave people behind in her single-mindedness. What Cole had done hadn't broken her. Her quest to destroy him had.

But she didn't want to be a jumble of dangerous shards of broken glass any longer.

Not a single person in the hall moved as Helena pressed the sword harder against Cole's back.

"Do it, sister. Kill me. Then you'll be no different from the monster you think I am." Cole's words sank into her. She didn't want to be a monster.

"I should," she growled. "You took everything from me." She turned the blade and leaned in, dropping her voice. "But you're wrong. I am not you." Growing louder once again, she said. "Drop your sword."

Eying the guards who each had their weapons pointed at him, Cole complied. Alex kicked the sword out of reach, and a guard pulled the knife free of Cole's belt.

"Treason sounds too good for you." Helena circled him, her sword skirting his waist until she faced him.

Cole's looks hadn't changed in many years. If she closed her eyes, she could imagine him as the brother who taught Kass to fight or who wore a mask to her name day ball in a show of support along with her other siblings.

"Did you ever love us, Cole?" she asked, not sure which answer she hoped for. "Were we ever your family?"

He swallowed. "I never stopped loving you, Sister."

She grimaced. "Yes, you did. You stopped loving me the moment you took my mother from me. I don't know why you did this, Cole. I don't care if Reed and Ian Tenyson forced it upon you or if you were behind everything. Because it doesn't matter. You are responsible for breaking Madra."

"Len..." He reached toward her.

She shook her head, tears clouding her eyes. "So, you don't get death. Cole Rhodipus, I place you under arrest. Murder. Treason. After this day, you will never see my face again. I won't visit you. If you die of illness, I will not mourn you. Because you are nothing. When we rebuild Madra's standing in the world, no one will think of you. We're going to have peace, Cole."

"That's all I wanted." The fight had left his eyes. "Peace from Father's wars."

Edmund's harsh laugh broke through Helena's thoughts. "Peace. You wanted peace?"

Helena lowered her sword and gestured to the guards. "Bind his wrists and take him away."

Two guards stepped forward to do her bidding, but before they reached Cole, he jerked back. Helena snapped her head around. An arrow protruded from Cole's throat.

He reached up in surprise. His lips moved but nothing more than a low gurgle escaped. Blood trickled from his lips, and he fell back, his head cracking against the hard floor.

"Cole." Anguish ripped through Helena as she dropped to her knees beside her still brother.

A single tear escaped her eye, rolling over the bridge of her nose. Why was she crying? Cole killed so many people. He almost destroyed the monarchy.

He didn't deserve her tears.

Yet, as more broke free, she couldn't stop them.

Her brother was dead. It was what she'd thought she'd wanted. Flashes of the young boy she'd known flickered in her mind. Cole and Quinn coming to the palace as children who'd just lost their mother.

Cole spinning her in his arms each time he returned from far kingdoms.

The twins joking with each other as they wedged her between them in the sitting room.

She'd lied when she said she wouldn't mourn his death. Commotion sounded around her, but she couldn't focus on it as she stroked Cole's pale face. He couldn't be dead. The brother who'd defended her to her father and protected her had to still exist. Somewhere.

Or maybe that Cole had died a long time ago.

Arms wrapped around her, and she buried her face in a familiar shoulder. Dell held on tighter.

She didn't know at what point in the fight he'd arrived, but Quinn stood behind him, using his body to hold Stev upright. She wasn't the only one who'd lost something. Both his brothers were dead. Kassander, Estevan, and Quinn lost Cole too.

She lifted her face to Estevan who had dropped the bow he'd used to shoot Cole. He'd seen what Helena couldn't. As long as Cole was alive, the peace she strived for wouldn't have been possible.

He'd done too much evil.

Estevan stumbled to the wall with the help of a guard. A piece of Helena's heart melded back together as Edmund finally managed the strength to stand on his own. Tears streamed down his face.

"I thought I'd lost you," Edmund choked out.

The guard release Stev, and he stumbled into Edmund, wrapping his long arms around him. "You kept them safe."

Edmund wound his arms around Stev's waist, careful to avoid his bare back and the wounds. "I promised." He pressed their cheeks together. "Besides, they're my family too."

A sob shook Estevan's chest moments before he claimed Edmund's lips with his.

Helena shook in Dell's arms, Edmund's words echoing in her mind. *They're my family too.* He was right.

She scooted back from Dell and stood, leaving Cole behind. Quinn stood back, his face white and his eyes trained on his twin.

Helena wrapped an arm around Kassander's shoulders, and the two approached Quinn.

"I gave him the bow." Quinn ran a hand through his hair, the same dark hair as Cole's. "I thought Estevan deserved... I let him kill Cole."

Helena took his hand in hers, stilling its trembling. "It was the right thing." She slipped her free arm around his waist. "We don't have to remember him like that. Let's remember the brother who never took anything seriously."

Quinn's laugh was barely audible. "He liked to keep us smiling."

"He always had time for me," Kassander spoke up.

The three of them fell into silence until Stev approached. "He was the reason I could help so many people. He stole the routes of food shipments from the merchant's council."

Quinn held out an arm as Estevan joined them. The four of them were all that was left of their once great family. Now what?

Helena breathed, trying to calm her frantic heart. She still had her brothers around her. She had Dell and Edmund. The pieces of her soul began sliding back into place.

"What's happening outside," she asked. How many of her people were dead?

As if the question snapped him back to the present, Quinn straightened. "I have to go." He shrugged out of their embrace, pulled his sword, and sprinted down the hall.

"This isn't done yet." Helena ran after him.

Outside, the courtyard looked as if a great battle had taken place. The fighting had stopped and stunned people tried to pick up the pieces of their lives. Some cried over bodies. Others collected swords from the fallen. A few wandered aimlessly.

Helena searched for where Quinn had run off to and

found him standing with Tyson and Camille. Relief shot through her as she took in the unharmed princess of Gaule.

Etta approached Helena, a grim smile on her face. "We took care of those loyal to Cole pretty quickly. Many of the guards flipped sides, but the rebels still suffered heavy casualties.

Helena scanned the bodies for any recognizable faces. Dell stood behind her, bent over the body of a tall woman.

"You're with Orlo at least, Catsja. Thank you for everything." He straightened and met Helena's eye.

Etta continued speaking. "Your cousin, Landon was apprehended and has been arrested along with any traitors who didn't turn to our side. They took him somewhere called the priests' holes."

Helena grimaced, remembering her days in that dank place. They'd have to find a better prison than that.

Quinn and Camille approached, their hands locked together as she leaned on him for support.

"We'll need to get you a new cane before you return to Gaule." Helena gestured to the girl's twisted foot.

Camille's brow creased. "I do not wish to return."

"Cam—"

"My kingdom signed a treaty with yours and I intend to honor it. Gaule and Madra will be allies."

Helena shook her head. "Estevan won't marry you."

"Then it's a good thing Stev isn't the one I'm in love with," she snapped, her face going pale as she realized what she'd said.

Helena stepped back, her eyes flicking from Quinn to Camille and back again.

The first light she'd seen in Quinn since Cole's first betrayal entered his eyes. He didn't smile. It would take a while for that. But at least there was hope.

Quinn nodded once. "Len, I'd like permission to honor the treaty."

She raised a brow. "I'm not the person you need to ask."

Surprise flashed across his face as if he hadn't thought about that. Estevan would become king of Madra—something they'd never thought possible after hearing of his death.

Dell pulled Helena away. "You would have made a good queen."

She bristled. "I never wanted the crown."

He pressed his lips to the side of her head. "I know."

The chaos of the day hit her suddenly, sending a wave of dizziness crashing over her. Dell gripped her arm as she stumbled.

"Are you okay?" he asked.

She tried to nod, but her entire body shook. "No. I'm not okay at all." She pushed away from him and climbed the steps before entering the palace.

The residence wing held many painful memories, but it was also where her family had been whole. Where they'd loved and supported each other. She walked through the halls, each step heavier than the last. Once she climbed the stairs and entered her family's home, she knew exactly where she needed to be.

Most of the rooms had been destroyed by the fire, but Cole had repaired them to look as they had before. She pushed open the door to the room where she'd always felt safe and half expected her mother to be behind the door. Or for Sophia to enter carrying tea.

She climbed onto the canopied bed identical to the one her mother had and sank into the plush white pillows, letting her mind linger in the past to avoid the realities of the present.

Twenty-Seven

Dell didn't understand how he'd gotten where he was. Growing up in a small village, he'd had nothing except his mother. When she died and his father came for him, he wasn't sure he'd survive the city, especially with a cruel stepmother and two conniving half-brothers.

But his father had been kind. In a single storm, that too was taken from the scared boy. He went from returned son to the stable boy within days of his father's shipwreck.

He swabbed the decks of ships, cleaned horse stalls, and slept with the animals. Unlike his brothers, he'd never had any ambitions other than to find a way out of the city.

And then he'd met her. Or them, really. Edmund and Helena changed his life.

Lenny. She'd come dressed as a boy and seemingly in need of saving. But he'd been the one needing to be pulled out of his lowborn life.

To be honest, he had no problem with his low status, only his family who refused to claim him as one of theirs, yet treated him as if they owned him.

Now, he was the only Tenyson boy left.

As he walked across the courtyard, a familiar face appeared. His stepmother had never been kind to him. She'd berated him and forced labor onto him.

But now she had nothing left. He swallowed every bit of pride he possessed and approached her.

"Dell." She lifted haunted eyes to his. "I'm... glad you're okay."

He scratched the back of his neck and looked away. "I'm sorry about Ian and Reed."

She sighed. "Those boys... They were my sons. I loved them and it was for that reason I told no one what they were up to."

His eyes widened. "You knew they wanted to take the throne?"

She hesitated a moment before nodding. "But they were my sons." Her eyes glassed over. "I can't help but wonder if I'd revealed their plans, maybe they'd both be alive now. Imprisoned, but alive."

Dell never thought he'd feel anything but hatred for the woman, yet as he watched her sunken face, sympathy entered him.

She nodded to herself as if coming to some conclusion. "The princess did the right thing. I'm Reed's mother... or was... but that wasn't him. He'd always been the more dangerous of the two boys. Too smart for his own good. But there was a time when his kindness was real. When I thought he'd escaped..." She trailed off.

"Escaped what?"

She rubbed her eyes. "The circumstances of being my son. I'm a hard woman, Dell. I take full responsibility for Ian. But Reed was supposed to be different."

"Is that why you joined the rebels? You thought it was your fault?"

She nodded and averted her eyes. "I don't expect any understanding from you. I know the kind of life I forced on you. But maybe... just maybe... you should consider yourself lucky. This is not the family you wanted to be part of, Dell. If you'd been one of us, you might have made different choices."

He shook his head. "No. I wouldn't have. Reed and Ian didn't do this because of you. They could have been different too."

A sad smile tilted her lips. "That's a nice thought, Dell. I only wish it were true." She met his eyes once more. "Your father would be proud of you." With those final words, she turned and walked across the rubble of the fallen gates, disappearing from view.

For the first time, he saw his stepmother as just a woman. A woman who'd lost everything. But he couldn't be for her what his brothers were. He had other people he needed to stand by. Others to now call family.

DELL LEANED FORWARD in his chair to get closer to the bed where Helena rested. She hadn't risen in the two days since the fight, not even to change her clothing. He studied her delicate features, stained with tears. Blood smeared across her slowly rising and falling chest. She didn't deserve anything that had happened to her, but if there was one thing life had taught him, it was that everything happens to make you stronger.

And Helena was the strongest of them all.

He brushed his fingertips down her cheek.

Outside those walls in the coming days, people would return the palace to a state of cleanliness as much as they could. The gate would take a while to repair. The palace guard who'd once pledged allegiance to Cole now put their efforts into removing the bodies of the slain.

Rebels had returned to their homes, safe for the first time in months.

And the people who would bear the scars of this day for the rest of their lives? They each tried to deal with it in their own ways. Quinn had ridden his horse past the gates, needing to be alone to mourn the man who'd been part of him. His twin. His new betrothal couldn't take the pain away from him. He hadn't returned in two days.

Estevan and Edmund were both being attended by healers throughout the day as they recovered their strength.

Kassander hadn't left Alex's side.

Voices drifted in from the common room and Dell stood, walking to the door to see who'd arrived.

Edmund leaned back on the couch, weakness still etched across his face. Alex sat at his feet with Kass not far.

"He's struggling, Alex." Edmund shook his head.

"Give him time." Alex put his hand on his friend's leg.

"I'll give him all the time in the world. He's the man... Alex, when I lost him, I lost a piece of my soul."

Alex nodded. "I remember the feeling well. Every time I lost Etta, it ripped me apart."

Edmund dropped his voice. "I think being here only makes it worse." He ran a hand through his hair and glanced to Kass who didn't seem to pay them any mind. "His own brother tortured him. How do you get over that? How do you walk the halls and not remember?"

"He isn't an ordinary man. Don't forget that. Estevan will be king. He must move past it."

A cough broke free of Dell before he could stop it, and both men startled. "Sorry, just coming to see what was going on?"

Edmund sat up. "We're waiting for Estevan to return from the healer."

In the absence of a Draconian with healing magic, Estevan's wounds were being treated the non-magical way with salves and potions.

Dell nodded. "How is he doing?" Helena and her brothers had avoided big family moments in the days since the battle. She'd had Dell checking on Estevan.

"Better today, I think." Edmund's lips tugged down. "At least his body is."

Just then, Quinn barged through the entryway, his hair mussed from the wind. He glanced around with wild eyes before calming and dropping into a chair. Camille entered behind him as if she'd been awaiting his return.

"How is the city?" Edmund asked.

Quinn was the only one who'd ventured beyond the palace walls. His face strained in consternation. "The people are jovial. They're marching in the streets to celebrate the end of Cole Rhodipus' reign and calling for a new monarch to be crowned."

"Estevan will be pleased of their support." Edmund sighed as if each reminder of Estevan's duty added more weight to his shoulders.

Quinn's brow furrowed. "It isn't Estevan they call for."

Each eye in the room snapped to his before Helena's voice spoke from her doorway. "What do you mean, Quinn?"

His eyes pinned her in place, and Dell would've sworn a hint of pride appeared in the dark irises. "They want you, Len."

She shook her head, sucking her lip between her teeth. "What... how... no. They can't. I'm just the princess."

Estevan had entered the room when they were all

focused on Helena. Her eyes found him first, and Dell followed her gaze.

The prince moved with the gait of a much older man, lumbering along as if afraid to hurt something. He lowered himself onto a chair, careful not to lean back.

Everyone in the room stayed quiet. Had he heard Quinn?

Helena's hands shook at her sides. "Estevan is meant to lead us."

HELENA COULDN'T HAVE HEARD Quinn right. The people calling for her? She'd never been more than a symbol to them. The mysterious masked princess, an icon of the tradition Madra loved.

Nothing more. Nothing less.

She searched the tired looking faces of her family as Etta and Tyson entered the room, stopping when they took in the seriousness around them.

"What did we just walk in to?" Tyson asked.

Estevan released a breath. "My brother stole the crown that was meant to be mine. My entire life, I've been raised thinking it was my future. When he took that away from me, I hated him." His eyes settled on Edmund. "But I soon realized it was because he'd taken everything else as well." He pushed himself to his feet, struggling with each movement, and walked until he stood in front of Helena.

"I'm sorry."

She sputtered. "What? Why?"

He searched her eyes. "I didn't see you. Before... everything. I loved you and wanted to protect you, but I didn't see you. Who you truly are. The strength you possess. And then you returned for me. You gave yourself up to save me. Even then, I did not understand."

"Understand what?" she breathed.

"You." He put a hand on her shoulder. "But I heard you. In your speech to the guards. You were right. Tradition has been used as a weapon wielded by kings. I'd forgotten, just as you told them, what makes Madra great. If we're going to get back everything we've lost, I can't be the one to rule."

She opened her mouth to speak, but he covered it with his hand. "Cole wasn't the only one who damaged our kingdom. Father created these circumstances. And I stood by his side. Yes, I did what I could to help the people, but what good is feeding them one day when father's policies meant they'd still starve the next? I should have fought him, but I was afraid. Of Father. Of the priesthood. You've never been afraid."

She pushed his hand away. "Stev, you can't do this." Tears hung in her lashes. "You can't put this on me."

He wiped a tear from her face with his thumb. "I can't be what Madra needs. I can't be hope. Not anymore."

"I don't want to be the queen."

He nodded. "I know."

She glanced around the room, searching for someone to back her up, to tell Stev he'd lost his mind.

But all she found was agreement.

She breathed heavily, settling her gaze on Quinn. He'd always been her ally—helping her sneak out of royal events and defending her to her father. The tiniest smile tilted his lips and seeing it was enough to make her heart stop.

She pushed out a shaky breath. "I will never forgive you for this, Stev."

He smiled. "You will."

Not for the first time, Helena sent silent thanks to Reed. She knew what would have happened if he hadn't prepared. She hadn't wanted to trust the man, but he'd proven to have her best interests at heart.

Where were the rebels? Reed had sent word about the tunnels and Helena expected them to storm the courtyard from inside the palace.

A platform sat at the base of the steps leading to the doors of the castle, erected for this very purpose. The courtyard spanning the distance from the palace to the gates was vast and packed with so many people they could barely move.

Each time a horrified gasp rose from the crowd, Cole turned heated eyes on them, and they quieted. This is what he wanted. Horror. Pain. It's what he thought Estevan deserved.

It was better than the deaths he'd given their parents.

Stev's face strained with his attempts to keep from crying out. He wouldn't give Cole that satisfaction.

A shiver wracked Helena's body, and she hugged her arms across herself.

A presence appeared beside her, and she looked sideways at Reed.

"I'm going to stop this." Reed stepped forward.

Helena gripped his arm. "No." She fixed her eyes on Estevan's face. If Cole didn't complete what he thought was necessary, he'd only do it again. This would never end.

"Helena, this isn't right. Cole is out of control. We can no longer wait for the rebels to arrive."

She lifted a hand and felt for the solid weight of the knife she'd slid into her bodice. Even as she watched the lash streak through the air before connecting, she didn't know if she could kill her brother. It had been so easy to think of

He stepped back, and she almost collapsed without his hands holding her up.

Tradition still had its place in Madra, and there was even one for this. Stev held up one hand and said the words every prince knew, but none had spoken in generations. "I, Estevan Rhodipus, cede my position in the line of succession for the throne of Madra. This decision is made with great thought and no coercion. Madra is a great kingdom and those after me in the line of succession will lead it well."

The air deflated from her chest. It was done. With witnesses. There was no turning back. Those words were as binding as any law in Madra.

Helena practically felt herself sliding up into a new position as heir to the throne. She straightened her shoulders and wiped her face. This wasn't finished. In Madra, in order for a new leader to take power, he or she must be wed. Both thrones demanded occupancy. It was another tradition Cole flaunted.

"Dell Tenyson," she turned. "How do you feel about the title of prince consort?" His title would be symbolic, holding no real power. She held her breath, waiting for an answer.

Dell frowned. Not the reaction she'd been expecting when she just proposed.

He shook his head and crossed the room, yanking the door open roughly and disappearing from view.

DELL CLENCHED AND unclenched his fists as he paced outside the door to the royal residence. The royal residence! Who in their bloody right mind would have expected him to be here? He was nothing. Nobody.

There was not a single person left in this world to spare a thought for him.

Except her. Irritation emboldened his anger. Helena had just asked him to marry her, hadn't she? He closed his eyes and leaned his forehead against the wall. He wanted her more than anything, but he'd never expected Estevan to give up the throne. Hell, he hadn't really known if they'd overcome Cole.

When they were in Bela, he'd imagined a simple life for them among the magic folk. The rolling green hills of the once forgotten kingdom had called to him with its peace.

Did a queen ever truly know peace?

Tradition. It was all that mattered to the Rhodipus line. They'd nearly driven Madra into the ground in pursuit of adhering to the old ways. Law stated an unmarried man or woman could not wear the crown.

As much as Helena and Estevan claimed they differed from their predecessors, they proved to be nothing but the same. And now, she expected him to marry her only because she needed a king.

There'd been no emotion in her voice during the proposal. Everything he'd felt for her... when she'd left him in Bela, she'd torn them apart. She couldn't piece them back together for no reason other than a crown.

A crown she didn't even want!

He'd heard every word Len said to the guards and again when she spoke to Cole before his death. He hadn't seen it before, but there was no doubt in his mind she was meant for this. The kingdom didn't yet know her, not in the way they knew Estevan.

But they would just as he did. He curled his fingers into a fist and slammed it against the wall. Their timing had never been right. All he wanted to do was take her away from here.

Away from the place where bad memories ran rampant. Where blood had been scrubbed from the stone floors again and again.

A light touch on his arm had his eyes snapping open. He twisted away from Helena as she watched him with guarded eyes.

He breathed heavily, noticing the hurt she wore like a shield. He'd caused that. He'd forced the walls around her into place.

But what was he supposed to do? Marry her out of some misguided obligation to the past? The priesthood was dead. They no longer enforced the rules of life in Madra.

"We need to talk." Her voice was small, and he hated the tremor in it. The Helena he'd seen over the last few weeks didn't waver.

As she stood before him, she was no longer that woman. Now she was the girl who'd stood nervously on the bank of the river, wringing her cap as he inched his body closer to hers. She became the defensive girl who yelled at him on a beach of black sand under the scorching heat of the sun.

Finally, he nodded.

She led him away from the ears of her family on the other side of the door. They descended the stairs wordlessly. He knew where she was taking him before they arrived.

The walled garden hadn't changed in the months they'd been away. It stood as a remnant of what was. Untouched by the war that changed Madra forever, its beauty was soothing. Flowering bushes lined the walkways with leafy overhangs shielding them from the sun. A cold breeze whipped the hair from Helena's shoulders, and she hugged her arms across her chest.

Dell shrugged out of his jacket and placed it over her shoulders.

"Thank you." She hugged it close.

The sleeves of Dell's linen shirt billowed out as he reached for her. He snatched his hand back when she gave him a cutting look.

They walked down the winding path to a stone bench that sat at the back. Vines twisted up the walls behind them.

Helena pushed out a breath.

"I'm sorry." They both spoke at the same time.

Dell cracked a smile and gestured for her to speak first.

She hesitated a moment. "I shouldn't have put you on the spot like that. Asking you for such a decision in front of my family was..." She shook her head. "I don't know what I was thinking." Steel entered her gaze as she turned to pin him with a stare. "Well, yes I do. I thought you and I..." She gestured between them. "I thought something that obviously wasn't true."

Unable to stop himself, Dell took her hand. "Helena... Len, I love you. I am in love with you. Please don't think I'm not."

She narrowed her eyes, pulling her hand away. "But you... you said no! I asked you to marry me and you said no."

"First, you never actually asked me to marry you. Second, I want to be with you for the rest of my life whether it be long or short. I've been lost to you since the moment you ogled me when I was naked in the river."

Her mouth fell open. "I did not ogle you. I... you..."

A smile tilted one side of his lips. "It's okay." He leaned in, pressing his lips you hers. "I ogled you when you were standing on the riverbank, dripping water and wild."

She put a hand on his chest to push him away. "Then why won't you marry me?"

"I'm going to marry you, Len. One day, I'm going to

marry the heck out of you. But it won't be to adhere to some tradition you don't even believe in."

She sighed. "No Madran monarch has claimed the throne unmarried. It's law."

He dipped his head to look straight into her dark eyes. "It's also law in this kingdom that a princess must be masked until her eighteenth name day. Do you plan on obeying that with your own daughter?"

She gasped. "Of course not."

"Then this law can be changed as well. Len, you don't need a king by your side to be a queen. You can lead your people on your own. I know you can because I believe in you, and they will too."

"Alone?" She swallowed nervously.

He cupped her cheek in his palm. "You're strong enough for this. Don't let anyone tell you you're not."

She leaned her forehead against his. "I think Stev is going to leave me."

He nodded against her. He'd had his own suspicions. Edmund and Estevan would return to Bela with Etta, Alex, and Tyson.

"You're not going to leave me too, are you?"

"Never," he breathed.

She pressed a tentative kiss against his lips. He responded instantly, wrapping his arms around her waist to pull her to him. She fit against him as if it was where she was always meant to be. Her arms wound around his neck as she deepened the kiss.

This time, it wasn't fire or passion that held them together. The warmth and comfort of knowing they had forever wrapped around them, allowing them to take their time, to savor each other.

Dell kissed a path to Helena's ear. "I forgive you for leaving me."

She leaned back, a smile on her lips. "We're back at this now?"

He shrugged. "You didn't need me. I see that now."

"You're wrong, you know." She put her hand against his face to turn him back into the kiss and spoke against his lips. "I'll always need you. No matter how strong you think I am, or how many guards I have at my back, you're all I need."

He hummed in the back of his throat, knowing she was everything to him. His best friend. His lover. His queen. Even life itself.

They'd fought battles and almost died. They'd faced betrayals and lost people they loved. Yet, they weren't broken. The glass shards had been put into the fire, melted, and hardened into something stronger than what was there before.

Epilogue

Helena stood in front of a portrait of her mother. Chloe Rhodipus looked radiant on the day of her coronation. Her marriage and coronation took place on the same day. It had been a marriage of alliance like Stev's would have been to Camille.

Camille stood beside her in an understated, yet elegant yellow gown. "Only months ago, this was supposed to be me." She gave Helena a sideways smile and leaned heavily on her cane. "If Cole hadn't betrayed the crown, I'd have married Stev and become queen of Madra."

Helena flinched at the reminder of the one brother who wasn't there for the biggest day of her life. In the weeks following his death, she'd tried to forgive him, to put aside her anger, but that meant letting the sadness inside.

What would her mother think of her on this day? She flattened her palms against the brilliant blue of her ornate gown. Silver threading wound through the bodice. It wasn't unlike the gown she'd worn to her name day ball.

She touched her face as had become a habit, feeling for

the missing fabric of her mask. But she was no longer the caged princess.

"What did you do," she began, "When Alex abdicated the throne of Gaule and you became your mother's heir?"

Camille chuckled. "I cursed my brother."

Helena laughed. She'd done the same in her moments of solitude.

"I imagine she'll need a new heir." Camille sighed. "Now that I am to stay in Madra."

"Quinn could return to Gaule with you should rule fall to you."

She shook her head. "He does not wish it and neither do I. I am not... beloved in Gaule. Though, my mother has fallen out of favor as well. I imagine she'll name Tyson the heir. He may not have been my father's son, but my mother is queen now so her line is royal."

A laugh burst free of Helena. "Does Ty know this yet?"

Camille smiled ruefully. "We'd know if he did because he'd have drowned the entire kingdom of Gaule with his magic just to avoid the throne."

They fell into silence until footsteps sounded behind them. Quinn wrapped an arm around each woman's shoulders. Helena leaned into him, grateful she wouldn't have to say goodbye to at least one of her brothers. Kassander would stay as well, but she'd been right about Stev. After the coronation, he was set to leave.

Edmund had stayed for the ceremony as well and saying goodbye to him would be just as difficult. Etta, Alex, and Tyson had already returned home, but wished her well. Lucky for them, Landon had brought Vérité to the palace stables before bringing Kassander to Cole. Helena doubted Etta would have left without her horse.

Kass appeared beside them and wedged himself in

between Helena and Quinn. "It's up to us now, yeah?" She looked up to Quinn.

He nodded. "When father sat on the throne, I never imagined we'd have control of Madra. I still feel like a child in this palace."

Helena laughed at that. Quinn was an army general. He'd led men into battle, but he'd always felt unsure of himself among these halls.

"Are you going to walk me into the hall?" She directed the question to Quinn.

Kass was the one who answered. "Of course I am."

Helena, Camille, and Quinn all laughed.

"I'm going to take my seat." Camille kissed Quinn's cheek and broke away from them.

"Give me a moment." Helena slipped out of his hold and walked toward the back door of the hall. Opening it just a crack, she found Dell immediately. As if feeling her presence, his eyes snapped to hers. She waved him toward her.

When he reached the door, she wrapped her arms around his waist. "Tell me I'm not going to mess this up."

He chuckled. "You don't need me to tell you that."

She swatted him away. "You're useless."

He grinned and caught her around the waist. His black jacket was embroidered with the same blue as her dress. He reached into his pocket and procured a small wooden carving.

He held the wooden crown between them. "You're going to be the best queen Madra has ever seen."

She took the crown, letting her fingers glide over the smooth dips and curves. "How do you know that?"

"Because I know you." He pressed his lips to the side of her head.

Music poured from the open door, signaling the start of

the ceremony. Dell left to find his seat again, and Stev's tall frame replaced his presence.

"Thank you." He nodded toward her. The words may have lacked emotion as most of Stev's words over the last few weeks had, but Helena read the meaning in them.

He needed a new start away from the place where so much had happened. He'd recovered from the wounds on his flesh, but the wounds on his mind and his heart would take much longer. She only hoped he found what he was searching for in Bela.

The string quartet played louder, and both doors flew open, revealing a hall teeming with people. Helena had made sure any in the city who wished could attend the coronation. With foreign trade resuming, many people were busy getting shops and ships operational again, but still, many had come.

She breathed deeply as Kassander stepped into the aisle first. He walked slowly in front as Quinn and Estevan each took one of her arms. Camille had joined Dell and Edmund in the front row. By the time Helena reached them, her heart beat so fast it threatened to burst free.

She smiled at them as she passed and climbed the three steps to the dais they'd built for this occasion. A seat for each royal rested on the platform.

There had been no remaining priests to perform the coronation, but since they were forgoing tradition anyway, it hadn't mattered.

The music stopped and silence stretched in the hall.

Helena knelt as her three brothers turned to face the crowd.

Estevan spoke. "Madra has long been a kingdom ruled by the past. On this day, we change the fate of our land. We look to what is in front of us instead of behind. Helena Rhodipus becomes a new kind of ruler, the first of a new generation.

She will change many of the laws we are beholden to only because we have always been. The first among these is that an unmarried monarch will sit on the throne."

His harsh eyes scanned the crowd. When no one objected, he turned to Helena and crossed to the table at the edge of the dais where a crown sat. Not her father's crown... She glanced up in confusion, but Stev forged ahead.

"Helena Rhodipus, do you promise to be a fair and just queen?"

She nodded. "Always."

"Will you put Madra first in all things?"

"Yes."

"Will you lead with compassion and understanding?" That was a new one.

"I will."

Stev lifted the crown. "This crown belonged to Chloe Rhodipus, our mother."

Helena shook her head. She didn't recognize the blue gems or crossing gold pieces.

Stev continued. "It was taken from her when I was a boy." Helena had heard the story. The priesthood forced her mother into a symbolic role instead of one with any real power. And they'd taken her crown? The only headpiece Helena ever saw her mother with was a delicate tiara.

"Helena Rhodipus." Stev handed the crown to Kass. "I crown you queen of Madra, one of the six kingdoms."

Kassander grinned as he set the crown on Helena's head. The weight that bore down on her differed from the weight of the mask. That had been a prison. But the crown was the ultimate freedom. She could turn Madra into the kingdom it was always meant to be.

Every eye in the room settled on her, asking her to make life better for them. And she would.

Dell had been right. A queen didn't need a king. One day, she'd have one. Dell wouldn't avoid the throne forever.

But for the first time in her life, she believed in her own strength. She'd returned to Madra determined to save her people or die trying. As she stood and turned to face the expectant eyes of her people, she knew she'd make that choice a thousand times more.

Because that was what a queen did.

She raised her hand to wave and a roar of applause echoed off the high ceilings. People stood, cheering for their new queen. Pride spread through Helena.

She met Dell's eyes. When he winked, her smile grew.

She may not have known it until that very moment, but she was always meant to stand here. The crown fit her as if it had been made for her. And her people's acceptance wrapped her in a cloak of strength, unbendable and immovable.

This was her time.

Madra's time.

Thank you for reading Glass Princess! Want more Fantasy and Fairytales? Noble Thief is now available.
It tells Tyson's story of love and duty and competing loyalties.

M. Lynn is a USA Today bestselling author of love. Yes, love. Whether it be YA romance (Under Michelle MacQueen), NA romance, or fantasy romance, she loves to make readers swoon.

The great loves of her life to this point are two tiny blond creatures who call her "aunt" and proclaim her books to be "boring books" for their lack of pictures. Yet, somehow, she still manages to love them more than chocolate.

When she's not sharing her inexhaustible wisdom with her niece and nephew, Michelle is usually lounging in her ridiculously large bean bag chair creating worlds and characters that remind her to smile every day - even when a feisty five-year-old is telling her just how much she doesn't know.

See more from Michelle MacQueen and sign up to receive updates and deals!

www.michellelynnauthor.com